D1475063

FINDING BLISS

FINDING BLISS

Dina Silver

amazonpublishing

The characters and events portrayed in this book are fictitious. Any similarity to real persons, living or dead, is coincidental and not intended by the author.

Text copyright © 2013 Dina Silver

All rights reserved.
Printed in the United States of America.
No part of this book may be reproduced, or stored in a retrieval system, or transmitted in any form or by any means, electronic, mechanical, photocopying, recording, or otherwise, without express written permission of the publisher.

Published by Amazon Publishing
PO Box 400818
Las Vegas, NV 89140

ISBN-13: 9781477807361
ISBN-10: 1477807365
Library of Congress Control Number: 2013903607

PROLOGUE

I checked the clock before tucking the last few strands of my long auburn hair under my swim cap. It was a quarter to three, which made my mother officially forty-five minutes late. At least Jacob Denny could tell time. He was my boyfriend then, in the seventh grade, and he'd come to watch me swim the hundred-meter butterfly with his older sister that Saturday. As the swimmers in the heat before mine were exiting the pool, the coach raised a finger and looked in my direction, indicating I had one minute before I needed to get up on the block. I scanned the entry doors for spectators and sighed because they remained closed and vacant. I paced the pool deck for another thirty seconds and then took my place at the head of lane number four, bouncing and shaking out my arms and legs before taking my position.

Just then, one of the large exterior doors at the opposite end of the pool flew open and my mother entered with another woman I'd never seen before. Every whisper in that arena was magnified, and their boisterous arrival was like sounding a bullhorn in a library. They were hanging onto each other, laughing and shushing as they made their way through the humid chlorine-infused air. No one moved but them. Everyone—in the bleachers and on the pool deck alike—was mesmerized. Not even the eighty-two-year-old security guard got up off his folding chair to stop them.

And then she spotted me.

"There she is!" Mom hollered to her friend and pointed. "I made it, sweetie!" She waved frantically at me across the length of the pool, and then held up her thumb like it was a cigarette lighter at the end of a concert. "Where's my camera?" she asked her giggling friend, and then smacked the woman on the arm, causing her to crack up further. Mom moved closer to the pool and shuffled through her large purse. "Got it!" she screamed waving it in the air.

I glanced over at my coach; his arms were crossed, and his eyes were fixated—like everyone else's—on my mother and her friend. The rest of the swimmers, who'd been in starting position only seconds before, were now standing up straight, leaning back on their heels, and shifting their gaze from me to the spectacle at the end of the pool. I lowered my chin and rolled my eyes over to where Jacob and his sister were seated in the bleachers two rows up. His mouth was agape.

The woman with my mother was stumbling in place as she applied lip gloss and watched my mom position the camera in front of her face with one hand while still waving at me with the other. "Good luck, Chloe!" she screamed.

She blew me a kiss and then took one more step before slipping on some water and tumbling, camera first, into lane three.

CHAPTER ONE

I checked the locks, pulled the shades, then fell asleep on the couch after putting the Reed twins to bed. Two hours later, I awoke to a crunching noise and nearly had a heart attack at the ripe age of twenty-one. Tyler, the Reeds' eldest son, was seated on the coffee table in front of me, eating a bag of chips inches from my face. I shivered when I realized it was *him*. Although we'd gone to the same high school, we'd never officially met.

But I knew exactly who he was.

As far as my hometown of Glenview, Illinois, was concerned, Tyler was the most physically gifted athlete on the planet, and had gone on to be the starting quarterback for Notre Dame after high school. He stood six foot three inches, had a body like a Greek god, and an ego to match. All of which were on display among the many photographs that peppered the walls and built-in shelves of the Reeds' home. Pictures of him kneeling on the field next to his helmet. Candid shots of him screaming with victory, fists clenched in the air. Newspaper clippings of his accomplishments framed with little placards on the matting. Chin held high in every shot, with his emerald green eyes gazing at me through the glass, mesmerizing and inviting. He was known for his good will as well. Tyler worked with inner-city kids in Chicago, coaching sports clinics and teaching the importance of physical fitness. His reputation had preceded him… and intrigued *me*.

Most of my income during my college years had come from babysitting and working as a summer girl for Tyler Reed's siblings, Sammy and Sarah, who were twelve years younger than he was. His football schedule kept him in South Bend at summer school and training camps, so we'd never crossed paths. It wasn't until eleven o'clock that night, lying bleary-eyed on the Reeds' couch, that I finally got my chance. And despite every sensible bone in my body, I'd already developed a full-blown schoolgirl crush on him.

Many women were attracted to him, so my fascination with a good-looking football star wasn't all that surprising. However, as an ambitious college-educated woman with hopes of revolutionizing the field of divorce law one day, falling for the handsome hometown hero was not what I'd have imagined for myself. I was much more practical than that. Besides, I was sure he had no idea who I was.

"You must be Chloe Carlyle," he said with a grin that put me instantly at ease. Tyler's eyes were as magnificent in person as they were on the mantel. His thick dark hair was longer than in the pictures and hung in loose strands around his face. A square jaw, long eyelashes, and a disarming grin rounded out this mythological creature.

I nodded as he continued chewing and rustling the bag of Cool Ranch Doritos with his giant hand. A combination of intimidation and infatuation caused my breathing to speed up. I pulled the rubber band off my wrist, quickly threw my hair into a ponytail, and then took a deep breath. "Yes, I'm Chloe, and I'm hoping you're Tyler," I replied. "If not, you'll have to excuse me while I call the police."

He laughed.

I took a deep breath and regained my composure. "There's left-over pizza in the fridge if you want? The kids only ate a few slices," I told him.

"Not anymore, there's not," he said. "So how much are my cheapskate parents paying you?"

The Reeds were one of the wealthiest families in our neighborhood. Dr. Reed was a well-known heart surgeon, and notorious for turning Tyler into the Astroturf idol that he was. He had even hired retired Chicago Bears players to coach Tyler privately during his years at Glenbrook South. Dr. Reed's sideline tirades were legendary, and rumor was they hadn't lessened any at Notre Dame. I'd heard he once pulled the coach's headphones off and screamed in his ear, for which he was banned from the field for a while. Afterward, he was required to attend each game with a security guard.

By contrast, his wife, Dixie, was a consummate Southern belle who hailed from Atlanta society—and whose penchant for passive-aggressive behavior was artfully hidden behind her batting lashes and Southern twang. I had met Mrs. Reed while volunteering at a PTA fund-raiser and offered my holiday babysitting services when I found out she still had two small children at home. The Reeds had a full-time nanny who worked daytime hours, and I covered everything else when I was home from school. Dr. Reed traveled a great deal, speaking at hospital conferences all over the country, and his wife accompanied him most of the time. She was also a board member at Evanston Hospital and the social chair at her country club, leaving little time for things like child rearing and housework. Nothing could tear her away from a commitment that included flowing Chardonnay and silent auctions, which had left me caring for their feverish, nauseated children on more than one occasion. My mother described Mrs. Reed as cold, but at twenty bucks an hour, I found her plenty warm.

Theirs was a world I longed to be a part of. Accomplished, married parents. Siblings to share a meal with. A beautiful home with two fireplaces and crown molding in every room.

But our upbringings couldn't have been more different.

I moved from Miami, Florida, to Glenview with my mother when I was a freshman in high school. I spent my years at Glenbrook South as the new girl. Not the shy, nerdy one—more like the tall, athletic swimmer with big dreams. I met my best friend, Grace, a couple of days after Mom and I moved into our new home. Grace and I were both tall for our age, a little too studious to be truly cool, and inseparable during those four years. I had big plans for myself even then, and went after straight As with single-minded purpose.

Swimming and studying were two of the many ways I managed to escape from my mother, who'd lost not only her Wedgwood china but also her joy for life in her divorce when I was two years old. She rediscovered both in a bottle of vodka a year later. Luckily for her, she was the product of a father whose grandparents had built a manufacturing dynasty and left generations of descendants with monthly trust-fund checks. Mom was set for life, with just enough money to keep a roof over our heads, ensure that she never had to work a day in her life, and provide a means to fund her shopping and alcohol addictions. As I got older and threatened to dent her stipend with demands like winter coats and school supplies, she began to parent me. "You can't always get what you want," she'd say. "It's time you learned to take responsibility for yourself and earn some money." She had no concept of what it took to hold down a job, but she was very proud of herself for insisting I get one.

When I was twelve, I realized she was an alcoholic. The day she tumbled into the pool in front of my teammates and classmates, I was stunned by everyone's reaction to her. Jaws dropped, heads shook, and whispers filled the air, lingering in my mind for months. I'd always thought that was just who she was. Fun, vivacious, full of life. Loud.

A week after that swim meet I was watching TV one morning when a commercial came on and asked, "Do you or someone you love have a drinking problem?" I turned and looked at my mother, who was on her second pack of cigarettes and fourth vodka martini, and dialed the number.

A therapist scheduled an intervention for the next day, which included said therapist, my uncle Justin, his fourth wife, and me.

"We're going to each present her with a hamburger," the therapist instructed us.

"I'm sorry," I interrupted. "Did you say hamburger?"

"Yes, Chloe, a hamburger. Your 'bun' will be your opening statement: the first layer of your speech where you'll simply state how much you love your mother and what she means to you. Next will be the 'meat,' where you outline—in your own words—what she's done to hurt you. Last will be another bun where you reiterate your love for her, and how you're willing to do whatever it takes to support her through her recovery."

"She's a vegetarian," I said.

However, my mother digested her four hamburgers and willingly checked into rehab that afternoon. Saying good-bye to her was one of the hardest things I've ever done, and I'll never forget the look in her eyes when she left that day. Addiction or not, she was all I had. I went to live with my aunt and uncle for three months, which I mostly spent worrying about my mom. I was overwhelmed with guilt and uncertainty—and scared I'd never get my mom back. And in some ways I never did. She emerged three months later with nothing to mask her unhappiness, and moved us to Glenview for a fresh start. Her lust for life had been sucked away. This new mom was sober and somber. And quiet.

"Your parents take great care of me," I told Tyler. "And I love Sammy and Sarah, they're a pleasure to be with." I watched him walk over to the TV where he grabbed two DVDs from the shelf. I couldn't look away. I'd been staring at pictures of him on and off for about three years, and there he was in his parents' living room, close enough for me to touch, without a piece of glass between us.

"Oh yeah, those two are a barrel of laughs," he said before sitting down next to me on the couch, bumping my knee as he settled in. "So what's your story?" he asked.

I sat up straight. "I'm just home for winter break. I'll be graduating college this year and starting law school at Northwestern in the fall," I said, my heart beating like it did after a long swim.

He scanned me from head to toe with a predatory expression that was somewhere between perplexed and amused. I could tell he was fully aware of the effect he had on most women, including me.

"You went to South?" he asked.

"Yes. I was a year ahead of you."

"Thanks, counsel, I figured that part out all on my own when you said you were graduating this year. You got a boyfriend?"

I rolled my eyes.

"Easy killer, I'm just making conversation," he said.

"Yes, I do."

"What's his name?"

"You really shouldn't talk with your mouth full."

Tyler swallowed. "What's his name?" he asked.

"Brian," I said and nervously picked at my nail polish. "His name is Brian, and we've been together for about a year." I was in a casual relationship with a guy named Brian at the time, but for some reason I felt compelled to make it sound more serious than it was when Tyler questioned me.

He nodded. "You like Brian?" he asked mockingly.

"It's really not your concern."

He shrugged his mile-wide shoulders and then stood. "I hope to see you around, Chloe," he said my name slowly, with deliberation. Then he grabbed a bottle of tequila from the bar and left the house. Gone as quickly as he'd appeared.

I exhaled and smiled.

CHAPTER TWO

The following summer, the Reeds asked me to accompany them to their vacation home in Lake Geneva for three weeks. Lake Geneva is a quaint little town in Wisconsin about an hour north of Chicago, but it feels worlds away. Highrises and buses are replaced with pubs and trolleys, while fish fries and boat rides are the town's most coveted delights. And although Lake Geneva has added a Starbucks and a Home Depot to appease some of its fastidious urban transplants, the place has still managed to capitalize on its biggest assets: fresh air, farmland, and Fourth of July.

Every summer the Reeds planned their summer vacation around the Fourth of July festivities at the Grand Geneva, a huge resort that anchors the town and used to be the old Playboy Club. These days it's a luxury resort boasting two championship golf courses, a spa, and walking trails. It may be the closest thing to the Berkshires in the region. Minus the mountains.

Mrs. Reed informed me that she and her husband would be in and out of town while I was there with Sammy and Sarah. I gladly accepted their offer, and looked forward to the break and the income after graduation. Despite being raised by nannies, Sammy and Sarah were two of the most well-behaved eight-year-olds I'd ever met. They knew their place and were fearful of the repercussions that came with misbehaving around their father. The kids and

I got along great because I let them do what they wanted when their parents were away, which was always, and they agreed to keep quiet about it. If they wanted to jump in the lake with their clothes on, I'd let them. If they wanted to sit in front of the TV and eat spaghetti with their fingers, I let them. If they wouldn't tell, neither would I.

Two days before we were set to leave, Mrs. Reed called me to go over some last-minute details.

"Hello, Chloedear," she said as though it were one word. "I'm just confirming that we'll pick you up Saturday afternoon around four o'clock, and then we can all have suppah together," she said in her unmistakable drawl. "Dr. Reed and I have to leave early Monday morning to head back into the city. He has a vereh important meeting, and then we'll return to the lake sometime midweek. You'll have the Jeep at your disposal while you're there," she said. Formalities were very important to her. Referring to her husband as Mr. Reed instead of Dr. Reed would have been like insulting her grandmother's sweet tea.

"Oh, I thought we were all leaving on Sunday?" I asked.

"No dear, I mean, I guess we could leave Sunday if that's better for you."

"No, no, it's fine, either day works for me, I just thought you'd originally said we were leaving Sunday, but Saturday sounds great. I'm really looking forward to it," I said.

"Wonderful, then. Bless your heart; you're so generous to accommodate our schedule. One more thing, our son Tylah is coming up Sunday evening to spend some time with friends who have a house down the lake from ours. I'm not sure how long he's staying, maybe three or four days, but I'm sure he'll stay out of your way. We hardly evhsee him when he's there."

My fingers clenched tightly around the phone, and I opened my mouth to answer her but nothing came out.

"Chloedear, are you there?"

"Yes, of course," I said finally.

"See you Saturday, then." *Click.*

We arrived at the Reeds' sprawling Victorian-style lake house that Saturday in the late afternoon, and the kids wasted no time jumping off the dock and floating around in oversized inner tubes. The house was a study in white. Not clean, contemporary, cool beach-house white; more like a wicker factory had sex with a garage sale. The house was dripping in lace curtains and flea market finds. The main sources of color were a collection of ceramic cookie jars displayed on the large, white built-in shelves that flanked the TV, and needlepoint pillows with quotes like "Friends Welcome" and "When I Count My Blessings, I Count You Twice," which adorned nearly every white seat cushion in the house.

The next day I took the kids into town where we got ice cream and watched fudge being made through the front window of the chocolate shop, then picked up a peach cobbler Mrs. Reed had ordered from her favorite local bakery. Tyler arrived that evening while we were all on the back patio having dinner. He walked out of the house holding a beer in one hand and texting with the other.

"Hello, Tylah, darling." His mother waved.

Sammy and Sarah shouted in unison, "Hi, Tyler!"

"Hey, squirts," Tyler said. "Got a burger left for me, Dad?"

Dr. Reed glanced at him and then turned his attention back to the grill. "Talked to Coach last night," Dr. Reed started. "He said your sprint times were down this week."

Tyler rolled his eyes and shook his head. "Good to see you too."

Dr. Reed placed his spatula near the grill and went to pat Tyler on the shoulder like one would greet a German shepherd; then he took the beer out of Tyler's hand and tossed it in the garbage. "One burger coming up," his dad confirmed.

Tyler glanced at his empty hand, and then at his mother.

"Let him have what he wants, Jim," Mrs. Reed said diffidently to her husband.

"He's got ten pounds to lose by next month. He'll survive on one burger," Dr. Reed said. "And stay away from the beer."

Tyler's mom looked back at him and smiled. "Your father's right, dear," she concluded, and then changed the subject. "You remember Chloe, darling," Mrs. Reed said, gesturing toward me with her hand.

He turned just in time to catch me staring at him.

"Yeah," he said, acknowledging me with a nod.

I smiled and then looked away. I wasn't a shy person, and had had a string of boyfriends. I was responsible for earning my own money, paying my own bills, and my confidence never failed me… unless, of course, Tyler Reed was around.

He took a seat at the table with us and began answering a barrage of questions from his brother and sister. He never looked at me, and I never took my eyes off him. The chair disappeared beneath his muscular build as he leaned back and rested his elbows on the armrests. I could see the edge of a tattoo peeking out from under his short sleeve. Sammy and Sarah hung on every last word about his practices and teammates, until their father chimed in and started to criticize Tyler for his unimpressive performance.

"It's embarrassing for me to hear from Coach that you're not meeting expectations," his dad said. "You've got appointments with three top agents next month, and every stat counts."

"It's embarrassing for me to have you call him every fucking day."

"Tylah Alexandah Reed, I nevah!" his mother shouted.

His father cut her off in the same tone. "Don't you dare complain to me! If you were performing like you should be, I wouldn't have to make the call every day. Do you have any idea what it's like for me to hear you're not playing as well as you should be? You have two months until you declare eligibility for the draft, and I will not tolerate anything less than stellar numbers."

Sammy, Sarah, and I sank into our seats and picked at our food as the two of them continued shouting at each other until Tyler abruptly stood and left.

Mrs. Reed sniffed away the unpleasantries and regrouped with her best happy-hostess smile. "Who would like some cobbler?" she offered.

The next morning, the Reeds left for the city, leaving me with Tyler and the kids. Which was much like leaving a cheetah and a gazelle alone in the house.

CHAPTER THREE

Mrs. Reed was right: Tyler did stay out of my way at first. Monday morning he grabbed a set of golf clubs from the garage, and then came back six hours later to shower before heading out again to visit a friend who lived across the lake. He eventually came home around three thirty in the morning. I did my best to keep the kids quiet during breakfast the following day and get them outside as early as possible without waking him. Around noon on Tuesday, the kids and I were at the dock at the bottom of the grassy hill picking up the mail, which was delivered to the lake houses by boat. We were sitting on the wood planks, and I was paging through a Pottery Barn catalog when I looked up and saw him. Tyler was at the top of the hill holding a coffee mug in nothing but a pair of cargo shorts. I waved, hoping he'd join us, but he just nodded and went back inside. That night as I was preparing dinner for Sammy and Sarah, he brushed past me to get to the fridge.

"Are you going out tonight?" I asked.

"Yeah."

"I'm making pasta; would you like some? There's plenty here," I offered.

"Sure."

Our eyes met up close for the first time, so I held his gaze as I spoke. "It'll be ready in about ten minutes," I told him.

He nodded and walked outside.

As the four of us ate dinner together in the kitchen, Sammy and Sarah did most of the talking. They were eager to tell him how we'd tried fishing off the pier with gummy worms to no avail. Occasionally I would steal a glance at Tyler when they had his attention and watch him balance his chair back on two legs, arms crossed over his expansive chest. It was seven o'clock, and he had yet to put a shirt on. Afterward, I cleaned up everyone's mess, and he left. I put the kids to bed and fell asleep on the couch watching TV.

Around one o'clock in the morning, I heard him come through the front door. I lay still, pretending I was asleep, and watched him go into the kitchen and grab a bottle of beer from the fridge before walking over to the TV and shutting it off. The room went dark. I couldn't help but wonder whether Mrs. Reed would think I was responsible for the missing beers or if she would even notice. I closed my eyes as he got closer and felt his hand on my shoulder a moment later.

"Hey," he whispered.

I opened my eyes to find him leaning over me.

"Want to take a walk?" he asked.

Holy shit, yes.

I nodded and sat up. Tyler walked back into the kitchen and grabbed two more beers, then handed me one as we started down the hill to the small dirt path at the edge of the lake.

"I don't want to go too far, with the kids asleep and all," I said.

"Okay," he said and sat down under the neighbor's oak tree. He leaned his back against it and stretched his long legs out in front of him before twisting open his bottle. "How've you been?" he asked.

"I've been good," I answered and sat cross-legged next to him, but facing the water. "Thanks for asking."

"You still with Brian?"

My eyes went wide. "Wow, I'm impressed you remembered," I said. "No, we broke up."

"What happened?"

I shook my head and began peeling the label off my beer. "He cheated on me," I confessed. Brian and I had begun to get serious our last semester of college, and dated for about four months before I walked in on him naked with his fraternity brother's younger sister who was visiting for the weekend. Needless to say, I couldn't wait to tell Brian's friend, and he couldn't wait to kick Brian's ass.

"Ouch," he said, oddly amused.

"Whatever. He was no prize…obviously."

"You're going to law school, right?"

"Yes, this fall," I told him. "How about you? Notre Dame treating you well?"

"Can't complain," he said and took a swig of his beer, nearly emptying the bottle in one gulp. "I have a year left."

"And then what? Are you hoping to be drafted?"

"We'll see."

"That would be exciting," I said.

"I guess."

"Is there something else you'd rather do?"

He shrugged. "I just don't see myself playing football forever. I'd like to maybe get into film one day."

"Acting?"

He took a sip and shook his head. "Directing."

"How very Hollywood of you," I said. "But it seems a face like yours should be in front of the camera, not behind it."

"It's likely not going to happen," he said.

"I bet Sammy and Sarah would love to see you play football on national television."

He laughed. "Notre Dame has played on national television."

I blushed. "Oh, of course they have."

"I gather you're not a fan," he said.

I took a sip of my beer before answering. "No, I'm not much of a football fan, but since I'll be starting law school at Northwestern this fall, clearly I'd root for them given the choice."

"We crushed Northwestern forty-eight to zero this year. Twice." He winked, and I slapped him on the arm.

"Something tells me you're not hurting for fans," I said.

"I'm not, but it's kind of nice to talk to someone who doesn't want to relive game highlights. It's typically all anyone asks me about. I like that about you. You're different...or just weird," he said and leaned away from me to avoid a second slap.

I laughed. "You're a shit. And if you're not careful, I'm going to make you tell me all about your stupid home runs or field goals or whatever it is you do besides flexing your bravado."

"You think I'm a thug."

I shook my head. "No, I don't."

"You do, I can tell."

"Technically, a thug is more of a common criminal or assassin," I said. "So, again, no. I do not think you're a thug. In fact, you're quite the opposite. Here you sit, a dark-haired golden boy, on the lawn of your family's summer home sipping beer and talking about playing college football at Notre Dame. There's nothing criminal about it."

He studied my face and then grinned.

I lifted a finger and stopped him before he could speak. "If you say I'm weird again, you will get slapped."

"You're weird," he said without hesitation.

We sat for over an hour talking and joking about his parents and siblings. He was much more clever than I'd initially given him credit for, and I was glad to see how much he cared for his brother and sister.

Tyler told me about his relationship with his grandfather, and how much he admired him. Dr. Reed's father, Billy McCutcheon Reed, had come to the United States from Ireland when he was twelve years old. He'd been sent alone on a ship to live with distant relatives in Bridgeport, a South Side Chicago neighborhood. From there he worked odd jobs, paid his way through college, and built McCutcheon Meats, one of the largest meatpacking industries in the country.

"What an amazing man," I commented.

"He's awesome. I play for him, not my dad."

Tyler talked about his teammates and, despite my lack of knowledge, entertained me with a few game stories. Last-minute field goal kicks, Hail Mary passes that didn't pan out, turnovers that won the game. I didn't give a shit about football, but he was eager to talk to me, so I listened intently and slowly drank him in like a milkshake. I should've been embarrassed by how strong my attachment to him was, but I was quite content to bask in his attention for as long as he was willing to give it. The more he opened up, the deeper I fell.

"This is nice," he said and busted me gawking at him again. We locked eyes for an incredibly peaceful yet intense moment, and I sensed those emeralds of his had so much more to reveal.

"How'd you get that scar?" I asked and pointed above his right eyebrow.

He shrugged. "Who knows."

I glanced back at the house. "I really should get to bed. Sammy's been waking up at an ungodly hour, asking for Cinnamon Toast Crunch."

Tyler stood and extended his hand to lift me from my spot on the ground. It was warm to the touch, so I loosely held on to his pinky finger as we walked. He cocked his head and smiled at my grip on him. There was an awkward pause when we both entered the house, before going our separate ways.

"Good night," I said.

Tyler smiled at me. "Night, Chloe."

I slept soundly that evening.

I made dinner for everyone the next night, too. Frozen family-style lasagna for Tyler and myself, and grilled cheese sandwiches for the kids. He thanked me afterward and took off for the night, leaving me with his siblings and longing for more time alone with him. I was cleaning up the kitchen, while Sammy and Sarah were watching a movie, when I started to panic about when he would leave the lake, and whether I would ever see him again. I put the kids to bed that night and was sitting out on the screened-in porch when it started to rain. I loved the rain. My mom and I used to sit by the window in her bedroom when I was little and have raindrop races. We'd each take our index finger and point to a drop at the top of the window, and then follow it down the glass to see whose would make it to the bottom first. She'd drink her martinis and laugh hysterically like a drunken sailor when her droplet would accidentally combine with another, forming a plumper, faster blob that would race past mine. Anytime it rained, I'd run to the window in her bedroom and scream with delight. Rain meant we had to stay inside, tucked under a blanket, watching TV on the couch. And if there was lightning or thunder, then I got to sleep in her bed. Sitting on the Reeds' porch, alone with my memories and affection for Tyler, inspired me to give my mom a call and check in with her.

"Hello," she answered. It was only eight o'clock, but I could tell by her voice that I'd woken her up with my call.

"Hi, Mom. I'm so sorry, did I wake you?"

"I just nodded off by the TV. It's been a really crazy day. When I got to the dry cleaners this morning, I caught the two women who work there talking about me. They abruptly stopped chatting as soon as I walked in, and I could tell they'd been whispering about me."

"I'm sure they stop talking to each other anytime a customer walks in, Mom. It's nothing to worry about."

"No, Chloe, this is *big*. Do you get what I'm saying?"

I thought for a moment before responding. "Not really, no. I think maybe you're overreacting. I'm sure they were just talking among themselves and stopped to wait on you. Why would they be talking about you anyway?"

She didn't answer me.

"Mom?"

"Yes?"

"Is everything all right? Is that why your day was so crazy, because of the dry cleaners? I don't think you have anything to worry about. Switch cleaners if they're bothering you."

"I can't just switch cleaners," she said like it was an absurd notion.

"Well, please don't let it bother you. I hate to think of you getting upset about something like that."

"How are you?" she asked.

"Everything's good. The Reeds' son Tyler is here," I said, subconsciously hoping she'd try to pry some information about him from me so that I could talk about him, but she didn't bite.

"That's nice," she said. "I really must be going."

"You sure you're okay, Mom?"

"Yes, but I really need to get off the phone."

"Okay, love you," I said.

I promised to call in a few days, and we hung up. That was the first time in four years that I'd felt the urge to ask her if she'd been drinking, but I didn't.

That night I couldn't sleep. Sometime after midnight, I got out of bed, walked outside to the back patio, grabbed a blanket and headed down the hill to the edge of the lake. I wrapped myself in the blanket and sat down in the grass. The moon was full and made the perfect night-light, illuminating the houses and piers that circled the water.

When I looked to my left, I saw him.

Tyler was standing about twenty yards away, smoking a cigarette. He must've felt my eyes on him because he turned around a second later. Once he noticed me, he flicked his cigarette into the lake and walked over.

"Stand up," he said.

I did as he instructed without hesitation. He smelled like beer, cologne, and tobacco. He studied me for a minute before speaking.

"You're always staring at me," he said with a funny grin.

I didn't respond since it wasn't a question, nor was it untrue. So I just stood there and continued to stare at him.

"Kind of like you are now," he added.

I eventually looked away and took a tiny step backward, which he negated by stepping forward. "Maybe you just think everybody's always staring at you," I said.

"Everybody is always staring at me. Especially you," he said. "I like it."

He took another step closer and erased nearly every bit of space between us. My heart started racing.

"What is it that you want, Chloe?" he asked, gently running a finger from my bare shoulder to my elbow.

I swallowed hard and began to fumble with the bottom edge of my tank top. He knew what I wanted. I wanted him, and he was fully aware of it. Was he taunting me? Making me look like the fool that I was? Clearly, he sensed my ridiculous infatuation with him and intended to act on it.

"You're drunk," I said. I turned and had begun to walk toward the house when he grabbed my hand and spun me around.

"Whoa, hold on, don't run away," he said, pulling me close. Tyler Reed was touching me. No, he was embracing me. My nerves had jumped into the driver's seat of my brain and were spinning the steering wheel in frantic rotations. Not to mention the brakes had gone out on my inhibitions.

Tyler kicked the blanket aside and wrapped his arms around my waist. I placed my palms on his chest, partly in defense…and partly because I could. With his right hand, he swiftly slid the rubber band out of my hair, looking bemused. Then he pulled away, causing my palms to fall off his upper body, and led me by the hand back up to the house. Nervous and eager, I followed him. Obviously.

He dragged me inside and released my hand. I stopped just inside the door and watched him walk over to the couch, where he motioned for me to join him. Neither of us said a word as I sat down next to him. My eyes were fixated on my hands, which I was wringing in my lap, when he leaned over and forced me gently down into the white cushions. I shivered despite the summer heat. His face was only faintly visible from the moonlight filtering through the bay window, and the muscles in his forearms flexed as they embraced me.

"Relax," he said softly.

I laughed nervously through my nose. As if.

"I don't want you to do anything you don't want to do," he whispered.

I nodded.

He slowly removed his shirt, exposing large tattoos on each bicep. One was a laughing skull; the other a ball of fire in the shape of a football. "I've wanted to kiss you since the day I saw you all curled up on my parents' couch. You were so nervous when I woke you up. It was adorable," he whispered. "And your hair…" he paused to drop his face next to my head and sniff before grabbing hold of my hair and pulling gently. "I like your hair down like this." He tugged again, and I moaned in surprise. "You should wear it down more."

I wanted to say something, but not only did I lack the ability to speak at that moment, I had no intention of interrupting him. Tyler Reed, my brass ring of desire, was lying on top of me whispering in my ear and sniffing my hair. I deliberately slowed my breathing down when he told me to relax. I could do this. Granted, all six feet three inches and two hundred–plus pounds of him were on top of me, but I could do this. He thought he knew me. But I was strong, and not as innocent as he believed. I wrapped my arms around his lower back and pulled him into me.

"I want to kiss you, Chloe, and I know you want me to."

I nodded again.

He leaned in and pressed his mouth against mine. Gentle yet deliberate kisses at first, with his lips absorbing every ounce of my desire for him. I nearly fainted when his tongue entered my mouth and slid over the surface of my teeth. His body was heavy and warm, and his hands began to tug harder at the roots of my hair, causing my chin to rise and my mouth to press even harder against his. I sank farther into the cushions, and he straddled me, kissing and stroking my breasts through my T-shirt. I reached up to unbutton his jeans when he stopped me. "No," he said. "Not yet."

I froze, deeply regretting my initiative. Was he rejecting me? Teasing me? Saving me? I was panting so heavily by then that I could hardly hear my own thoughts. I grumbled with disappointment and released my grip on his pants.

"Not yet," he whispered.

If I'd opened my mouth, I would've blurted out how much I wanted him. How desperate I was to have him. It took every ounce of self-restraint to bite my tongue and maintain my dignity. He took my hand and stood, elevating my head from a "Bless Your Heart" needlepoint pillow and my little slice of heaven, then led me to my room off the kitchen.

"Good night," he said and kissed me softly on the lips before shutting the door behind him. I stood alone in my room reeling from withdrawal.

The next morning he was gone.

CHAPTER FOUR

A week passed with no word from or about Tyler. That first day I thought maybe he'd gone for an early morning run. But by noon, I realized he'd taken his car and left. The Reeds returned, and I was thrust back into surrogate mother mode. Although they were technically back, the Reeds were hardly ever around. After the first week, even Sammy and Sarah stopped feigning excitement whenever I'd announce that their parents would be back soon. Dr. and Mrs. Reed had mastered the art of being absent even when they were present.

In the meantime, I was going crazy wondering where Tyler was, and why he'd left so abruptly without saying good-bye. I found his cell number in the Reeds' address book and, against my better judgment, texted him.

Hi, Tyler, this is Chloe's phone, just wanted to make sure you're okay? I sent it two days after he vanished, but got no response.

His disappearing act left me devastated. I was embarrassed and angry by what had happened between us and yet, at the same time, felt almost as if I'd dreamed the entire thing. I wallowed for four days, berating myself for being so stupid and naïve. Vowing never to let Tyler Reed or anyone else use me like that again. Then on Sunday, the start of our third week, I overheard Mrs. Reed talking on the phone.

"That's fine, dear, of course," she said and then paused to listen. "What time tomorrow?" Pause. "Okay, you'll join us for suppah on the Fourth, of course, buh-bye."

As soon as she set the phone down, I walked up and asked her, "Are you having company?"

"Indeed, we are. Tylah will be back tomorrow night. Just in time for the Fourth of July celebration at the Grand Geneva."

I lit up with anticipation. I would finally have my chance to tell him off—if he dared to face me, that is.

"He's bringing his girlfriend, and I expect they'll be here two or three nights," she said.

My light went out. "His girlfriend?" I asked instantly and with such disbelief that it sounded as though I'd never heard the word before.

"That's right. Her name is Sadie Kennedy Stiles, and she's the daughter of one of my sorority sisters, if you can believe it. She goes to school at the University of Wisconsin. Her mother and I were on the homecoming court at Tulane togethah for three years in a row," she said before grabbing her Chanel tennis bag and heading out the door without another word.

The tuna melt I'd had for lunch began to make its way back up my throat. I was trapped in that house, and the worst part was that Tyler knew it. He had me caged up like an animal for his enjoyment, and I had no escape. My temples throbbed with humiliation. I had to find a way out. There was no way I could face him as he paraded another woman into that house.

"Excuse me, Mrs. Reed!" I shouted, running after her down the driveway. "I was actually going to ask you if I could skip dinner with the family tomorrow night. There were a few shops in town that I passed with the kids yesterday that I'd love to check out on my own, if you don't mind?"

She tilted her head and considered my request. "Why, of course, darling, if you'd rathah not spend time with us and the children, you can certainly have some hours to yourself."

"Oh, it's not that I don't want to be with you all…"

"That's quite all right, but you mustn't miss the Fourth of July party."

"Never," I said, relieved that I had successfully excused myself from at least one dinner with Tyler and his girlfriend.

By late afternoon the next day I'd made myself nauseous with dread. I awoke with a searing headache and refused every bit of food that was offered to me. I begged the kids to go horseback riding, but of course they wanted to stick around the house and wait for Tyler to show up. I was down by the lake toweling them off on the dock when Tyler and Sadie arrived around five o'clock.

"Children!" Mrs. Reed shouted from the top of the hill. "Tylah's here!"

And so it began. My attempt to avoid and ignore another human being who was sharing the same confined space with me and six other people. Mission impossible.

Sammy and Sarah shed their red-and-navy-striped Polo beach towels and ran through the grass up to the house. I sat on the dock and must have folded those towels a dozen times each. Rinsed the inner tubes twice, and flipped through a magazine I'd already read. After twenty minutes of killing time, I heard Mrs. Reed again.

"Chloedear, can you pull the Jet Skis in and then get the children dressed for dinner? White outfits, please, and be sure to braid Sarah's hair."

"Sure thing," I yelled back and gave a thumbs-up. I'd never pulled the Jet Skis in by myself before, but was ridiculously thankful for the time-consuming task. Dr. Reed had struggled with them a few times, but I was determined to get it done on my own and to take as long as possible doing it.

The Jet Skis were already tied up near the shore, so I started by backing the trailer down to where they were floating at the water's edge. Once I was close enough, I grabbed the rope attached to the first Jet Ski and began to pull. It didn't budge. I attempted to shift the front end of the Jet Ski by shoving it with my rear end a few times, but it was clearly stuck in some mud or sand. I tried tugging the rope again. Still nothing. I had just paused to wipe the sweat off my forehead when I heard his voice.

"Looks like you could use a hand."

I lifted my head, but did not turn around to face him.

Tyler loaded the first Jet Ski onto the trailer with ease. I watched him for a moment and then swiftly headed up the hill without a word.

I scurried into the kids' room, brushed and braided Sarah's hair, located Sammy's sandals, helped them pick out coordinating white outfits, and then sprinted to my room. Ignoring my beach clothes and damp hair, I grabbed my purse, let Mrs. Reed know I would see her later that evening, and darted out the garage door before Tyler had finished with the Jet Skis.

I strolled the two main streets of downtown Lake Geneva, apprehensive and lonely. I missed being with the kids and hated Tyler for putting me in this situation. I sat for almost an hour on a park bench trying to come up with a reason to leave and never return, but I couldn't do that to Sammy and Sarah. I could say I was sick, but Mrs. Reed would simply insist on having me see a local doctor. I could say my mother was sick, but it was unlikely that Mrs. Reed would consider that a valid reason for her to be burdened with her own children. Or I could stick it out. I had only a week left, and I could suck it up and be the bigger person. Why should I let Tyler get the best of me? Why was I hiding from him when he was the one who should be ashamed of himself?

I drove back to the house, set myself up in the TV room, and waited for the family to arrive home after dinner. At nine o'clock

I heard the garage door open and waited for all of them to walk through the kitchen. I glanced up and saw only Sammy, Sarah, and their parents.

"We missed you, Chloe!" Sarah said, running over to me.

"Aww, I missed you, too, munchkin."

"Did you make the most of your time alone, dear?" Mrs. Reed asked as she plunked her bag down on the kitchen countertop.

"I did, thank you so much."

"Buy anything for yourself?"

"Just a coffee and some fudge," I said.

"Not too much, I hope. I read an article in the *New York Times Magazine* about how chocolate can trigger enzymes that lessen our ability to focus. We wouldn't want to lose our focus…or consume too much chocolate, now would we?" she said batting her lashes.

I nodded and then shook my head.

"Well, you're going to love the Fourth of July event tomorrow night. There'll be fireworks and activities for the kids and a huge outdoor barbecue for all of the guests."

"I'm really looking forward to it," I said as she gathered her needlepoint bag and reading glasses from a basket near the couch. "Where's Tyler?" I asked and nearly slapped my hand over my mouth once I realized my subconscious had failed me.

"He and Sadie went to meet some friends for ice cream."

"Hope it's not chocolate," I said with a wink.

"Indeed," she said. "I expect they'll be home late."

I'll be up, I thought to myself and slid the rubber band out of my hair.

CHAPTER FIVE

I'd fallen asleep on the couch again, and awoke at one thirty in the morning to the sound of keys in the front door. I heard a few snorts and giggles that were followed by some muffled whispers. I sat up and faced them so that I could get my first glimpse of Sadie. She was hanging on his elbow with her purse strap falling off her shoulder. Her pixie haircut was bleached so white that it glowed beneath the two sconces in the foyer. I had to concede that she was attractive—despite the fact that you could see her hair from space. She was very slim, and her petite body was swaying as she leaned into Tyler's side looking up at him.

"Oh, hey, Chloe," Tyler said, averting his eyes.

"Hey." I stood and walked over to where they were standing. Tyler shoved his hands in the front pockets of his jeans and glanced at his feet while I did what I did best—stared at him.

"Sadie, uh, this is Chloe, our summer girl."

She said hello and extended her minuscule Barbie hand, but I pretended not to notice. Instead, I kept my eyes on Tyler. Clearly, their "ice cream" had been spiked.

I took a deep breath like I was about to begin telling them a long story, but then changed my mind. "Good night," I said, smiled at Sadie and walked to my room. I could hear her mutter something that rhymed with *bitch*.

Tyler was sleeping on the pullout couch since Sadie was staying in his room, so I made sure to be up early the next morning. I began the day by unloading the dishwasher and slamming cabinets before sunrise. Mrs. Reed came in after about five minutes of clatter and placed her hand on my shoulder.

"Aren't you a peach, thank you, dear, but Tylah's still sleeping, so why don't you do that later? Dr. Reed and I are meeting some friends for golf today, so we won't be back until before dinner," she told me. "I'll need you to have the kids dressed for the party in their red, white, and blue clothes by five."

"No problem," I said.

"Perhaps you could take them to the resort pool today? I know how much the children would enjoy having lunch by the pool. Unless, of course, there's something else you had in mind. It's up to you."

"No, that's a great idea. I'll take them to the pool. Have a good game," I said, then grabbed a mug of coffee and headed down to the lake. It was barely six thirty in the morning and a murky fog hung over the placid water. I picked up a rock and tossed it in to alert the fish of my presence. My thoughts were a mess. Half of me was determined to find my voice and give Tyler a piece of it, while the other half wallowed in humiliation. What a fool I had been to think he'd be interested in me. I shook my head and took a sip of my coffee. I had to muster the strength to get through the next week. I owed it to the kids and Mrs. Reed not to fall apart. Why should I? Tyler didn't owe me anything. It wasn't like he'd cheated on me. He'd only used me because I let him. It was my fault, and I wasn't going to let it happen again. Just then a rock sailed over my head and ripped through the glassy water in front of me. I turned around to see Tyler standing barefoot in the dewy grass in a white T-shirt and sweatpants, with spiky bed-hair. He looked beautiful, and the sight of him made my chest hurt.

I turned back around.

"I'm so sorry," he said from behind me. His voice was low and tired.

I nodded.

"I mean it, Chloe."

I nodded again and felt tears pooling in my eyes. *Noooo! You mustn't break!* I told myself. "It's fine," I whispered loud enough for him to hear.

"No, it's not. I…"

"Ty-lah!" Mrs. Reed shouted from the house. "Your father asked you to move your car, now! For heaven's sake, he's waitin' on you."

I spoke before Tyler could finish his sentence. "Just go," I said. And he did.

I tried calling my mom again that morning but there was no answer.

I was cleaning up the dishes from the kids' breakfast when I overheard Tyler in the TV room telling Sammy that he and Sadie were going on a boat ride with some friends. I stayed in the kitchen until they left the house, and then took the kids to the pool at the Grand Geneva, which was a ten-minute drive from the Reeds' house. We sat in our towels and wet bathing suits and ordered club sandwiches to be brought to our chairs. Then we came up with a contest to see who could stay in the hot tub the longest without passing out. After that we dove for quarters and golf balls in the shallow end before ordering virgin daiquiris and frozen chocolate-covered bananas for dessert. Once they were good and waterlogged, we headed home to dress for dinner. I was putting a load of laundry in the machine when Sadie approached me.

"Yay! I'm so glad you're doing laundry. Can I throw these in too?" she asked, holding out a pile of pink clothes to me.

"Sure," I said, lifting the lid of the washer for her to toss her stuff in.

"Thanks. Just let me know when they're done," she said.

I sneered at her, which wasn't really fair, but I didn't care. "When the dryer stops running is when they'll be done," I informed her.

She lifted her chin to indicate she understood.

The five of us were forced to share a car on the way back to the Grand Geneva to meet Dr. and Mrs. Reed for the Fourth of July festivities. Tyler and Sadie sat in the front, and the kids and I sat in the back. Twice, Tyler's eyes connected with mine in the rearview mirror.

We spun through the revolving door of the lobby and were presented with red, white, and blue beads that we were to hang around our necks. We then walked through the expansive lobby area, down three steps, and outside onto the hotel's grand patio where over a hundred families had gathered to celebrate the holiday and wait for the fireworks to light up the sky over the golf course. We located Dr. and Mrs. Reed at a large round table that had been reserved for all of us. Tyler sat directly across from me with Sadie on his right, and I sat between the kids. As soon as they started fidgeting, I reached in my bag and handed them each their own iTouch. As they went into zone-out mode, I leaned over and feigned interest in whatever game they were playing. Meanwhile, Tyler and Sadie participated in the adult conversation with his parents. My neck was stiff, and my palms were sweaty. I was concentrating so hard on not thinking about him, that he was all I could think about.

I excused myself to the bathroom, reentered the main building, and walked quickly down a long hallway leading to an empty ballroom. I propped myself up against a wall and tilted my head up to the ceiling. I closed my eyes and took a few deep, deliberate breaths. Tyler was standing in front of me when I opened my eyes.

"Oh my God, what the hell, Tyler?"

"What are you doing back here?"

"Trying to get away from you for two minutes," I snapped.

He took a step closer, and I turned my gaze toward the corridor to make sure no one was stomping in after him.

"Listen," he started, taking hold of my right hand. "I want to talk to you."

I yanked my hand away from his. "What is there to talk about? You are insane; it's that simple. I have a few more days here with your family, and then I get to go home and never have to see or think about you again. So please leave me alone and let me do my job and get through this without you or Tinker Bell getting in my way."

He leaned forward until his shirt collar was less than an inch away from my mouth. I swallowed what little saliva I had left in my dehydrated throat. "Please, Tyler," I whispered, eyes cast downward. "Please just leave me alone."

His breath was warm against my ear when he spoke. "I want to talk to you. I realize this is a bad time. I'll come find you later," he said and walked away.

I exhaled and stood there, wishing he would come back and give me all of his attention again.

Before walking back to the table, I filled two plates with hot-dogs and potato chips for the kids. After dinner, Sammy, Sarah, and I grabbed the blanket we'd brought and went to claim our spot on the grass for the fireworks show while the Reeds went to join their friends at the bar. Tyler and Sadie came over to where we were sitting to say good-bye.

"No!" Sarah scolded him. "You have to stay for the show; that's why we're here, Ty."

Tyler glanced at Sadie, whose expression indicated she had no intention of spending one more minute with his family.

"Sorry, squirt, we're going to meet some friends in town."

"You suck," Sammy said before turning his attention back to his handheld device.

I tried not to smile.

Once the sun went down, the kids and I snuggled together and ooh'd and aah'd as a kaleidoscope of lights burst across the night sky. We each picked our favorite fireworks. Mine were the ones that exploded into starry glitter after bursting onto the dark canvas. Sammy liked the ones that started out like a snake, and Sarah preferred the finale to anything else. After the show, I dragged the two exhausted, saccharin-filled kids through the lobby bar like rag dolls in search of their parents. It was time to get them to bed. When I found Dr. Reed, he handed me his keys, said they'd get a ride back with friends, and dismissed me by turning his back on us.

I almost never had any direct contact with Dr. Reed, so I cleared my throat before speaking. "Excuse me, Mr., I mean, Dr. Reed? Sarah wanted to say good night to her mom, do you know where she is?" I asked him.

"Outside with the other women," he said over his shoulder.

"Okay, thank you."

Sarah overheard her father and instantly began whining at the thought of traipsing back outside through the crowd to find her mother. "I don't want to go out there; you go get her, Chloe," she said defiantly and refused to move.

I leaned in close to her since we were standing next to Dr. Reed and three other brooding men holding cigars and brandy snifters. "It'll just take a sec, okay? We'll go back outside, say good-bye, and then go home."

"No! We were just out there!"

I knelt before her. "Sarah, you're too old to be acting like this. Let's just go quickly, and the sooner we find her, the sooner we can head home," I said, pleading with my eyes and my best everything-will-be-fine smile.

"Do. You. Mind?" I heard Dr. Reed say above me.

I could tell by his eyes that he was pissed. I stood up, embarrassed. "I'm so sorry. They wanted to say good-bye to Mrs. Reed…"

"I don't care, just get them out of here."

I nodded and grabbed Sarah's hand. "Yes, of course, I'm so sorry."

Once we were back home, I calmed the kids down with Swedish Fish and two episodes of *The Simpsons,* and then put them to bed. Mrs. Reed had come home in time to say good night to them and asked me why we'd left without saying good-bye. Once Sammy and Sarah were asleep, I found Mrs. Reed reading out on the patio. I stuck my head out to let her know I was going to bed.

"Come sit for a moment," she said.

I hesitated and then slid into a nearby wicker loveseat adorned with an "I'd Rather Be Golfing" pillow.

"I just wanted to say what a wonderful help you've been this summer, Chloe. We're sure going to miss you next year," she said.

"Thank you. I'm going to miss the kids a ton. You'll have to promise to e-mail me lots of pictures."

"Of course, dear," she said, then closed her book in her lap and smoothed the shiny jacket with her French-manicured fingers. "I expect Tylah will miss you too."

My smile faded. I raised my eyebrows and met her gaze. "Um, yeah, it's been great to get to know him better. I mean, we really haven't spent much time together, but you all have been so kind and generous," I said.

"He's a wonderful boy, Tylah. So talented and charming."

I nodded in agreement.

"He's worked so vereh hard to get where he is. We wouldn't want anyone or anything to get in his way or hinder his chances in the draft. Would *we?*"

I shook my head.

"He's always been surrounded by people of superior caliber. I know you wouldn't want him exposed to any unsavory elements," she lowered her chin. "I'm sure your mother would agree."

I sat as though frozen, recalling the one time that my mother had fallen off the wagon. It had been a Friday night during the summer before my junior year of college, and I'd been at the Reeds' house watching the twins. I got a call from our neighbor, saying that my mom was sitting in her car in our driveway with her head on the steering wheel. My neighbor had tapped on the window, but Mom only turned her head. Frantic, I called Mrs. Reed's cell phone, but she never answered, so I had to take Sammy and Sarah with me in their pajamas to unlock the car and drag my poor mother to bed. Apparently, she was about to drive to the 7-Eleven to get a pack of lighters when she passed out. By the time I drove the kids back, the Reeds were home and panicked. I explained the situation to Mrs. Reed and sat through an hour of questions and insults that she cleverly masked behind a false façade of concern.

"Naturally, we all want what's best for him. For Tylah to stay focused and free of any unnecessary distractions. But I know you're far too busy with your duties here to get in his way," she concluded.

I refocused my gaze on her. Her eyes had narrowed slightly, but she hadn't lost her signature, patronizing grin. "I don't understand," I spoke with trepidation. "He's with Sadie," I said, feeling the need to identify the real meaning behind her lecture.

She continued, ignoring my segue. "He has a big future ahead of him. There are many people counting on him, and he has many expectations for himself, of course."

I nodded again, but she wasn't done.

"I know how he is, how easily he can lose sight of things if he doesn't stay focused. The draft is next year, and there's a lot riding on his commitment to the team this fall. It's all so *vereh* exciting for him," she went on. "*We* don't want to see him get distracted," she cautioned me, lashes fluttering.

Maybe she needed to put her glasses back on. Did she think Sadie was seated across from her? No, there was no way to mistake that Lite-Brite head for anyone else. I shifted uncomfortably in my seat, causing the wicker to crackle and calling attention to the awkward silence. *Best to ride the wave of denial,* I thought. "Oh my gosh, no, Mrs. Reed, it's not like that between Tyler and me," I said, waving my hands like I was swatting away fruit flies. And it wasn't. Maybe if she actually knew how cruel he'd been to me, she'd be acting a little more sympathetic rather than staring at me like I'd taken a blowtorch to her needlepoint bag. "I'm so sorry if you got that impression."

"I know we both want what's best for Tyler," she said, eyebrows raised.

I swallowed the lump in my throat. "Indeed," I answered.

She smiled. I think.

After a few seconds, I realized she'd said her piece and was dismissing me. I pressed my palms together. "Thanks again for everything. The kids and I had a lot of fun tonight."

"Good night, dear," she said in a cryptically cheerful tone as I stood up and walked away.

CHAPTER SIX

I was shaking when I got to my room. I shut the door and slid to the floor with my back against it. Only a few days left. I clasped my hands behind my head and massaged the back of my neck while I replayed the events of the evening in my mind. Mrs. Reed had just chastised me for distracting her son, when all the while Tyler was the one ambushing me and derailing *my* focus. I wished I wasn't so desperate to know what he wanted to say to me, but I was. His eyes were all over me at dinner, and based on my little chat with Mrs. Reed just then, I wasn't the only one who'd noticed. Every time I looked up from my plate, I could feel his eyes on me. However, I'd only dared to meet his gaze twice.

I shook off my conversation with his mother and tried to regain my composure. It was not my responsibility to defend myself to her. I'd done nothing but take exceptional care of her children that summer while she played golf and took mint-julep-induced naps every afternoon. I put my pajamas on and got into bed. As soon as I leaned back, I heard the sound of paper crinkling beneath my pillow. I sat up, lifted the pillow, and found a piece of notebook paper folded in half.

Meet me at the lake at midnight.

A shiver shot through me and landed in my stomach. I ran my finger over the words he'd scribbled in blue ballpoint pen and then looked at the clock. A quarter to eleven.

I smiled and studied the note for a few seconds longer; then I folded it back up and placed it at the bottom of my duffel bag near the closet.

I rolled my eyes and sighed. I'd already let Tyler inside my head farther than he deserved. Was I willing to do it again? I was trying to be content with the memories of the couple nights we'd shared together. A simple summer fling that flared up and then died out just as quickly. Big deal, so I didn't get the guy. I had more important things to think about, including managing *my own* expectations. He wasn't the only one who didn't need any distractions.

I got back into bed and wrapped myself beneath the white sheets. Everything in the room was white down to the digital clock, which played mind games with me every time the illuminated numbers changed.

Eleven o'clock. *Goddamn it. Would he be waiting down there for me? I hated to be rude and ignore him. Not that I owed him any sort of courtesy given his behavior.*

Eleven fifteen. *I should be the bigger person and just go down there and tell him to "focus" his attention elsewhere.* Yawn.

Eleven thirty. *I hated to leave him wondering if I was going to show up or not.* Double yawn.

At 12:20 a.m. I woke up and leaped out of bed like a jack-in-the-box. My body shook from suddenly disrupting its brief slumber. I grabbed a cardigan, slipped on my flip-flops, and walked gingerly through the kitchen and outside. He was there. That massive shadowy figure sitting down at the end of the dock could only belong to one person. I closed the screen door behind me slowly so as not to rouse the rusty hinges. If I'd had any intention of blowing him off, ignoring his handwritten distraction, and moving on with my life, there was no trace of that reasoning as I skipped down the hill and padded toward him with anticipation. Once again the moon was full. He stood when he heard my flip-flops slap against the wood surface of the dock.

"I thought maybe you were playing hard to get," he said.

"I fell asleep."

He smiled and took my hands in his. "Are you nervous?" he asked.

"No," I lied.

He ran his thumb over my knuckles. "I know you asked me to leave you alone, but I felt that I owed you an explanation and an apology," he said. "I was planning to bring Sadie up all along. What I hadn't planned on was you."

I looked up at him, and our eyes clicked like magnets in the dim light of the midnight sky. *I'm the crazy one*, I thought to myself. I was falling in love with this boy I barely knew…and boy, was I in trouble. All I could concentrate on was the pattern of his thumb stroking the back of my hand like a pendulum sending shock waves from my wrist to my heart.

"When I heard you were going to be here with the kids this summer, I changed my initial plans and decided to come a week earlier, alone."

The cheetah.

He continued. "I know a lot about you, Chloe. My mother talks about you all the time. How sweet you are, how smart you are, how strong and determined you are. I had to find out for myself."

The gazelle.

"And?" I said.

"And she was right for once. But she hadn't mentioned how pretty you are," he said. "I enjoy watching you play in the lake with the kids. You always take a few extra seconds to let your hair down and adjust your suit before diving in the water."

"So you've been staring at *me*?" I smiled.

"And those legs of yours." He paused and looked down. "Maybe I'm selfish, but Mom—and you—had me intrigued," he said, taking a step closer. He wrapped his arms around me and rested them on my behind. His shoulders were back, and his head was tilted forward gazing down at me. All I had to do was lift my chin and we would kiss. I had his undivided attention, and his lips could be mine again for a moment. It was my move, but I couldn't bring myself to do it.

I averted my eyes. "I may be all of those things, but I'm also afraid," I said. "I'm a little out of my comfort zone with you."

"What are you afraid of?"

"Of being naïve, of looking stupid, of getting hurt."

He bent down to my ear and whispered. "I don't want to hurt you. I want to kiss you."

My best friend, Grace, used to tell me I had no filter when it came to expressing something I felt passionately about. That I never possessed the ability to repress my thoughts or emotions, and I could tell that lack of restraint was about to become an embarrassing problem.

"I want to kiss you, too, Tyler. I've wanted to kiss you since before I met you." I paused. "But I know how this is going to end. I'll be left wanting more—more than you can give, most likely—and you'll be with Sadie by the time the sun comes up."

He shook his head. "Sadie and I are just friends."

"Just friends? It seems like more than that to me. Does Sadie know how you feel?"

"Yes."

"Does your mother?" I asked.

"Sadie and I hang out, that's all."

"Well, you should probably continue 'hanging out' with her since she's your guest and your mother has your china pattern picked out already."

"Then why did you come down here?"

I snorted with laughter. "Because I wanted to, because..." *Don't say it!* "Because I can't resist you, and you know it." *Blabbering fool.*

Tyler's hands released their grip on me and found their way behind my neck. He cradled my head and pulled my mouth onto his tongue in one seamless motion. His fingertips pressed into my skin and then moved to my loose hair where he grabbed the roots and pulled back, forcing my tongue farther down his throat. He had just started to guide my body to the ground when we heard the screen door slam above us.

CHAPTER SEVEN

Dixie Reed stood just outside the porch with her arms crossed. The silhouette of her robe like a long black cape wafting behind her.

"Fuck," Tyler whispered when he saw her.

"Oh my God," I said softly. "Is there any possible way she doesn't see me?"

"Nope."

"I'm so screwed," I said with my hand over my mouth in dismay.

Tyler laughed and held my other hand. "Relax, I'll handle it."

"No, you won't. She literally just warned me about you."

He blinked. "She what?" Tyler turned his face away from the house and back to me.

"She...nothing," I said. "Let's just get out of here." I began to walk up the dock toward the grass when Mrs. Reed turned and went inside. There was nothing she needed to say. She was clearly aware that her presence was enough of a shakedown. I breathed a microscopic sigh of relief, but it didn't last long.

Tyler latched onto my bicep with his right hand. "What do you mean she warned you about me?"

I threw my hands up and then waved at the air between us. "This, Tyler, she cautioned me about this. About becoming a distraction for you...as if I'd been doing anything to get in *your* way. Maybe she was trying to do a good thing by telling me to leave you alone, you know?" I thought for a second. "Maybe she's attempting to protect both of us," I said, though I doubted she had my best interests in mind when she'd told me to stay away from him.

He moved his face closer to mine. His eyes looked liked his father's had in the bar only a few hours earlier. He was pissed. "I don't need any protecting and neither do you. Especially from her. You're a big girl, aren't you?" He asked as he latched his arm around my waist.

I nodded like a child.

"So why is she getting involved? She and my father need to stay the hell out of my life."

I had no answer for him. All I could think was that the screen door was going to fly open again, and this time that ninety-pound glow-in-the-dark Q-tip would be standing there holding a pair of shearing scissors with my hair's name on it.

Tyler wrenched my hand away from my side and placed it on the scar above his eye. "You wanted to know how I got this," he snapped. "Ask me again!"

I shook my head no.

"Ask me, Chloe."

I looked at the scar and then into his eyes.

"Ask me," he repeated.

"Where did you get it?"

"I got it from him." He pointed vaguely toward the house. "He threw a frozen can of Red Bull at my head. The edge of the lid landed right here, just above my eye, and sliced open my skin an inch wide," Tyler said. "I fumbled a snap that day."

I sighed.

"You want to know about the two on my back?"

I shook my head. "I need to go. This is crazy," I said softly, trying to free myself from his grip. My eyes and cheeks were burning. "Please, Tyler, I don't know what you want from me, and I don't care. I need to go inside and figure out how I'm going to face your mother in the morning, and you need to do the same with Sadie. I'm willing to take the blame for all of this because I should have known better. Whether you do or not, I *do* know better. I never should've let myself get involved. I never should've put myself in a position where people could get hurt, especially me. I'm sorry about your dad, I really am, but it sounds like we both have enough of our own problems. There's no sense in upsetting everyone to try and make this work. I don't think you have a clue as to what you want, and I can't be tossed around while you figure it out," I said, and he released me.

"I think it's you that I want, Chloe."

"You think, but you don't know." My eyes were shifting from him to the house. "And you're being selfish and unrealistic. We're both being unrealistic. Your girlfriend is asleep in the house for God's sake, and I'm going to law school in a few weeks." I sighed. "I like you, Tyler, you know I do. I've liked you for so long, and wanted this so badly that I'd actually convinced myself that you were capable of feeling the same way about me. Only I just let my infatuation for you go too far—and I thought it might end like this."

He bit his bottom lip and furrowed his brow. "You think you know me, but you don't," he began, teeth clenched. "And you think you *know better*, but you obviously don't. You're no different than anyone else. You bought into the same fantasy everyone else does, so don't beat yourself up about it." He shook his head, briefly pointing a finger at me. "Only I expected you to be different."

I threw my hands up and then crossed my arms. "That's not fair, and you know it. What on earth would you *expect* me to do? You get close to me, seduce me, fool around with me…and then vanish only to reappear with Sadie at your side. Who, by the way, is still here!" I reminded him. "Honestly, Tyler, are you so self-centered that you have no concern for either of us?"

He thrust his head back and ran his fingers through his hair. "I'm sorry," he said. "I left you that note because I wanted to apologize, and I did. I'm not sure how I let things get out of control between us, but my feelings for you are real." He grabbed my elbows in a vice grip. "I like you, a lot, and I promise I wasn't using you," he said and gently shook me before letting go and allowing the blood to flow freely again through my arms. "I'm the asshole."

I sighed heavily and then ran up the hill before he could talk me out of it. Which he easily could have done.

I was ashamed of myself and on the verge of tears when I returned to my room. My only consolation was that we were leaving Lake Geneva in a few days. I climbed under the covers and wiped my useless tears away. Tyler would head back to Notre Dame for preseason training soon, and I would start law school and leave him and the Reed family behind me once and for all.

CHAPTER EIGHT

The next morning was painful. Mrs. Reed, who usually had a daily tee time at eight o'clock, was still seated at the breakfast table with the kids and me at nine. She was quiet in her robe, scrolling through her phone and sipping her green tea while Sammy and Sarah debated how they wanted to spend their day.

"We could have lunch at the place with the chili cheese fries?" Sarah suggested.

"Or we could go to the pool and have daiquiris again?" Sammy said.

"Nonalcoholic, of course," I mumbled.

Tyler sauntered in during our discussion and grabbed the orange juice from the fridge.

"Tyler, can you come to the pool with us today?" Sammy asked excitedly.

Mrs. Reed shot me a look, and then turned to face Tyler. He looked at her and answered Sammy.

"Sure, squirt," he said.

I gulped.

Mrs. Reed set her phone down on the table. "Why don't you take Sadie to play tennis instead," she suggested. "I'm sure she would love to see the courts, and then you two can have lunch at the club. I bet she would enjoy the Cobb salad; they use duck bacon. I'll call and reserve a table for you."

"The pool's fine," Tyler told her.

"Yay!" Sammy cheered. "Can you throw me in?"

Before Tyler could answer, Mrs. Reed spoke again. "Of course, well, you won't be needing Chloe then. You and Sadie can take the children, and she and I will stay here and organize my closet. I'm in such a state over getting everything ready before we leave, and I would be so grateful for the help," she said, and then looked my way. "Could I trouble you for some help, Chloedear?"

I'd rather stick your antique needle threader in my eye. "Of course," I said.

Sadie bounced in just as Tyler was about to speak.

"I'm sure Chloe's really dying to organize your shit, Mom. But I do need her there because Sadie and I are only going to stay for an hour or so. We're meeting some people for a late lunch at Popeye's."

Popeye's was a Lake Geneva institution that had been around for over forty years. It sat at the edge of the lake in the center of town and was known for a large outdoor deck and the fried perch.

"Well, I just read an article in *Country Living* that said too much fried food can lead to permanent belly fat," Mrs. Reed added.

My head whipped back and forth between Tyler and his mother as they decided my fate.

"I can help organize!" Sadie chirped. "I love stuff like that."

I lifted a piece of toast to my mouth in hopes of suppressing my grin.

Mrs. Reed smiled at her. "You all go have fun and do what you like," she said and retreated to her bedroom.

"What time are you going to the pool?" Tyler asked me.

"We're leaving in about half an hour."

He chugged his juice, leaving the empty glass on the counter next to the sink. "See you there," he said and walked out of the kitchen with Sadie in tow.

It was eleven o'clock by the time Tyler waltzed out onto the pool deck alone. Heads turned as he passed. It was hard for anyone not to stare at a real-life Adonis, especially one who looked every bit the celebrated college quarterback that Tyler did. He wore striped board shorts, a fitted heather gray T-shirt, Ray-Ban sunglasses, and a small, white towel draped loosely over his shoulders. The kids and I were in the shallow end having an underwater breath-holding contest when he shed his shirt and flip-flops and jumped in. As soon as he was in the water, throwing the twins in the air as easily as if they were pizza dough, I retreated to my deck chair. Behind my sunglasses I watched the joy on their faces as he wrestled and roughhoused with them for nearly an hour. No one was immune to his charm. That day in the pool, the center of Tyler's attention, the kids were the happiest I'd seen them all summer. And I knew exactly how they felt.

When Tyler attempted to exit the pool, they clung to his back like little monkeys, and he had to shake them off. He wiped his face with a towel and sat down on the chair next to mine, elbows resting on his knees.

"I don't know how you do it all day, every day with them. That was exhausting," he said, his wet hair slicked back, eyes squinting toward the sun.

I laughed. "Trust me, I'm not nearly that much fun. I throw coins in the pool, that's about the extent of it."

He sniffed. "Look, Chloe, I'm leaving today after lunch to drive Sadie back to Milwaukee. Then I'm heading to Glenview for a couple nights before I have to go back to school for some preseason shit."

"Where is she?" I asked.

"Getting her nails done."

I nodded slightly. "You can do better than her."

"Can I?" He smiled. "Hot law student better?"

"Maybe," I said.

He looked away for a moment before resuming eye contact with me. There was a sense of uncertainty between us. I could feel it zapping my brain, daring me to say something meaningful. I gazed into his eyes with the same challenge. *Tell me something, Tyler. Tell me what I want to hear.*

"So I guess this is it," he said. "I'll see ya around."

I exhaled. "I guess so." I angled my head and smiled. "Have a safe trip, Ty."

Tyler leaned in and gave me a kiss on the cheek that lasted a beat longer than a peck. I gently touched his damp shoulder before he pulled away and stood. Heads turned once more as he walked away. I heard my mother's voice as he strode out of my life, "You can't always get what you want."

Tyler's departure brought out my least favorite emotion: hopelessness. Just like when my mom came back from rehab. A low-grade sense of despair that was out of my control. I knew there was a connection between us, but not much I could do to save it if he was just going to walk away.

By the time the kids and I arrived back at the house, tired and sunburned, Tyler and Sadie were gone. The house felt empty and cold, devoid of excitement. I began to pack the kids' clothes and toys into large Rubbermaid containers, which would be picked up by a freight company that Monday. I left out only what they'd need to get through the next couple of days. Sarah and I were in the kids' room folding her T-shirts when Mrs. Reed interrupted us. The tension between us had dissipated because she was a master at putting on a happy face and ignoring situations that gave her displeasure.

"Dr. Reed has been called in for an emergency at the hospital, so he and I are going to be heading home this evening," she said. "And we won't be coming back."

"Oh?" I asked, confused.

She leaned on the doorframe, her hands folded behind her back. Sarah went about her business, unconcerned with her mother's schedule. "Since we were planning on closing up the house and leaving in two days anyway, Dr. Reed suggested that you stay here with the kids. Someone needs to meet the freight company on Monday with our things, and then you can drive Sammy and Sarah home in the Jeep afterward."

Hallelujah. I couldn't have been happier to learn of the revised Reed-free plan and the chance to ride out my last couple of days without those two.

"Of course, it's my pleasure. We'll be just fine," I reassured her, trying to contain my glee. "Don't worry about a thing; in fact, I can even go through your closet for you and get your things organized into bins with my little helper here," I said, patting Sarah on the head.

"Wonderful, thank you," she said and pulled a small wrapped gift out from behind her back. "I have a little something for you."

Sarah jumped up to grab it from her and ran it over to me.

"That's so nice, thank you. You didn't have to get me anything."

"Open it!" Sarah urged.

The package was small and soft and felt like a gerbil covered in wrapping paper. I tore through the paper and discovered a tiny needlepoint pillow with a ribbon sewn to the top; the message read, "Find Your Bliss."

Anywhere but here, I thought to myself.

"Find. Your. Bliss," Sarah read aloud over my shoulder.

"You can hang it on your door handle," Mrs. Reed said, stating the obvious.

"That was so kind of you to make this for me, thank you so much."

The next morning, the kids and I went into town, rented bikes, and rode around the lake. We had a late lunch consisting of gelato, homemade fudge, and Frappuccinos. Afterward, we went back to the house and watched a movie while I braided Sarah's hair into cornrows. When we woke up on Saturday, I made toast and scrambled eggs loaded with cheddar cheese and bacon bits, and we took our plates down to the dock and threw bread crumbs into the water. Sammy had wanted to have breakfast with the fish before we left. I did my best to revel in my carefree state of mind those last few days, knowing that the pressures of law school would soon consume my life, but being in that house only reminded me of being with Tyler. I missed seeing him walk through the front door and throw himself onto the couch. I missed him tossing the kids in the air. I missed the giddy anticipation of seeing him turn a corner and smile when he saw me. I missed our late-night talks and basking in his undivided attention. I was surprised by just how much I missed him in only a few short hours.

The kids and I whiled away most of that afternoon digging for worms and trying to catch one of our breakfast guests with Dr. Reed's dusty fishing poles from the garage. After dinner in town, we came home and revived our fishing efforts to no avail until the sun went down. Sammy was "head baiter" since I had little interest in holding a worm, let alone piercing one.

"Tomorrow's our last night here, so why don't we decide what we want to do?" I asked them.

"I want to do a night swim at the Grand Geneva; you promised we could do that before we go," Sarah reminded me.

"Is that okay with you, Sammy?" I asked him.

"That's fine."

"What about horseback riding? Anyone want to do that tomorrow? We could go for a ride in the afternoon since the stables are near the resort, and then go to the pool afterward," I suggested.

Sarah nodded.

We packed up the fishing gear, and I let them spend a half hour in bed with their handheld video games while I sat and read my book on the floor of their bedroom. At nine thirty I said good night, turned off the lights, and gently closed the door on my way out.

When I turned around, Tyler was standing right in front of me.

CHAPTER NINE

He placed his hand over my mouth as I gasped with raw fear, sparing the kids the terror of hearing me scream. My eyes were still wide as he pulled his hand away and placed a finger in front of his lips. "Shhhh."

My heart was racing as I followed him down the hall, through the den, and into the kitchen trying to gather my thoughts and make sense of what was happening. Before I could speak, he pressed my back up against the counter and kissed me on the mouth.

"Are you crazy?!" I said, pushing him away. "You scared the shit out of me. I could've had a heart attack."

"You look like you're in pretty good shape to me," he said, beaming wickedly.

I took a deep breath and shook my head at him, but couldn't help from smiling. "What are you doing here?" I asked.

He stepped forward, wrapped his arms around me, and squeezed. A full-on emotion-filled embrace. No kiss, no wandering hands—just pure, unadulterated intimacy. I rested my cheek on his chest, and we stood there for what seemed like a lifetime. He was back. Just when I'd resigned myself to missing him forever, he was back in my arms, and until that moment, I had no idea it was possible to feel so happy.

Tyler was the first to pull away. "I have something for you," he said and grabbed a plastic bag from the breakfast table.

"What's this?"

"Open it."

I untied the handles and pulled out a Notre Dame football jersey and pennant.

"You're a fan now," he said. "It's official."

I hugged him again.

Tyler took the bag and its contents from me and placed them back on the table. Then he took my hand and led me down to the lake where we sat on the lawn and looked up at the sky and discussed star formations like two little kids. He leaned in and placed a hand on my face and then kissed me. His touch was gentle and sweet, yet demanding. He then laid me down in the grass and explored every inch of my body under the moonlight, desperate to discover every curve. He kissed the soft pillow of skin behind my knees while mumbling something about my legs. His mouth traced the small of my back. His thumbs pressed into the base of my neck, and we made love on the hill for hours. I could not get enough of him. His smell, his skin, his touch. My body ached for him if he pulled away for even one second. Around three o'clock in the morning, we woke up naked and cold, grabbed our clothes, and scurried into the house. Tyler was unable to keep his hands off me as I awkwardly attempted to dress in front of him on the dark back porch.

"What are we going to tell the kids?" I asked as he was inhaling my hair from behind.

"About what?"

"About why you're back here, you fool."

"They don't give a shit. Tell them I came back to toss them around the pool one more time," he said.

I smiled, thinking about how much joy that simple gesture would bring them. "What about your mother?" I asked, my smile fading. "I'm guessing you know that your parents are gone."

He backed away and threw himself onto the couch. "Whatever," he said with a wave of his hand. "I'll tell her I forgot something and decided to stay the night."

I sighed and did my best to convince myself that she was his problem, not mine.

"Come over here," Tyler said.

I walked over and sat on his lap. We kissed on the couch for another hour before falling asleep.

"Tyler?"

"Chloe?"

"Ty?"

"Chloe?"

"Ty!"

Sammy and Sarah were standing in front of the couch, repeating our names.

"Holy shit," Tyler mumbled. "What time is it?"

"Oh my God!" I yelled like my hair was on fire. "Oh my God, I'm so sorry. We were up late last night talking because Tyler forgot something and came in the middle of the night to get it, and we were totally just talking on the couch, and he just decided to stay, you know, because it was so late and he didn't want to get back in the car when it was super dark because, you know, how I'm always saying how dangerous it is to drive late at night and guess what: Tyler is going to throw you in the pool today!"

The three of them were staring at me like—well, like my hair was on fire. Tyler burst out laughing, and I slapped him angrily and avoided making eye contact with the kids.

"Who wants pancakes?" I asked no one in particular and headed for the kitchen.

The four of us spent the day at the pool, and Mrs. Reed never bothered to check in, so I never had to lie to her about anything. Tyler picked up some steaks in town and barbecued them for dinner. Afterward, we made ice-cream sundaes and put a movie on for the kids.

"Tyler and I are going down to the dock," I told the two poltergeist-like figures transfixed in front of the TV. Sarah nodded, thankfully.

Tyler was waiting for me with two beers.

"What are you going to tell your mom?" I asked as I joined him on the edge of the dock with our legs swinging over the side.

"Nothing."

"Surely you don't think those two are going to keep quiet about you coming back here," I said, pointing up at the house with my thumb.

"I'm not worried about it."

I shrugged. "Well, as your most ardent new fan, I'm certainly glad you came back."

"Me too," he said and reached over and swept some of my hair from my shoulder.

I thought about broaching the dreaded "what are you thinking" conversation, but I knew better than that. Tyler was going back to Notre Dame and likely entering the NFL draft. He would have legions of commitments and women and responsibilities that would overshadow anything that had happened between us over the summer. And me, I was heading off to law school, well aware of the demands that were ahead of me. I wanted to ask him if he would be thinking about me half as much as I'd be thinking about him, but I didn't want to go down that path, because what good could come of it? I was glad to have him back even for a short time. And while

I may have been victim to his charms, I was no victim. I'd gotten exactly what I wanted.

"Sadie made it back okay?" I asked.

"I don't want to talk about Sadie."

"That's fine, but despite all signs to the contrary, I do have somewhat of a conscience, and I don't want to get between you two," I said, lying blatantly. I wanted badly to get between them, but I was more interested in getting him to open up to me.

"It's not what you think; there's really nothing between us. She's just a girl."

"What am I?"

He leaned to his side and ran a hand through my hair. "You're a woman," he said and then kissed my ear and left his mouth there. "A gorgeous, smart, fucking sexy-ass woman."

I curled my shoulder to my ear and smiled. "Flattery will get you everywhere."

Tyler wrapped his arm around my shoulders and placed his lips atop my head. He stayed there for a long time before speaking. "I'm going to miss you. I'm going to miss all of this. Being up here with you is like another life."

The freight company arrived the next day as scheduled and loaded up the truck with various bins, duffel bags, and sporting goods. Tyler supervised that activity while the kids and I packed up the Jeep with snacks and a few remaining possessions before the sky opened up and it started to pour. Tyler quickly hugged the kids and then embraced me after they'd climbed into the car. Our conversation was rushed due to the rain, so I jumped in and opened the window halfway to say good-bye.

"I'll call you," he said, shoulders hunched, water dripping from the rim of his baseball hat.

I placed my palm on the window and nodded. Tyler ran to his car and waved before driving away. The fear of never seeing him again was debilitating.

I drove the kids home in silence, thanks to the portable DVD player, but my mind was exploding with countless memories of my time with Tyler at the lake. My summer had begun with very few expectations other than relaxing and spending time with the kids, but my priorities had taken a drastic turn once Tyler became part of the equation. I shook my head at the thought of how quickly my plans for a quiet, stress-free summer had turned into such an emotional maelstrom. My heart ached as I wondered if he was disappearing from my life all over again.

I dropped the kids off at their house around noon, hugging them until they begged me to stop, and managed to get out of there before Sammy announced Tyler's return to the lake.

The real drama began when I walked through my own front door and found my mother facedown on the garage floor.

CHAPTER TEN

She lifted her head from a huddled position on the cement ledge in front of her car with a Diet Coke in one hand and a cigarette in the other. She stood up as soon as she saw me, arms flailing, eyes glassy and wild. "Don't tell them I'm in here," she snapped angrily. "Go back inside, Chloe!"

I looked over my shoulder and then back at her. "Mom, are you okay? Don't tell *who* you're in here. What is going on?" I asked, frightened, and tried to grab hold of her arm.

"Would you be quiet already? They're going to find me!"

I jerked my head around quickly and studied the garage. It was empty and stifling from cigarette smoke. I needed to get her out of there. I lowered my voice and got close enough to smell her breath. Nothing. "Mom," I began cautiously. "Can we please go inside and talk about this? You're scaring me."

"If we go in the house, they'll see us through the front window."

"Who will see us?" I asked.

"The three federal agents who've been following me and drugging me." She emphatically held up a ziplock bag filled with bottles of her prescriptions for Paxil and Ambien.

My mother's daily routine consisted of opening a can of Diet Coke and watching the *Today* show in the morning, *General Hospital* and *Ellen* in the afternoon, and whatever was on CBS in the evening. If she felt adventurous, she might leave the house and pick up Subway for lunch. On Sundays, she did her weekly trip to the grocery where she'd stock up on enough bread, Muenster cheese, and Diet Coke for the week. The only drugs in the house were her antidepressants, sleep aids, Tums, and Advil. I had years of experience dealing with drunkenness, but insanity was beyond me.

I shook my head in disbelief. She wouldn't stop moving. She was pacing the floor of the garage and shooing me to go back inside. I stood there for two minutes before running in the house and calling Grace.

"Thank God you're home," I said, nearly panting. "My mom has lost it. Something is seriously wrong with her. Can you please come help me?"

"I'll be there in fifteen minutes."

By the time Grace arrived, I'd been able to lure my mom back into the house by promising to close the blinds and lock the doors, and by agreeing not to touch the bag she was cradling. Grace and I spent over an hour trying to reason with her.

"Should we call the paramedics?" Grace asked me.

"I'm afraid she'll completely self-destruct if strangers come in here and try to take her away. We need to find another way to get her to the hospital," I said, and then it came to me.

"Mom, I have an idea," I said, following her as she walked in circles around the house, pausing only to light a cigarette and peek behind the curtains. "We need to get you to the hospital and have you tested so that we can find out what the agents are drugging you with."

She agreed.

As soon as the three of us walked into Evanston Hospital, my mother started telling anyone who would listen, "They're trying to drug me."

It was enough to make the nurse at patient check-in look up from her computer screen. "These two are drugging you?" the nurse asked, pointing at Grace and me.

"No, the federal agents. They came into my house and replaced my pills with drugs. They even stole clothes from me and rearranged my pantry."

The nurse shifted her gaze to me. I pointed my right index finger toward my head and began turning it in circles.

"Okay, ma'am, let's get you into a room."

The three of us were taken to a room and waited forty-five minutes for a doctor to come in and observe her. It took him only fifteen minutes to determine that she was having a nervous breakdown and needed to be admitted to the psych ward for observation. He brought Grace and me into the hallway to talk to us.

"We'd like to admit her and get her off the drugs she's carrying around, and on some antipsychotic medication as soon as possible," he said.

"Okay," I mumbled as Grace wrapped an arm around my shoulder.

"The only thing is that we can't keep her against her will, so we're going to need to get her to admit that she's either a harm to herself or to others."

I could see her through the narrow window in the door, waving her hands around while talking to one of the nurses. She looked delicate and scared, and my heart broke for her.

"Do you want me to talk to her?" I asked. "I think she'd be more comfortable with me."

"No, no, our staff will sit down with her. Once she admits she's in danger of hurting herself or someone else, then they can sign the papers on her behalf."

I nodded and followed him back into the room.

When I looked into her eyes, I realized she was not going to go down without a fight. The psych team's questions were very pointed and direct, but she danced around all of them like a prima ballerina.

"Have you had suicidal thoughts?" they'd ask.

"Well, wouldn't you if you were being drugged against your will?" she answered.

"Are you depressed?"

"Wouldn't you be depressed if you were being followed and people were breaking into your home?" she'd say.

"Have you thought about killing yourself?"

"I'm a good Christian woman. I would never do something like that."

Four hours later, they'd won. She was beaten down and exhausted and begging for a cigarette. She eventually caved and admitted she'd had thoughts of suicide, and once she realized they had goaded her into saying it, she was *pissed*. I burst into tears as they took her away to the psych ward, kicking and screaming obscenities at me and everyone around her. To say it was the lowest point of my life would be a grandiose understatement.

Grace took me home and made some coffee while I sat on the couch in silence and watched raindrops race down the window.

"Do you want me to have my mom come over?" she asked.

I shook my head no.

When it came to our families, Grace and I had one thing in common: a nonexistent relationship with our biological fathers. But that's where the similarities ended. Grace's mother and her husband, who'd adopted Grace as a baby, were madly in love and functioned admirably as a nuclear family with no bombs. Grace's family had also become the closest thing I had to loving relatives in this world.

"How did this happen?" Tucked next to me on the couch, she finally had a chance to ask me.

I sniffed. "She was hiding on the floor of the garage like a frightened kitten when I got back from the lake. Who knows how long she'd been there or would've been there had I not found her today. She sprung into defensive mode as soon as she realized she wasn't alone."

Grace tilted her head to the side. "Had she been drinking?"

"No, I don't think so. I didn't smell any alcohol on her. And I did a quick check around the house and can't find any bottles. That's the worst part about it. I think she's sober."

Grace and I had met in my first week after I moved here from Florida. I'd been jogging past her house one day as she was shooting hoops in her driveway. I introduced myself as the new girl, and she asked me if anyone had ever told me I looked like Julia Roberts. I said yes, but not very often. We bonded over our height and our biological fathers' absence. Since mom and I had moved to Glenview right after her stint in rehab, Grace was aware of what my mom and I had gone through. I opened up to Grace early on about what most of my childhood had been like, and how I was comfortable talking about it, but not comfortable living with it any longer. On more than one occasion, I had packed a bag for the weekend and taken refuge at Grace's house. There were always family movie nights on Fridays and family dinners on Sundays. Her parents had what seemed to me to be the perfect relationship; yet, spending time with them didn't make me jealous, it made me motivated.

"I'm so sorry you had to come home to this."

"Me too," I said, rubbing the back of my neck. "I'm supposed to move into my own apartment tomorrow. How can I possibly leave her alone at a time like this?"

"You will; you have to, Chloe. Your new place isn't far away, and it's even closer to the hospital than you are now."

"I can't just abandon her."

"She'd want you to stick to your plans."

I nodded, but I wasn't convinced.

"I mean it, you go move your stuff and check on her tomorrow when you're done. Do you want me to get Patch and his friends to help you? I'll get my mom to pay him, and he won't be able to say no. My little brother can't resist cash."

"No, thanks, I'm fine. It's a furnished studio, so I really just have a few boxes and suitcases."

"Okay, let me know if you change your mind." Grace leaned in, gave me a squeeze, and then sat back. "So tell me about your summer up at Camp Reed. From the few texts you sent me, it sounds like you had a great time," she chided me. "I'm dying to hear about everything."

I had only given Grace a glimpse into what had happened between Tyler and me for two reasons. One, I didn't want to give her all the details via text, and two, I was worried about getting ahead of myself and making too big a deal about it. Once he came back with Sadie, I was relieved I hadn't told Grace every sordid detail.

But now, sitting with my best friend, my sister, my family, I wanted her to know. "I think I'm in trouble."

She leaned back and cocked her head. "Why, what have you done?"

"Fallen for the wrong guy."

I spent the next half hour picking chipped nail polish off my fingernails and bringing Grace up to speed on what had transpired at the lake. That Tyler and I had been left alone for a few days and that he'd kissed me. Then he disappeared and returned with Sadie, only to confess that he had feelings for me while she was asleep in the house. Finally, I told Grace how he eventually took Sadie home and came back to surprise me with sex in the yard. More than once. Hell, Grace and I used to joke about the crush I had on him. My one-sided schoolgirl fascination. As I told her the whole story, it occurred to me what a cliché it all was. By the time I was done talking, Grace's expression was more frightened than mine had been when Dixie "Maleficent" Reed had busted me swapping spit with her prince.

"Why are you looking at me like that?" I asked.

Her mouth was agape. "I just can't believe it."

"I know, right?" I said, motioning like I was about to high-five her and celebrate my one-night stand, but she left me hanging. "Grace, it's fine."

"It's really not. He shouldn't have taken advantage of you like that."

"Whoa, he did *not* take advantage of me. I wanted him, you know I did."

"But he should know better," she said.

"Also, he has a girlfriend," I said and burst out laughing at the absurdity of it all.

She stared at me like I was huddled in the corner of the garage, hiding from federal agents. "I really don't know why you're laughing, Chloe. He took advantage of you, and I don't like it one bit."

I wished she would stop saying that, so I cleared my throat and went in for the kill. The one thing she hated more than anything. The one statement that always sent her flailing into back-pedal mode. "I shouldn't have told you," I said and stood up.

She shot up after me. "I'm sorry, but you know I'm only looking out for you, and he seems like a real shit. I can see in your face that you're completely smitten with him."

She was right.

"Please, Chloe, look what you just came home to. You have so much going on, and you start law school in a couple weeks...I just don't want to see you get hurt. You know that," Grace said and then gave me a good long hug.

"Love you," I said.

"You too."

The next day I moved my stuff into my new apartment. I'd barely set down the last box when I had to dash out to meet with my mom's doctor at the hospital. I hadn't had anything to eat because nothing could fill the hole in my stomach.

"How is she?" I asked, sitting across from him at his desk.

"She's doing much better. We gave her some Seroquel, which is typically used to treat symptoms of schizophrenia, although we've diagnosed her with delusional disorder."

"What's that?" I asked.

"Patients who have delusional disorder appear to function normally, but make unusually odd choices based on their delusional beliefs."

"Such as spending an afternoon on the garage floor to avoid imaginary law enforcement? Or whispering to the women at the dry cleaners not to wait on the man behind her in line because he's one of them? Or hanging bed sheets over every window even though the blinds are already closed?"

"Precisely," he said. "We're going to adjust her medication for the next few days to see where she functions best, but then she will be free to go."

I let out a breath that I'd been holding in. I was so relieved to hear that she'd be going home soon. Mom hated being out of her element. "Okay, thank you, doctor."

"Do you live at home?" he asked.

"I'm starting law school, just moved into my apartment today actually, but I feel terrible about leaving her." And I did. The guilt of having left her alone all summer was tearing me up, and the thought of doing it again, combined with the image in my brain of her huddled on the garage floor was almost too much to bear. "What if she skips her medication, or refuses to take it? She has no one to look after her."

"If she stops taking her meds, well, then she'll have to live with her paranoia and delusions. There isn't much we or you can do to force her unless she becomes a danger to herself or to others."

I massaged my forehead and sighed. "I just don't know what I should do. I really don't think I can live with myself if I abandon her at a time like this. I don't feel right about leaving her alone again."

The doctor took his glasses off, placed them on his desk, and lowered his chin. "You want to know the truth?" he asked me.

"Please."

"I've dealt with many cases like your mother. Some much better; some much worse." He paused, struggling for the right words. "Your mom is like the *Titanic*: if you stay with the ship, you'll go down, too. Those people who clung to the boat ultimately perished. You need to get yourself on a lifeboat and get as far away as you can," he said. "I'm not telling you to desert her completely, but once you save yourself, you'll be able to care for her better than you could now."

I nodded with instant clarity, then hugged him and thanked him for giving me some perspective. As he spoke, I knew he was right. Though I didn't like thinking of my mother as the *Titanic*, I knew that neither of us had a chance at a better future if I shelved my goals to stay home with her.

I drove back to my new apartment and began the process of moving in. I placed my soap dish on the bathroom sink. I unwrapped and hung my new shower curtain. I folded my sweaters and T-shirts and put them neatly away on the shelves in the closet. When I got around to unpacking the last of my duffel bags, I found Tyler's note.

Meet me at the lake at midnight.

I smiled. I didn't care if he'd taken advantage of me because, for once in my life, I'd felt like the luckiest girl in the world. I'd enjoyed every last minute of it, and given the chance would've done it all over again. How can you be taken advantage of if you're a willing participant? I neatly folded the note and placed it in my sock drawer before cleaning up the rest of my stuff. Once I was done, I hung the "Find Your Bliss" mini-pillow on my door handle and wept.

CHAPTER ELEVEN

I spent that first week sorting out my class schedule, buying my books, stocking my cabinets with snack food, worrying about my mother, and jumping at the phone every time it rang, hoping it was Tyler. My time in Lake Geneva already seemed like a distant memory or a story I'd read in a novel years ago.

Ten days after admitting my mom to the hospital, I picked her up and took her home. She stared silently out the window for most of the drive and made sure I watched as she walked in the house and threw her medication in the trash.

"I tell you I'm being drugged, and you turn me over to people who give me more drugs," she hissed as she lit a cigarette.

I walked over to her and embraced her. "I love you, Mom. Please call me if you need anything, okay? Please," I said, then got into my lifeboat and headed back to my new apartment.

I woke up the next morning exhausted. My concern for my mother, coupled with a rented mattress, was no recipe for a good night's sleep. I walked to a nearby convenience store to pick up some toilet paper, dish soap, and a few other things I needed. When I got back, I rearranged the furniture, scrubbed the countertops, vacuumed the floor, and Windexed every surface that wasn't covered in fabric. Once I was finished, I grabbed my cell phone and sat on the floor with my back against my borrowed bed. Tyler was back at Notre Dame already, and likely up to his kneepads in practices and agent negotiations, but I was itching to bask in his attention again if only for a second. I stared at the phone, trying to formulate the perfect sentiment when it hit me. Not too sappy, not too needy, just letting him know that I was thinking about him. He said he would call me, but he hadn't. I just wanted to connect with him.

I'm staring at you, I texted.

Two hours later, as I was getting into bed, he texted me back.

I know, and I still like it.

He'd just sent me the message, so I knew he was sitting somewhere with his phone nearby. I needed to hear his voice and have him whisper in my ear again. I had told myself repeatedly that he didn't take advantage of me, not because I couldn't live with the fact that he did or didn't, but because I wanted so badly to believe that he cared for me like I cared for him. He'd consumed nearly all my free thoughts for the last ten days, and I wanted to know if I'd affected him the same way. I thought about calling Grace first, to get her opinion on whether I should call him, but then I remembered that I wasn't in fourth grade and dialed his number. It was almost midnight.

"Hello," he answered on the fourth ring.

"Hey, it's Chloe."

"Hey, beautiful." He sounded worn-out.

I had no agenda when I dialed. I hadn't planned on asking about Sadie or questioning why he hadn't called me, although I would have loved some insight into both. I simply wanted to hear his voice.

"Well, I just wanted to give you a quick call. I moved into my new place and was thinking about you, and, well, that's it. Hope you don't mind."

"Of course I don't mind," he assured me.

"I had such a great time with you this summer." Commence verbal diarrhea. "And since I'm not the strong, silent type, I just wanted to let you know that I've been thinking about you a lot and would love for us to try and stay in touch. I know it's hard and both of our schedules are going to be crazy—"

"Yeah, of course," he interjected. "I just don't know anything right now. The season is just starting, and I'm training like a dog, but I like hearing from you."

I nodded slightly as he spoke. "Of course, yeah, I totally understand. Good luck with everything, and hopefully you won't mind me pestering you on occasion with a text here or there."

"Not at all."

"Great," I chirped. "Sorry I woke you, and I guess I'll see you around."

"I hope so," he said.

We ended the call, and I crawled into bed frustrated and mortified. His tone was warm, but his words were cool. I was surprised by how much I needed to hear his voice, and by how disappointing it was. I was furious with myself for hanging my hopes on him like every other swooning cheerleader out there. I replayed every tender moment we'd shared at the lake over and over in my head, trying to determine where things had gone wrong between us, but I came up short. I wanted to cry like a baby, but I didn't. I was determined to hold my head high and take it for what it was regardless of how deep my feelings were. I wasn't the first girl to fall for Tyler Reed, and I wouldn't be the last. He was on the path to superstardom, revered by decades of Notre Dame football fans who no doubt believed that Tyler and his teammates routinely broke bread with Jesus Christ himself. Tyler needed to focus on his game and his career and not be distracted by late-night phone calls and relationship drama. It made perfect sense that he would want nothing to do with my problematic mother and me. That he should be surrounded by people of superior caliber and free of exposure to "unsavory elements."

Anything else would be delusional.

CHAPTER TWELVE

A week later, classes were in full swing, and I had a grueling schedule that left me with little time for anything other than reading court cases and attending lectures. I had classes in constitutional law, civil procedures, criminal law, and an elective in divorce law. My mind was full, and I was thrilled to have my focus back where it belonged.

A guy by the name of Cameron Sparks lived across the hall from me. He was also an overwhelmed law student, and we quickly became close friends and study partners. Cam was from Miami. He was nice-looking, stood about three inches taller than me at five foot eleven, and insisted on wearing flip-flops regardless of the season. Cam was unlike me in just about every way. Laid-back, unaffected by self-imposed pressure, and not easily distracted by obsessions over college quarterbacks or delusional parents. Anytime I had one of my weekly panic attacks—brought on by a phone call from my mother, coupled with the amount of studying I had looming over me—he knew just how to rein me in and keep me grounded. More often than not, his remedy included guacamole and margaritas.

One Friday night in October, I got a text from Tyler around eleven o'clock. It was the first one he'd sent me in a month. Cam and I were sprawled out on the floor of my apartment studying when Tyler's name flashed across my phone.

"Everything okay?" he asked when my eyes widened.

"Yeah, fine, I just got a text from a guy…this guy I know."

Cam elevated his left eyebrow. "A boyfriend-guy?"

I shook my head. "No, just a guy I hooked up with this summer, but definitely not a boyfriend-guy," I said and smiled.

"You like hook-up guy though, don't cha? And you want him to be boyfriend-guy, I can tell. Neighbor-guy knows all," he said, patting himself on the shoulder.

I laughed. "I was crushing on him pretty hard over the summer, but he couldn't be more wrong for me."

"You've read the text five times. What does it say?"

"It says neighbor-guy needs to mind his own business."

"That's oddly coincidental," Cam said.

I lifted my phone from the floor and read the text aloud. "It says, *I miss you and the lake*," I told Cam.

"Skinny-dipping? Sounds serious."

"Well, it's not," I said.

I crossed my legs, placed the phone facedown next to me, and proceeded to tell Cam every detail about Tyler and our summer at the lake. I loved chatting about it, and we both welcomed a break from reading family law contracts. Cam laughed when I concluded my story and told him that Tyler was a football player at Notre Dame.

"What's so hilarious?" I asked and smacked him on the leg.

"Nothing," he said, trying not to smile. "Why aren't you still together?"

"Because we're not."

"Not many girls would let go of a *Notre Dame* quarterback." He said the school in a very la-di-da manner.

"I'm not many girls," I said, smacking him again, then laughed along with him. "Fine, he dumped me. Sort of. It didn't work out." I admitted.

"He sounds like a real shit," Cam concluded.

"He's just got issues, but he's not a bad guy. His parents are a little screwy."

"Whose aren't?"

"Amen."

I tried not to think about Tyler too often, but distance hadn't done much to lessen my affection for him. "It's fine, really," I said. Although anytime Tyler's name was brought up, it was hard for me to concentrate on anything else. Images of him emerging from a swimming pool dripping wet could easily erase three chapters of divorce law readings from my memory in mere seconds. I'd done what little I could to make peace with what transpired between Tyler and me, but his text catapulted him back to the front of my mind.

"Are you going to text him back?" he asked. "Something equally profound, like *I miss you and cake,* maybe? You could start a rhyming thread."

"Can we please just get back to work?"

When Cam was in the bathroom around one in the morning, I texted Tyler back.

Miss you too, I typed, and bit my lip before hitting send.

Cam came out of the bathroom and called me out. "I took an extra-long piss so that you could text him back and think you were getting away with something."

"I have nothing to hide from you, I just told you the entire story."

"Did you secretly text him while I peed?"

I smiled. "Yeah."

Cam was funny and honest and adorable and naturally brilliant. My whole life I'd gotten great grades because I worked my ass off to get them. Cam was one of those people who'd sleep through class and still get an A on the final exam.

By the time December rolled around, we were inseparable.

A week before winter break, I was studying for finals when he knocked on my door. I opened it to find him standing there with a Dominos pizza box and a six-pack of Corona.

"Hola!" he shouted, pushing past me. "When is the last time you made your bed?" he asked as he threw himself on top of it.

"You're under strict orders to leave me alone for the next three days," I said, hands on hips.

He opened the box to tempt me.

"Ooh, stuffed crust." I drooled and sprang toward the pizza.

"It's just a quick carb break, and then I'll be out of your hair."

Cam joined me on the floor where I was sprawled out with my books, and we ate and drank well past the point where I should've stopped. "See, now I'm useless. There's no way I'm going to pick up those books again."

"Good, come out with me, then."

"Just because your brain functions on another level, does not mean everyone else's does. I have to study."

"Come on, it'll be fun. You've been locked up in here for a week, and I know your test isn't for two more days," he said with a mischievous grin.

"Okay, fine, but only because you're cute," I said, and he was. Cam was twenty-two years old, but looked like he was seventeen. Zac Efron on the outside, and Bill Gates on the inside. He was a passionate thinker, always spewing ideas and theories that would undoubtedly change the world one day. Law school was unlike college in that I spent my time with a much smaller incestuous group of people. And every first-year female at Northwestern was head over heels for Cam Sparks, except for me. Because as much as I hated to admit it, I was still pining for his polar opposite.

"See, I knew you thought I was cute," he said, pointing at me.

"I tell you all the time, Cameron."

Cam had kissed me once during midterms. We'd been at the campus library for five hours, and then gone back to his apartment for some food and a quick break. It was late, maybe eleven o'clock, and I came out of his bathroom to find him leaning against the opposite wall waiting for me. He didn't say a word, just pushed himself off the wall, grabbed the back of my neck, and kissed me. He tasted like spearmint, and I kissed him back and forgot where I was for a moment. When he was done, he stepped away from me in the tiny hallway and looked really happy with himself.

"Sorry," he said post-kiss.

I hadn't realized my hand was on my mouth, so I removed it and smiled. "It's okay. Do you feel better now?" I teased.

"You have no idea," he said, and that was it. He'd never made another move.

I'd thought about that kiss nearly every time I chewed a piece of gum—but I cherished my relationship with him and wasn't keen on crossing that line. We were so great together that I never wanted to do anything that would threaten our *thing*. Our sweet, quirky, flirty, irreplaceable friendship thing.

"Speaking of people who think you're cute, why don't we go knock on Amanda's door and bring her with us to the bar? That way you can get laid and leave me out of it."

He smiled and crossed his arms. "Look at you talking shit. I like it," he said. "Amanda has blue-cheese breath, and I have no interest in hearing about how many problems her parents are having with their building permits on Long Island."

Cam's parents were both schoolteachers in Florida and had struggled through years of tax cuts and union strikes. They had retired with barely enough to care for themselves by the time Cam went to college at Duke. While he was there, he started an environmentally friendly online T-shirt business called Green Tees, which netted him $8,000 a month after he branched out to several other universities. He targeted campus events and fraternity parties and printed their logos and slogans on organic cotton shirts with water-based inks. He sold the business to Adidas his senior year and made enough money to pay off his student loans, cover his law school tuition, give him a nice nest egg to crack open one day, and send his parents on a Caribbean cruise for two weeks.

"Fine, let me grab my coat," I said.

Cam and I walked over to Bar Louie, had a few more beers, and each ordered a burger and fries.

"Have you decided whether you're going home for the holidays?" I asked him.

He shook his head.

"You're welcome to come with me to my friend Grace's house if you stay in town," I told him.

I'd spent every Christmas since high school at the Reynolds' house. Sometimes my mother would join us; sometimes not. Ever since law school had started, I'd driven home on Sundays to bring Mom dinner. Some nights we would sit in silence and watch TV for a couple hours; other nights we would eat dinner as soon as I arrived and then she'd ask me to leave so that she could organize her closet. I never quite knew what I was in for when I'd arrive at her house. There were times she made me feel like an unwanted intruder. While other times she presented me with a new sweater and asked me to curl her hair. If she was acting nervous, I'd simply drop off some food and magazines, take a quick turn around the house—snuffing out any cigarettes she'd left burning in various rooms, kiss her on the head, and leave. It was always unpredictable, never easy.

"I'm going to drop a gift off for my mom, and then head over to the Reynolds' house around noon on Christmas day. It would be great to have you with me," I said. Cam knew enough about my mom's situation not to be surprised that I wasn't spending the day by her side exchanging gifts and decorating gingerbread cookies.

"Thanks. I'll let you know," he said.

By the time the dust had settled after finals week, my apartment was strewn with crap. Loose pages of printed cases and statutes. Empty pizza boxes and cans of Red Bull. Piles of laundry and damp bathing suits growing toxic mold. The mess was embarrassing, but I was relieved just to have survived my exams. Christmas day I spent the entire morning cleaning my apartment and clearing my mind. I had known that law school was going to be a challenge, but I hadn't realized it would nearly kill me. Cam knocked on my door just as I was about to drag the last bag of garbage to the chute.

"When are we leaving?"

I laughed. "You're coming with me, I take it?"

"I'm with you."

"Why don't we drive separately since I have to stop and see my mom first," I said.

"I'll come with you."

I placed the bag of garbage on the floor and ran my hand through my hair. "I don't know, Cam. She's always such a mess, and I don't know how she'd feel about having a stranger in the house. Guests are not a welcome part of her routine."

"I totally get it," he said.

"Do you? Because you know it's nothing personal, right? I mean, bringing you home would be a normal mother's dream," I said.

He nodded and put his hand up. "Enough said. Give me the Reynolds' address and tell me what time to be there and what to bring."

"Be there at noon, and I'll text you the address. As for what to bring…I don't know, wine always works."

"What are you bringing?"

"A coconut cake from The Fresh Market; it's my favorite."

"You're bringing your favorite cake to someone else's party?" he asked.

"Your sarcasm and weak attempt to derail me with your even weaker sense of wit is about to get you disinvited and left alone on Christmas—not to mention, no coconut cake."

"I'll see you at noon." He smiled and walked away like he hadn't a care in the world.

CHAPTER THIRTEEN

Every time I put the key in the door of my mom's house, I did so with trepidation. She'd been sober for over eight years, but even then I never trusted the sturdiness of her wagon. Not for one day. Now, with her new illness, I just prayed that I would find her on her indented couch cushion with a Diet Coke in hand, watching TV—and I released a huge sigh of relief when I did.

"Hi, Mom, Merry Christmas," I said as I entered the front door, which opened into the living room/TV room/family room/den/study/office, basically the only room in the house that wasn't a bedroom, kitchen, or a bathroom.

"Hi, honey."

I placed two grocery bags on the kitchen counter and shouted out to her. "I brought you a vanilla pound cake, and some brie and crackers."

"Did you get Caffeine-Free Diet Coke?"

"Yes," I said. Mom had a vicious Diet Coke habit. She'd drink six of them in the morning, and then switch to Caffeine-Free Diet Coke at noon so that she could sleep. Which was really a nonissue considering the number of Ambien she went through.

The house smelled like an ashtray. A huge, full, dirty old ashtray. She'd cut back to a pack a day, but she hadn't curbed her habit of leaving lit cigarettes all over the place. Rather than carry a cigarette around with her, she preferred to just have them burning throughout the house to greet her as she entered a room.

"Mom," I said to the side of her face, which was fixated on the television. "You're going to burn the house down."

"I'll be just fine as long as no one comes in."

"If you burn the house down, your clothes will burn with it." I tried jarring her by threatening the one thing she cared about, but we'd had that exchange many times before and nothing ever changed. "I brought you something."

She turned to me. "How kind of you."

She unwrapped the box, inside of which was a Northwestern Law sweatshirt. "Thank you. I'm very proud of you," she said.

Her words were her gift to me. Despite my mother's mood swings and illnesses, I knew she loved me and that there was nothing else she wanted more than for me to be successful.

"Thanks, Mom, I love you," I said and hugged her while she lifted the remote and changed the channel. "Are you sure you don't want to join me at the Reynolds' house today?"

"I'm more comfortable here."

"Do you want me to curl your hair for the holiday?" I asked.

"Not today. I'm going to dress later this afternoon," she said, eyes fixated on the TV. "They're playing *A Christmas Story* at two o'clock," she said.

I smiled and gave her a kiss on the cheek. "I'm heading over to Grace's house, okay? So I'll see you in a week or so. Love you."

"Okay."

"Please be careful with your cigarettes," I said and walked out the door. I'd given up long ago trying to understand her and attempting to talk her into things she didn't want to do. But every Sunday, and especially on Christmas, I couldn't help but feel a little bit sad walking out that door.

I left my mom and headed for the only place that had ever felt like home to me. I was a few minutes late and entered through the garage door into the kitchen to find Cam and Sydney, Grace's mom, standing over the stove tasting bits of the enormous ham she was cooking. Upon my graduation from college, Grace's mom had insisted I call her by her first name, which felt insubordinate and wrong, but I'd acquiesced. Cam already had his sleeves rolled up, with a glass of wine in one hand. He greeted me by tapping his watch and mouthing, *what the fuck?*

I gave him the evil eye, and then a kiss on the cheek. "Sorry I'm late," I said and embraced Sydney. "Merry Christmas, I see you've met my friend Cam?"

"I have," she smiled and looked at him for a second. "In fact, he brought your favorite coconut cake."

"He did not!" I screamed. "Why you little piece of—"

Cam interrupted me with a hug and cracked himself up. "I couldn't resist," he snickered into my ear.

My eyes were wide with mock fury, but I couldn't suppress my laughter. "Well, now you have two," I said to Sydney, handing her a large brown bag from The Fresh Market as soon as I'd composed myself.

Just then, Grace walked in with her boyfriend, Jack. Sydney and I were waiting for Grace to reciprocate our greetings, but her eyes were doing a body scan of Cam instead. Finally, she looked away and winked at me.

"Grace, this is Cam. Cam, this is Grace," I said, going through the formalities.

"It's so great to finally meet you," Grace said and walked over to embrace him. "I've heard so much about you."

"Well, it's all a pack of lies. I'm not nearly the nerd Chloe makes me out to be."

"Yes, you are," I mumbled.

Cam shook Jack's hand, and then pointed at me and whispered to him loud enough for everyone to hear. "She thinks I'm cute."

I shook my head, filled a basket with rolls, and helped Sydney with some last-minute preparations as a few other guests arrived. Cam took a seat at the kitchen island while Grace and Jack went to greet the rest of her relatives in the den.

"So Cam," Sydney began. "Where are you from?"

"Florida."

"And you're going to be a lawyer like Chloe one day?"

Cam grabbed a handful of shelled pistachios from a three-sectioned serving dish in front of him that also held pecans and cashews. "We'll see. I want to have the law degree for when I start my own business, but I likely won't practice. I'm planning on getting my MBA as well. A friend from Duke and I are working on building a new POS software to streamline the checkout process for major retailers. He's the tech guy, and I'm everything else."

Sydney looked at me, and I shrugged. "Nerd." I nodded.

Just then a pistachio flew through the air and hit me between the eyes.

Once both sets of Grace's grandparents had arrived, we were all seated. Between the Reynolds' dining room table and an additional card table, there was room for everyone. The buffet was adorned with gourds and colored platters brimming with honey-baked ham, creamed spinach, broccoli casserole, mashed potatoes, Swedish meatballs, and Pillsbury crescent rolls. Next to that was a smaller dessert buffet with Sydney's mother's famous reindeer cookies, a chocolate Yule log, and two coconut cakes. It was a happy time, and I was content to be surrounded by people who loved me and made me laugh. I was seated next to Cam and admired the way he charmed the table with stories about trips to exotic locations and tales of getting arrested for leading environmental protests. We all hung on every word.

After dinner, the women cleaned up while the men went into the den and watched football. The old-fashioned predictability of it all brought me so much comfort.

Grace and I were wiping down the counters when she finally asked me about Cam. "He's adorable," she whispered. "Have you never mentioned what he looked like or have I not been paying attention?"

Grace had moved to her own apartment in downtown Chicago after graduating from Purdue University and was living in the Bucktown neighborhood, where she was teaching preschool.

"You've been busy wiping butts and making crafts," I said.

She threw a dish towel at me. "Don't be snide, you know I wipe noses too."

"I'm kidding, I actually envy you. I miss the days when little people looked up to me and believed that I held the answer to every random question in their spongelike brains. I bought a couple of gifts for Sammy and Sarah that I'm going to run over to their house later tonight."

"They'll be so excited to see you. Is Tyler home for break?"

"No. I stalked his Facebook page, and it looks like the team has to stay together in Indiana since they're in the Rose Bowl next week."

"My dad said there was an article about him in the *Tribune* last weekend," she told me. "Have you heard from him?"

I shook my head. Notre Dame hadn't played in—or been eligible for—the Rose Bowl since 1925. Tyler's name had been all over the local press.

Grace went about rinsing wineglasses in the sink while I dried large ceramic platters. "Why don't you send him a text and wish him good luck in the game?" she suggested.

"I could, I mean, I'm capable of it—but why bother?"

"Or better yet, forget him altogether and hook up with Cam."
She clapped. "He's *really* cute, Chloe."

He was reasonably good-looking, if you liked that slim, hairless
Abercrombie & Fitch thing. But my relationship with Cam was so
much more important to me than that. He was the calming force
that I'd needed so badly in my life. To complicate things by sleeping
with him would mean losing what we had, and that was way too
precious to me. What if it didn't end well? What if I repulsed him?
And let's be honest, I was nowhere near over Tyler, and to finally
admit that defeat was depressing.

"We spend so much time together, I would hate to compromise
what we have. Cam's pretty much the only reason I've been able to
survive this first semester," I said.

She came closer to me and, keeping her voice low, said, "Well,
it hasn't gone unnoticed by my mom and me that he has a thing
for you."

"A thing? Really, Grace. What, a hard-on?"

She laughed. "For someone you spend so much time with, he
sure does stare at you a lot."

We finished the dishes and hit the dessert buffet. It was a tradi-
tion in the Reynolds' home that dessert always be served on paper
plates so that Grace's mom could enjoy her holiday sugar fix without another round of dirty dishes. At about five o'clock Cam and
I expressed our profuse gratitude and left. It was snowing when we
walked outside to our respective cars.

"Domino's pizza back at my place in an hour?" he offered.

"I'm stuffed," I said, pulling my faux-fur-trimmed hood over
my head.

"You'll be hungry in an hour, that's how it works. Your body…"

I leaned in and silenced him with a kiss on his cold cheek. "I have some gifts to drop off for these two kids I used to sit for, and I might be a while, but I'll knock on your door when I get back."

"Do you want to drag me along to that house too?"

I shook my head and zipped up the remaining inch of my coat. "This one I need to do by myself."

CHAPTER FOURTEEN

s I drove over to the Reeds' house, I was apprehensive and flooded with memories of Tyler. I knew that walking into his home was going to dredge up all the emotions I'd been trying so hard to suppress. But I was eager to see the kids and grateful to have had a day with good friends. When I'd called Mrs. Reed the week before, she'd said to come by anytime after four o'clock. I pulled in through the open iron gates at the entrance of their driveway and parked behind three other cars about halfway up the circular drive. My car hadn't had time to warm up, so I was shivering as I grabbed the gifts from my backseat and ran across the wet, crunchy gravel to the front door. I rang the bell, and then bounced on my toes, breathing down the front of my coat while I waited.

Tyler opened the door.

By the look on his face, I could tell his mom hadn't mentioned that I'd be stopping by.

I couldn't help but form a toothy cartoonlike grin at the sight of him. If my eyes could have popped out of my head as my tongue unraveled to the ground, that's exactly what would've happened. I placed the bag of gifts on the floor, stood on my toes, and wrapped my arms around him. He buried his face in my hair and lifted me off my feet.

"It's so good to see you. I thought you weren't going to be here?" I questioned, back on solid ground but still wearing my giddy smile.

"Is that why you came, because you thought I wasn't here?"

"Had I known, I would've come earlier. I came to see Sammy and Sarah, and give them some gifts. You're just the Christmas bonus." *Thank God I didn't bring Cam with me*, I thought to myself, removing my jacket.

"You look fantastic," he said.

Tyler hadn't seen me in much more than tank tops and sandals, but that night I was decked out. I wore all black: a sequined top, a leather miniskirt, opaque stockings, and boots. Had I known he was going to be there, I would've worn my hair down, but instead it was in an updo, flanked by long sparkly earrings.

"Thanks, Ty; you're not so bad yourself." Tyler's hair had grown longer. He had it slicked back, and it hung just past the collar of his white tailored dress shirt. His sleeves were rolled up, and his hands were tucked in the pockets of his tweed pants. He looked glorious.

"Congratulations on the Rose Bowl, by the way. I'm so proud of you," I said, handing him my coat.

"Thanks. I'm heading out first thing tomorrow morning. We're only allowed twenty-fours hours away from the team for Christmas."

"That must not be enough for some of the players. You're lucky you live only a few hours away."

He nodded.

"Chloedear," I heard Mrs. Reed coo from behind me. "Merreh Christmas."

"Thank you," I started and turned toward her. "I brought some gif—" The sight of Sadie standing next to her interrupted my sentiment and knocked the happy-holiday wind right out of me. I swallowed and willed myself not to look back at Tyler. I lifted the shopping bag I'd brought with me off the marble floor. "These are for Sammy and Sarah."

God dammit, why didn't I bring Cam with me!

I wanted to drop the bag and head for the door with some excuse about not being able to stay, but once again in the company of Tyler and his "friend," I was trapped. There was no way I was going to get out of there quickly. I hadn't seen the kids in months, and I'd promised them I would spend some time with them.

Mrs. Reed extended her arm and waved me toward her. "Come dear, they're eager to see you."

I held my neck firmly as if it were in a brace, not allowing myself to turn even one inch in Tyler's direction. He was left holding my coat as I walked away from him. Sadie asked him to refill her wineglass and floated past me without a word. All I wanted to do was give the kids my gifts and run. Sammy and Sarah were in the finished basement wading through the presents they'd opened that morning when I found them. I nearly burst into tears when they ran to me.

"Oh my goodness, it's soooo good to see you two," I said in the midst of a group hug.

"We miss you, Chloe," Sarah said.

"I miss you, too, and I'm so sorry I don't come see you more. School has been really busy, but I'm going to try and be better about visiting next year, okay?"

They both nodded and averted their eyes to the bright red shopping bag in my hand. "I brought you both something, but I can't stay long. Are you ready to open them?"

They nodded and clapped, and then tore through the wrapping paper. Sammy got his own brand-new fishing pole, and Sarah got a pair of swimming goggles with a built-in waterproof flashlight on top for night swimming. They were elated and spent the next twenty minutes showing me everything else they'd received that day. I should've been rolling around with them and playing with all their new toys like I'd planned, but instead I was desperate to get out of there.

Sammy placed three toys in front of me and asked me to help him open them. I began tugging on the first box, which led to a thick layer of plastic. Once I'd nearly sliced off my thumb removing the tier of the vault that surrounded the encased remote-control car, I was then faced with what looked like cable ties securing the thing to the base of the box at seven different points.

"Jesus, is this made of fourteen-karat gold?" I whispered under my breath. "Can you get me a pair of scissors, Sammy?"

He located the scissors, I began cutting at the ties, and the car finally came free. Once the car had been removed from the box, the cables still hung from seven different points on the body of the vehicle. I struggled to pull each of the seven wires through the underbelly of the car. My armpits were sweating by the time I was done. I spied the rest of the toys Sammy wanted me to open and shook my head. I was so infuriated that I was in the dungeon of the Reeds' house on Christmas day, trapped and alone just as I'd been last summer when Sadie had appeared at Tyler's side in Lake Geneva.

"Have your brother open those for you. I need to get going," I said to Sammy and stood up in a huff.

At six thirty, I said good-bye to the kids. I hesitated at the bottom of the stairs before heading up, wondering how I might sneak out without saying good-bye to anyone else. But I needed my coat.

I walked up the carpeted stairs, which led to the hallway just outside the kitchen. Thankfully, Mrs. Reed was talking with one of the catering staff near the sink. "I'm heading out," I said, barely loud enough for her to hear.

Mrs. Reed dismissed the caterer and rushed out to meet me in the hall. "Would you like to stay for pie?" she offered.

"No, thank you, I had dessert already. Do you know where Tyler put my coat?"

She folded her hands in front of her. "Wasn't that just lovely that he was able to be home for Christmas?"

I nodded. "Yup, that's so great. He took my coat from me when I walked in," I said.

"I just can't tell you how happeh I was to have him here with the family for the holiday. Being with family is so important during these times."

"It sure is."

"Speaking of family, how is your mother doing? You know I'm on the board at Evanston Hospital, and I was wrecked to hear about her recent troubles. You must be terribleh worried while you're off trying to conquer the world of law. Bless your heart, it must be so difficult for someone with such a full curriculum to be able to care for her. Tylah was so worried when I told him all about it this evening."

Deciphering the meaning behind Dixie Reed's famous digs was never a problem. It was fending them off that was the real challenge, like standing still, unflinching, as someone repeatedly slapped you in the face.

"Thank you for your concern," I said and began to walk toward the front door with her traipsing behind me.

"I read an article once in *Parade* magazine that said children of alcoholics have a genetic predisposition to become addicted to alcohol themselves. I'm sure you're being vereh careful. We wouldn't want to carry on that legacy."

I stopped walking, took a deep breath, and then turned to face her, but not before stepping in nice and close, emphasizing the four inches in height that I had over her. "You're always looking out for me, aren't you?"

"Why, of course, dear."

"Then could you help me locate my jacket?"

She stepped away and returned with my coat. "I'm sure you'll want to be polite and go say good-bye to everyone."

"Don't be so sure," I said and left.

By the time I reached my apartment, my hands stung from repeatedly smacking the steering wheel during the drive home. I entered my apartment, slammed the door, and collapsed onto my couch. A minute later there was a knock at the door.

"It's Santa," Cam said, his voice muffled through the cheap wood.

"Go away, I've been naughty!" I shouted.

"Even better," he said and knocked like a woodpecker until I let him in.

"Why do you still have your coat on?" he asked.

"Do I?"

"You're acting weird, but I'm going to go with it. I shall now use my undergraduate psychology minor to probe you with a series of questions that will lead me to the information necessary to extrapolate what is bothering you."

I defiantly whipped off my coat and fell back on the couch.

"Phew," Cam said. "Because, honestly, I don't have a psych minor."

"Tyler was there," I said.

"Hunky football Tyler?"

I nodded. "And guess who else was there with him?"

"John Heisman?"

"This bleached blonde idiot girlfriend of his, Sadie."

Cam had a look on his face like he wanted to laugh, but knew better than to mock me right then. "From where I sit, a bleached blonde idiot girlfriend is exactly what I would imagine a hunky Notre Dame football player to have with him."

I threw my hands up, wide-eyed, and pointed at Cam. "You're correct! It's exactly what's expected of him. He's lived his entire life doing what's expected of him, and never what he wants. He doesn't want her."

"How do you know? Do *you* have a psych minor?"

"Because he wants me," I said as I sank lower into my seat and then buried my face in my hands. "But I'm a distracting, troubled, non-pedigreed working stiff who bleeds red instead of blue." I raised my head up. "But I know he wants me, Cam…at least he led me to believe that."

He smiled at me with pity. "And you want him."

I nodded. "I wish I didn't, but I do."

"Are you going to cry?"

"Maybe when you leave."

At one o'clock in the morning I was awoken by the sound of my phone vibrating on my nightstand. I nearly hurled it at the wall when I saw Tyler's name on the screen, but I couldn't resist hearing what he had to say for himself.

"Hello," I answered groggily.

"Give me your address."

"No," I said after a short pause.

"I can't stop thinking about you," he said. "I had no idea you were coming tonight; my mom never mentioned it. I need to see you."

"What difference would it have made?"

"I don't know, but when I saw you at the door, all I wanted was to be with you, and I knew you were going to freak out when you saw Sadie. Her whole family was there, in the back den, and I was hoping you'd see that when you came to say good-bye," he tried to explain.

"Well, then, why didn't you come down to the basement and talk to me?" I asked, rubbing my eyes. "You know what? It doesn't matter. I don't care. I'm in bed, and I need to put this whole thing behind me. As the saying goes, 'Out of sight, out of mind.' Not, 'I show up on your parents' doorstep, and now I'm on your mind'!" I paused to take a breath and calm myself down. "Look, it's not like you owe me any sort of explanation. I would've loved to spend some time with you. Even ten minutes. But once again, I'm left with the short end of the stick. Merry goddamn Christmas, Tyler."

"Chloe, I'm on the highway headed for Evanston. Give me your address," he repeated. "Please."

"You're calling me from the car?"

"Yes, and I have to be back on the road heading for South Bend by six, too, so give me your goddamn address."

I sighed before answering, "It's 912 University Drive, apartment 2C."

"I'm on my way." *Click.*

I bit my bottom lip. My heart was racing and fluttering and aching and clapping with excitement. I got out of bed, brushed my teeth again, and changed out of my flannel plaid twinset into a black thermal V-neck and boxers. Tyler said he wanted to be with me, and he was on his way to making it happen. I'd waited so long for him to make his move that I didn't care if it came about by accident.

So I waited.

And waited.

At two o'clock I dialed his phone. No answer.

At three o'clock I went and knocked on Cam's door.

I heard the chain lock drop against the door before he opened it with one eye shut and the other squinting. "What's up?"

"Tyler called me two hours ago and said he was driving here to come see me," I told him.

"Score one for the team."

"He was coming from his parents' house in Glenview, which is a twenty-five-minute drive, tops, at this hour, and he hasn't shown up and isn't answering his phone. I'm freaking out."

"What time is it?"

"It's after three," I said. Just then my phone vibrated in my hand, and Tyler's name flashed on the screen. "It's him!" I shouted, and Cam closed his door.

"Tyler?" I answered frantically, running back inside my apartment.

"Is this Chloe Carlyle?"

The sound of a woman's voice startled me. "Yes, this is Chloe."

"There's been a car accident, and your name and number are coming up as the most recent dialed on the victim's cell phone."

CHAPTER FIFTEEN

Many years ago, when my mother first got out of rehab, she came home with a slew of new advice. Familiar sayings like "You can't always get what you want" and "Be happy with what you have" were replaced with things like:

"One must learn and grow from misfortune."

"There's a reason we don't get too many second chances in life, because if we did, we'd never learn to appreciate anything."

"Mistakes happen for a reason."

I was ten years old when I first learned that I was a mistake. My mother had been working as a receptionist at a dentist's office in Boca Raton when she began dating one of the patients. He was a used-car salesman who was getting some bridgework done. They'd gone out maybe two or three times before she got pregnant and convinced his God-fearing conscience to marry her. Two years later, another woman who'd purchased a convertible Mustang from him convinced his conscience to divorce my mother and marry her instead. "Accidents are often filled with unexpected blessings," Mom had tried to convince me. And although "unexpected," there was nothing about Tyler's accident that could be considered a "blessing."

The blood drained from my face. "Is it Tyler; is he okay?"

"He was brought to the emergency room at Evanston Hospital. I don't have all of the details. Are you related to Mr. Reed?"

"No, I'm a friend of the family."

"Do you have a phone number where we can reach his parents?"

"Um, yes, give me a sec." Shaking, I ran to my laptop and looked up the Reeds' home phone number. I rarely used it, but I figured they might not answer their cell phones late at night. "It's 847-555-1017. Can you please tell me if he's okay?"

"I'm sorry, Miss, I don't have any more information. Thank you for your help," she said and hung up.

I collapsed onto the floor and sat with my hands over my nose and mouth. *Oh my God. Oh my God. Oh my God.* I repeated over and over in my head. Tyler was hurt. He was on his way to be with me, and now he was hurt. He would miss the Rose Bowl. He may never play again. He may never walk again. *Oh my God. Oh my God. Oh my God.*

I stood up and ran back to Cam's.

"Tyler's been in an accident; the hospital just called me!" I cried out when he opened the door.

"Holy shit, what happened?" he asked.

"I don't know, he was on his way here, and when he never arrived, I just assumed he'd blown me off, but then he wasn't answering his phone, and I don't know what happened." My eyes were blazed with panic. "They brought him to Evanston Hospital. Do you think I should go over there?"

"Why was he coming to see you?"

"I don't know," I told him, hugging my body with my arms.

He lifted his hand to wipe a tear from my cheek. "It's going to be all right. What about his parents?"

"I gave the hospital their home phone number, so they must be getting the call right now. Oh my God, Cam, I hope he's okay!?"

"I'm sure he's going to be fine. Why don't you go to the hospital and see for yourself. Do you want me to go with you?"

I shook my head.

"Then call me as soon as you know something." Cam leaned in and gave me a peck on the cheek. "Try and relax."

I got dressed and drove frantically, trying not to get in an accident myself as I sped to the hospital. When I arrived, about forty minutes after the call, the tired woman at reception directed me to the E.R. waiting room on the ground floor. The Reeds had not arrived yet. I walked up to the nurses' station and inquired about Tyler. A nurse told me very little other than that he was in surgery and she'd let me know when he was admitted to a room. I fell asleep waiting.

At about nine thirty in the morning, the nurse woke me up and said Tyler was on the fifth floor in room 514.

"Thank you," I said. "Has anyone else asked for him?"

"His mother."

I took the elevator to the fifth floor and saw Mrs. Reed in the hall. She was talking to one of the hospital staff with her arms crossed in front of her. I ran up to her, poised to embrace her when she stepped backward as if I were diseased.

"Please see to it that only family members are allowed in," she said to the male nurse standing between us.

"Of course," he said.

"Is Tyler okay?" I asked, crazed in my desire for information.

Instead of answering, Mrs. Reed pursed her lips and looked at me as if I were a stranger. I had cared for this woman's children, taught them how to ride a bike, bandaged their skinned knees when she was playing golf, and here she was glaring at me with such distaste. She took one step closer to me and tilted her head before speaking. "I thought I told you to stay away from him," she said in a low, foreboding tone befitting any Disney villain.

I shook my head in dismay. There were no words to express the depth of my confusion. Apparently, her aggression was not always so passive.

"Do you have any idea what you've done?" she asked, eyes narrowed.

I placed my hand defensively on my chest. "I don't know what you think is going on between Tyler and me, but before tonight I hadn't seen him since the summer. I had no hand in this."

"Then why on earth are you here?" she asked. A fair question.

"I…they said I was the last call on his phone. He called me and asked to come over tonight. I tried to talk him out of it." I paused. "For God's sake, is he okay?"

"No, he's not okay. His arm is destroyed, and his season is over. Which means his career is *over*."

I mourned the loss of his Rose Bowl performance for a moment, but I cared little about his football career. I had raced down there to see if he was alive. If he was in a coma. If his eyes could still light up a room through a pane of glass. If having his undivided attention could still make me feel like the luckiest girl in the world. Was he in pain? Was he scared?

"How dare you lie to me," she snapped. "It's no secret that you're the cause of this disaster. You have no business here, and it's time you leave," she whispered angrily and then crossed her arms. The nurse looked up from his notes and made eye contact with me.

Her hostility left me stunned. I opened my mouth to speak but changed my mind. This was not the time to challenge her, so I turned and walked out through the large double doors and took the elevator to the lobby. However, I had no intention of going home. I walked out into the snow and across the street to a Starbucks, where I sat for two hours drinking peppermint lattes before heading back to the fifth floor of the hospital. My mind was spinning. I was sick about Tyler, not knowing whether he was bruised or on his deathbed. And I was pissed at his mother for treating me like some common nuisance. My nerves shook from a toxic combination of caffeine, sugar, and stress.

Only a few people were milling around the halls when I got off the elevator. I cautiously walked toward Tyler's room and looked around for the nurse I'd seen earlier with Mrs. Reed. Neither of them was in the hall, so I ignored her discriminatory demands and knocked gently on Tyler's door. There was no answer. When I knocked again, the door floated open.

"Hello," I whispered and took a microscopic step into the room. Still no answer.

I looked over my shoulder into the brightly lit hallway before taking one more step forward and closing the door behind me. Tyler was alone and asleep. The top of his head was wrapped with white gauze, and his right arm—in a cast that extended from his shoulder to his hand—was elevated by a hanging noose. *Not the arm,* I thought. A gentle beeping noise was the only sound.

Seeing him lying there brought me to tears. His face appeared so young and childlike despite his enormous frame. I sat down tentatively on the edge of an armchair in the corner of the room and folded my hands in my lap. I stared at his arm, suspended next to him, and prayed he would recover from his injuries. Gone was the confident, invincible Adonis, and in his place was a vulnerable, beat-up boy with angry parents. I sprang to his side when I heard a muffled sound come from his mouth.

"Tyler." I laughed with relief as his name crossed my lips. "Tyler, it's Chloe," I said.

The corner of his bruised lips curled into the hint of a smile. "I know who you are," he whispered.

"You scared the hell out of me. What happened to you?" I asked.

He closed his eyes and said nothing. Just moaned.

"Should I get the nurse in here?" I asked. "Are you in pain?"

"I fucked up," he said, his words barely audible.

"Shhhh," I said, lightly brushing some hair off his forehead. "It's going to be okay."

"No, it's not." Tyler sighed arduously. "It's over; everything is over."

Just then there was a knock on the door, and a nurse came in followed by two police officers.

CHAPTER SIXTEEN

Three days passed before I returned to the hospital. By then I'd learned that Tyler had been charged with driving under the influence, because he had a blood alcohol content of .09, when the legal limit was .08. One hundredth of a point kept him from returning to Notre Dame, and an unhappy triad injury kept him from ever playing football again. He spent four weeks recovering in the hospital and carried his parents' resentment and humiliation on his shoulders like a two-hundred-pound barbell. Just like his car crash, the entire course of his life changed in an instant. His identity as a revered football hero was stripped away, and everyone who had previously adored him disappeared. Except for me.

Every other night I drove to the hospital with my books and case studies and sat in his room reading and studying while he watched TV. On the few occasions that his mother came to see him, I would make myself scarce.

Exhausted did not begin to convey the depths of my fatigue. Between caring for my mom, attending classes, and visiting Tyler, I was in a permanent fog. Cam left a note on my door one night after about three weeks of that routine asking me to stop by when I got home from the hospital.

"Hi, stranger," he said when he opened the door. He held a cup of soup in his hands.

My mind had been pulled in so many directions, but Cam was still able to ground me, and seeing him made me feel like everything would be okay one day. He opened the door wearing an "I run with scissors" T-shirt that made me smile and relax my shoulders a notch. "Hi, Cam, I'm so sorry I missed the study group on Tuesday."

"No worries. You look like shit though."

"Thank you."

He shrugged and took a slurp of his soup. "Come on in."

Cam had the only one-bedroom apartment on our floor, and he was a neat freak. Everything had its place. No small appliances were allowed to live on the countertops; no garbage was allowed to sit in the can for more than six hours. There wasn't so much as an errant pencil languishing on a desktop. I plopped onto his couch and put my feet up on his coffee table. A move that was discouraged yet permitted.

"I'm worried about you, girl," he said.

"Me? I'm fine. I thrive on drama. It's normality that really scares me. In fact, the day my mother calls me and tells me she's on her way to Talbots before dropping off a tray of homemade seven-layer bars at a Junior League luncheon is the day I jump off a bridge."

Cam relaxed into a beanbag chair across from me. "You look exhausted. The circles under your eyes have circles."

"Is that the best you can do?"

"Okay, wait. The bags under your eyes are so big they each need their own bellman," he said.

I pretended like I was yawning.

Cameron tilted his head, looking concerned. "Does he appreciate you?"

I knew exactly whom he meant, but before Cam asked me, I hadn't ever really stopped to think about whether he did or he didn't. I cared a great deal for Tyler, and I wanted to be with him. It was that simple. After a week in the hospital, he'd thanked me for coming, and said it was the only thing he looked forward to. After two weeks, he'd asked me to lie with him in his bed.

"Climb up here," he'd said one night about half an hour before visiting hours were over.

"I'm too big to get up there with you."

"Please," he said as he struggled to shift himself over to make room for me.

"Stop, you're going to hurt yourself. I'll scoot my chair really close to the bed."

"I want you next to me, not on the chair. Get those gorgeous legs up here now."

I breathed a small sigh of defeat and carefully reclined next to him. First I sat, then I rested my body on my elbow and swung my legs up until I was barely on the edge of the bed. Tyler turned his head so that there was no more than an inch of space between our faces.

"I wanted to feel you. You're so warm," he said.

"Are you sure this doesn't hurt?"

"I'm sure. Give me your hand."

We wove our fingers together and rested our cheeks on each other. His labored breathing made me sad.

"I'm so sorry this happened to you," I whispered and squeezed his hand.

"Shhh, it's okay."

"I'm so sorry," I repeated. "I know how hard this must be for you. I can't imagine how you're able to deal with your father through all of this. And your teammates, they must be—"

"Shhh." Tyler let go of my hand, wrapped his arm around my shoulder, and kissed me. His lips were dry and soft, and I melted into them without moving another muscle for fear of hurting him.

From that day on, I'd climb into his hospital bed, and we'd kiss once the lights were off and the nurses had finished checking on him for the night. There was nothing awkward about it. Sometimes, as we lay there half-naked, our bodies and lips pressed tightly together, Tyler would tell me how I was healing him and beg me to stay the night.

I smiled at the thought of his needing me. "I think he does appreciate me," I finally said to Cam.

He nodded, but his expression indicated he wasn't convinced. I knew Cam had feelings for me that went beyond friendship, but I also knew I was in love with Tyler, and I made no secret of that.

"He's obviously going through a rough time, but he knows how much I care about him, and it helps," I said.

Although Tyler was recovering physically, the things that had defined him as a person were gone. He'd been sensationalized for his entire life and was struggling to figure out who he was without football. Granted, I was enamored with him, but after the accident there was a part of me that wanted to build him back up and, in the process, unearth another side of him.

"I just don't want to see you get hurt," Cam said.

"Thank you for that."

"I mean it, Chloe. You didn't have any relationship with the guy before the accident, and now you're like his only caregiver. Or girlfriend? Or I don't know what. What does he say about it?"

I shrugged. Cam could tell I was uneasy about his questions.

"I'm not trying to be a dick, I swear. You know that, right?"

"I know."

"I just want to make sure you're not putting all your energy into him without getting something in return," he said.

I averted my eyes. "Is that how you feel about me?"

He snorted with laughter. "I don't put all my energy into you."

I removed my feet from his table and leaned forward. "If I haven't told you how much you mean to me, then I should be ashamed of myself. Having you in my life has been such a gift, and there's no way I would have survived the last few months without you. However, I might not have gained five pounds if it weren't for you and your penchant for stuffed-crust pizzas, but it wouldn't have mattered anyway because I never would have survived."

"Pffft, you'd be fine with Amanda's shoulder to cry on, she and her trust fund can handle any crisis."

"I mean it, Cam. If you think I'm taking advantage of our friendship for one second, you let me know, and I will fix it."

Cam rolled his head and stretched his neck. "I do not feel taken advantage of. I'm only looking out for you. I can tell that you want to fix him, and I just don't want your efforts to be for naught. I don't know him well enough—or at all—to say whether he deserves you or not, so all I can hope is that he appreciates how much you care for him."

"I really think he does," I said, trying to convince myself as well.

CHAPTER SEVENTEEN

By the time my graduation from law school rolled around, Tyler and I were preparing to move in together to a condo he'd bought in the city. After our rather unusual hospital-room courtship, our relationship had blossomed into the real deal. It was a happy, romantic time for us, and it wasn't long before we fell into a comfortable routine. Though my head swam night and day with constitutional law, contract law, family law, and intellectual property law, Tyler was unfailingly sweet and supportive and kept me grounded. Some nights he'd watch sports at my apartment while I'd study with my feet resting on his lap. Other times he'd surprise me at the law library with a chocolate shake and cheese fries.

Tyler's relationship with his parents had gradually become less strained as ours grew more serious. Upon his recovery, he'd taken a job at McCutcheon Meats to appease his father, and his mother—being an expert at ignoring anything that displeased her—never brought up the past. My mother remained the same, but thankfully drama-free, and my life was on track to become more than I'd ever dared to hope for.

Everyone on our floor threw a huge party after graduation, even though we all knew the real work was ahead with the bar exam looming over us. But the night of our party, we were all in great spirits and got drunk off our asses. Cam and I spent most of the evening retelling old stories that made us laugh beer out of our noses and whispering private jokes to each other one last time. Saying good-bye to school was easy. Saying good-bye to Cam was another story.

I purposely messed up his apartment by dancing around and throwing empty plastic cups all over the floor just to annoy him, and he let me. We sat on the floor in the hallway with a few other friends and played poker. Cam sat across from me and sent me secret signals indicating what cards the people next to him had. We ended up winning $125 from Amanda's trust fund.

The next morning I woke up with a wicked hangover. I ran out to grab a Quarter Pounder with cheese to refuel before packing up the last of my things. Tyler came by around noon to help me move, and was amused to find the note he'd written me years before in Lake Geneva lying on top of a stack of papers.

"Don't mess with my note," I said as I saw him holding it. "It's proof that you want me."

He placed the note back on the dresser and came over to the sink where I was standing; then he wrapped his fingers around the base of my neck and pulled my lips to his. He lifted me off my feet and then proved how much he wanted me one last time on the floor of the kitchenette. We were lying naked amid a pile of crumbled newspaper when there was a knock at the door.

"Shit," I said and scrambled to get my clothes back on. "One sec!" I yelled to the door.

Tyler grabbed my ass as I was getting dressed and made very little effort to pull his pants up.

The woodpecker-tapping began when I took too long, and Cam was leaning against the doorframe when I finally opened it.

"Am I interrupting something?" he asked before looking past me and realizing that he was.

Tyler walked past us with two large boxes in his arms. "T'sup, Cam."

"I could use a hand too," Cam yelled after him.

I threw my hair back up into a ponytail. "You want to come in? There's actually room to sit now that Tyler's here to help."

"No, no, I just wanted to say good-bye," he said.

"I thought you were leaving Friday? You're not even packed."

Cameron fished a small box out of his jeans pocket and offered it to me. "Tic Tac?"

"I'm good."

He popped two mints in his mouth and began sucking and talking simultaneously. "I'm going to New York to visit a friend, then coming back and packing up this weekend. Get your tears out and your hugs in quickly, because I'm leaving"—he paused to check the time on his phone—"now."

I launched myself at him and hugged tightly.

"I'm going to miss you something good, Cameron Sparks," I said.

"I'm going to miss you too."

"Please call and text me all the time, okay? Be like really, super annoying about it."

"I promise," he said.

I let go and put some space between us. "Maybe we can get together when you're back from New York? I can help you pack up your stuff."

"Sure, I'll give you a call."

We stood there, suddenly awkwardly distant, as though the three years we'd lived and breathed each other every day had never happened.

I leaned in and gave him one last squeeze, and then pulled away. I didn't want to let go of him and was surprised by how sad I was. "You're cute," I said.

"I know."

CHAPTER EIGHTEEN

Studying for the bar exam was like training for the Olympics, only there was just one medal: gold. You either passed or you didn't. No second place, no consolation prize, and in my case, no job unless I passed. I'd been working for two summers as a law clerk at Goldin & Bass, a midsize firm in the city that specialized in divorce and family law. That summer I'd been given six weeks off from my job to prepare for the exam. I enrolled in a bar review course, and attended classes there five days a week, four hours a day. After class, I went straight to the library, and spent another seven to eight hours on class assignments and studying. Training for the exam began to take a toll on my mental and physical health. There were times when I'd be reading a case study and start hallucinating. Words would rise off the page and turn into insects right before my eyes. I lacked sleep, vitamins, food, liquids, exercise, sex, and just about everything else. Tyler ceased to exist, and I hadn't seen or phoned my mother in weeks. The only thing I could afford to care about was passing that test, and for some cruel reason, three years of law school had done little to prepare me for it.

During one of my last weeks of classes, I came home from the library at eleven o'clock and woke Tyler by accident when I knocked the toothbrush holder onto the bathroom floor.

"What the hell was that?" he yelled at me.

"I'm so sorry," I said, peeking my head into the bedroom. "I dropped the toothbrush cup on the floor."

He looked at the clock. "Jesus Christ, some of us have to work." And then I lost it.

"Do you have *any* idea what I've been going through? No wait, let me rephrase that—you have no idea what I've been going through. I'm up to my ears in books and reading and class assignments and stress and worry and guilt, so much so that I'm starting to see things that don't exist. I can't even form a thought without arguing the other side of it in my head! How dare you make me feel as if I need to tiptoe around here because 'some of us have to work'!"

My heart was racing. I could feel my body trying to stop shaking and return to normal. All I wanted was to crawl into bed and get the minimal amount of sleep I needed to stomach the next day's routine.

"Shut the fuck up," Tyler mumbled and pulled the comforter over his head.

His reaction nearly knocked me off my feet. He'd never spoken to me that way before, and he was well aware of the pressure I was under. Had he reached his limit of being supportive? Was it too much to ask of him to ride out this wave with me? I would never treat him like that if the tables were turned. I cried myself to sleep on the couch and made sure I was out of the house before he woke up.

The next day I attended my prep classes, but went over to Grace's apartment afterward instead of the library. I had four missed calls from Tyler, but hadn't returned any of them. He'd thrown me off course, and I resented him for doing anything that might risk my grade on that exam.

"Come on in," Grace said when I arrived.

"I haven't had a drink in three weeks, but I'm praying you have a bottle of wine."

"I teach preschoolers for a living…you know I have wine. So what happened?"

I threw my backpack on the floor, placed my laptop on her coffee table, and collapsed on the couch. "I blew up at Tyler last night. He gave me attitude when I accidentally woke him up, and I exploded."

Grace uncorked a bottle of Pinot Grigio, poured us each a glass, and joined me. She had always taken care of me. Whether I was having a breakdown about my mother, or complaining that I would never succeed in my career, or arguing with Tyler. I could always count on Grace. Though she liked Tyler a lot at this point, she'd always remained a little skeptical of him. I think she thought I was more invested in him than he was in me, but she'd welcomed him into the fold with open arms because she knew he made me happy. "I'm sure he knows you're under a ton of stress with the bar, and he's not going to be mad at you. Have you talked to him today?"

"He's called, but I haven't returned his calls."

"Just call him back. You're no good at playing games."

"That's just it, I'm not even trying to be stubborn and aloof. I don't even have time to *think* about making him suffer, much less act on it. I'm at the breaking point, and I can assure you, if I don't pass this test the first time, I'm going to move to Mexico and braid hair on the beach."

She snorted mid-sip. "I hear Playa del Carmen is nice," Grace said.

"Don't laugh, you know you'll be first in line."

"Well, you're not increasing your chances of passing the test by getting distracted over this. Finish your wine, and go home to your boyfriend so that you can get back on track."

"How are things with you and Jack?"

"Same old, same old."

Grace and Jack had been dating since well before I'd started law school. On the one hand, he was a respected young dentist who was due to take over his father's successful practice one day. On the other, he was the perennial child. He'd had the same group of friends since kindergarten, and as much as he loved Grace, he loved sports more. Watching sports, playing sports, talking about sports, thinking about watching and playing sports. He was about as interested in getting married as she was in playing fantasy baseball. But she wanted a family one day, as did I. Sometimes, we'd split a bottle of wine and imagine our picture-perfect lives together: as neighbors in Glenview, with our kids running back and forth, splashing through the sprinklers while we barbecued and sipped sangria in the backyard. Only then I'd remind her that I'd be at work most nights until ten o'clock, frantically begging her via texts to relieve my sitter and watch my kids for a few hours until Tyler or I could get home.

"He'll come around, Grace, and soon enough you'll be picking his dirty underwear up off the floor, wishing you were still single and living in the city listening to me bitch all night over a bottle of wine," I said.

I got home around seven o'clock. Tyler opened the door as I was fishing for my keys.

"Come here," he said and held out his arms.

My lips tightened, and I fought back tears as thunder sounded in the distance.

He pulled me close to his chest. My body convulsed with exhaustion, pressure, worry, fear, and self-doubt. Then I began to cry.

Tyler rubbed my back, wiped my tears, then pulled away and led me to the kitchen, where he had prepared dinner. "Don't ignore my calls. At least let me know you're okay," he said to me.

"Fair enough."

He pulled a tray of lasagna out of the oven, one that his mother had brought when she'd visited our apartment the first—and only—time. In addition to a homemade lasagna, she'd brought a six-pack of paper towels, some nuts (for guests, she instructed), a glass bowl to put said nuts in, four martini glasses that were hand-painted in pink and green leopard print, and a tiny cardboard box with scented soaps perched on a small pile of hay.

"I made the lasagna and picked up a salad," he said.

"Fancy."

"Thought you'd be impressed," Tyler said, spooning two servings onto plates.

"It looks amazing, Ty, thank you," I said and embraced him from behind. He placed the spoon down and turned around, clutching me like we'd been apart for days and kissed the top of my head.

"I'm starving," I announced.

"Have a seat. I'll bring everything over," he said as he uncorked a bottle of wine.

We didn't own a table and chairs yet, so I took a seat on one of the two stools at the island that separated the kitchen from the family room. Tyler grabbed the two glasses of wine and joined me. He looked tired and beat up. I knew he still missed having a passion for something. Whether football had been his true passion or not, he'd been committed to the game and accustomed to its accolades. It was hard for Tyler to live without praise and adoration once he'd gotten used to having them around. The drudgery of answering e-mails and dealing with disgruntled customers was no comparison to the glory days of performing your work in front of bleachers packed with cheering fans.

"A toast to you," he said, raising his glass. "The most beautiful and intriguing woman I've ever known. All that I know about happiness, you have taught me, and everything good in my life can be traced back to you. I know I act like a complete thug most of the time, but I really don't know where I'd be right now without your support. I love you, Chloe."

He rendered me speechless for a moment. Tyler was a man of few emotions, who mostly repressed his feelings like dirty secrets. The look on my face went from pleased to elated in an instant.

"I love you too," I said and leaned in to kiss him. Tyler was and always would be a bit of an anomaly to me. One night he's snapping at me, and the next he's professing his love over a semi-home-cooked meal with words I've never heard from him before. As much as he praised me for making him happy, deep down I still questioned whether he was capable of loving me as much as I loved him. But that night, I simply basked in his kind words. It was exactly what I needed.

"Only a couple weeks left until the big test," he said and began to eat.

"You'll have me back in no time."

"I'm fine, Chloe, don't let this asshole get in your way."

"I won't," I said and smiled. "How's work been?"

He took two bites of his pasta before answering. "It's a job."

"Have you ever thought about what else you'd like to do?" I asked.

"I'm fine where I am."

"No, you're not. I know you hate working at McCutcheon, and there's no reason you have to stay there. As soon as the bar exam is over, I'll be back to work, and making enough money to pay the bills around here. You can take some time and look for something else."

"I have every reason to stay there. My grandfather would be disappointed, and my father would kill me if I left, to name two."

"Your father hasn't bothered to reach out to you in three months," I said. "I know you're miserable there, and I know you could be great at something else. You need to figure out what's going to make you happy and go after it. It's not fair that you should be punished the rest of your life."

He looked at me with a blank, unreadable expression. "I don't want to talk about him," he said, shaking his head.

"Why don't you at least look into some graduate film classes at Columbia College or Loyola? You could take them at night if you don't want to quit your job. Your cousin Mitch...doesn't he work in the industry? I remember your mother saying something about him having a job in production. You should call him."

Tyler nodded, scooped another piece of lasagna onto his plate, then pushed his plate away and looked at me, hungry for something else.

"No more pasta?" I asked.

"Stand up."

"Why?"

"Just do it."

"I need to finish some reading before bed," I said even as I stood.

Tyler lifted me up onto the island and wedged himself between my legs. He pressed his mouth onto mine, and I bent forward and melted into him, losing every ounce of motivation to do anything but stay wrapped in his arms. Tyler stopped abruptly, with my legs wrapped around his torso, leaving me wanting more. "Don't move," he said. Holding my hands at my sides, he kissed me everywhere else. When he loosened his grip, I draped my hands around his neck and kissed him right below his ear. "I love you, Tyler."

CHAPTER NINETEEN

It was the morning of Friday, October 15th, and I was at work, curled up on the bathroom floor of the ladies' room with my head in the toilet. After the second time I threw up, my brow was moist with perspiration, but my stomach felt a little better. The Illinois State Bar Examiners were supposed to post the exam results on their website at midnight the night before, but hadn't done so. By nine I'd been awake for over twenty-four hours, spilled an iced mocha on my skirt, deleted two important e-mails, and cried in front of the IT guy. At ten o'clock, I got an e-mail alert that the results were finally posted.

I opened the e-mail and stared at the link that would take me to the test results for twenty minutes before closing the e-mail and calling Tyler.

My voice and hands were shaking. "Hi," I said.

"What the hell, have those dickheads posted scores yet?" he asked, fully aware of my need for a straitjacket.

"I just got the e-mail, but I haven't looked yet."

"Well, take your time. Have a scone or two and maybe you can get around to it sometime after lunch."

I cracked open a bottle of water and took a sip in order to tame the nausea while my head pounded like the inside of a bass drum. "I'm trying to, but I can't."

"Open the goddamn e-mail, Chloe. I know you passed, you know you passed; we've been over this. Now let's find out together. I'll stay on the phone, but you need to do it now."

"Okay," I said. "My hand is shaking so badly I can barely click the mouse. All right, e-mail is open. I'm clicking the link now. I'm into the website. I'm going to the results page," I gave Tyler the play-by-play as I scanned through the list of names and nearly wept for the people with FAIL next to their names until I got to mine, sandwiched between Sean Carlson and Megan Cartwright.

Carlyle, Chloe: PASSED

I blinked my eyes and read it twenty times while Tyler waited in perfect silence. "I passed."

"Shit yeah, that's my girl!" he screamed into the phone. "I'm so proud of you! I can't wait to celebrate with you later."

Tears and snot and sweat and relief drained out of me as I laughed and cried and shook with pure joy. I sniffed into the phone, unable to speak.

"I love you, and I'm so happy for you. We're going to celebrate tonight, so come straight home, okay?" he said.

"Okay," I muttered into the phone.

"I love you, Chloe."

I wiped my face and let myself revel in the good news for a few minutes before calling my mom.

"Good for you," she said when I told her. "That's great news. You told me how hard you were studying."

"I did, yes, thank you. It means I can keep my job."

"Thank goodness for that," she said.

Although I never asked her for money, she was always insinuating that I would. I'd tell her I was going away for the weekend to visit a friend, and she'd say, "Well, I hope you can afford it." Or I'd tell her that I was off to Macy's to buy winter boots and she'd say, "I've been saving up for a new pair myself." Always diverting me from daring to tap into her precious monthly stipend.

"I have some news of my own," she told me.

I grabbed a tissue from the box at the corner of my desk and patted my nostrils. "Oh yeah?" I said, assuming she'd bought new throw pillows or the woman at the dry cleaners had cut the sleeves off all her shirts.

"I'm moving back to Florida."

I paused. "You're what?"

"I'm moving back to Miami to care for my brother."

"Why can't Justin's wife look after him?"

"She left him."

"When?" I asked.

"Two years ago."

I placed my elbow on the desk and rested my forehead in my fingertips. "Why didn't you tell me?" I asked, even though I knew what her answer would be.

"I did tell you," she said, as I'd predicted.

Things would go into her head like a roach trap and never come out. And when and if her bits of knowledge did escape, she assumed I was well aware of every detail. It was pointless to argue—I knew that—but I was incapable of not defending myself.

"You never mentioned that to me," I said.

"Well, she left as soon as he got cancer. Took his dog and never came back."

I lifted my head for a second and rolled my eyes. "He has cancer? What kind?"

"I don't recall."

"Mom, surely one of his kids can help him or he can get some in-home care. Do you really want to leave your house here?"

"Florida is nice and warm, and it's where my brother is. And so long as these people around here mind their business and don't follow me down there, I can go and take care of my family in peace."

There was never any point in arguing with her. Ever since I'd tricked her into going to the hospital years before, she'd given little weight to my opinions. She still blamed me for that day. For humiliating her and calling attention to her in a negative manner. For leaving her home and her belongings unattended. She would never see that my efforts were out of love, because she would never acknowledge that she had a problem. She'd forgiven me the best she could, but not completely.

"I'll miss you, Mom."

"You can help me pack. I could really use the assistance. I can't trust movers to come into my home and pack everything up without stealing my things."

"I have to work, but I can help you during the weekend if you give me some notice. When are you planning on leaving?"

"Maybe in a couple weeks. You can help me pack before then."

"Mom," I spoke slowly. "I'm happy to help, but you need to give me notice, and I can only help on the weekend. So please let me know what day you'd like me there."

"All right, I'll call you back," she said, never keen on using her phone for too long. I'd begged her to get a cell phone, but she said they were too easy to trace.

I hung up with my mom and suppressed any thoughts regarding my obligations to her and whether this move was a good idea. Something I'd become quite adept at. My boss's office was a floor below me, so I took the elevator down to his office and knocked on his door. My job at Goldin & Bass was contingent on my passing the bar, so I was eager to give him the good news.

"Congratulations," he said.

"Thanks, Ron."

"I know what a load of stress that takes off your shoulders."

"You have no idea, well, I mean obviously you have some idea… yes, I feel like a new person," I said, beaming.

"Be sure and let H.R. know so that we can set you up with permanent employment here. I assume you're interested in staying?"

I laughed. I'd been working at Goldin & Bass for three summers by then, and the job market was vicious. Thousands of people standing in line for the same chance, the same handout, the same opportunity to hone their craft. And if you got out of line for any reason, there was someone behind you waiting to take your spot in an instant. Need to pee? Better hold it. Need to sleep? You're weak. Need to spend time with your family? Well, there's a singleton in line with no family who will work for less.

"I'm very interested in staying, yes."

"We're lucky to have you on board. We'll put together a formal job offer for you and get you all set up."

"Thank you," I said and returned to my desk.

I breathed easier and stood straighter. My stomach, which had plagued me for months with nausea, cramping, and stabbing side pains, had finally settled.

There were two texts from Tyler when I got back to my desk.

I love you.

Come straight home after work.

I placed the phone in my purse and looked blissfully around the office. Behind me were the familiar sounds of phones ringing, faxes coming through, fingers pecking at keyboards—the sounds of freedom.

The sky was black at seven o'clock when I left the office and headed home. Tyler had insisted we celebrate regardless of the exam results, only I can't imagine that I would've gone along with his plan had I failed. I grinned with excitement as I put the key in the door, picturing balloons and flowers and champagne waiting for me on the other side, but the house was dark when I walked in.

"Hello?" I said, thinking Tyler and Grace and a gaggle of friends were hiding somewhere to surprise and scare the shit out of me.

A few more steps. "Hello? Tyler?"

I set my computer case on the floor, put my hands on my hips, and tried to decipher the emptiness before walking toward the kitchen, which was the only illuminated room in the apartment. As I approached, I noticed the desk lamp from our bedroom was sitting on top of the island, shining its light on a wooden box with a heart engraved on the top. I looked at it curiously and smiled. I flipped the wall switch and turned on the overhead lights. I took the box in my hands and opened it. Inside was a familiar, folded piece of paper.

Meet me at the lake at midnight.

CHAPTER TWENTY

I placed the note on the counter and smoothed it out with my hands. I imagined him tearing through my stuff looking for it, and then gloating once he'd found it among my socks and underwear. That piece of paper represented the very start of our relationship, and was my first glimpse into Tyler's affection for me. Just then I noticed another piece of paper stuck to the fridge with a magnet from a local realtor that read DO WHAT IT SAYS. I stood perplexed. Was he at his parents' lake house in Wisconsin? I grabbed my cell to call him, but hesitated. If he had some sort of surprise planned, I didn't want to ruin his fun, but I also didn't want to drive an hour and a half to Lake Geneva if he was just trying to embarrass me by unearthing my cherished keepsake. Just then I got a text from him.

Are you home?

Yes, I texted back.

Then do as you're told.

I smiled and ran to get my things. It was only eight o'clock, so I had plenty of time.

I left the house at ten thirty, yawning but excited. The drive didn't take as long at that hour, so I stopped at the Brat Stop—known to serve the best bratwurst sandwiches north of the Illinois border—on the way there to kill some time. I was determined to follow his instructions and arrive exactly at midnight.

About five minutes before midnight I pulled into the driveway of the Reeds' lake house. I hadn't been there for three years, but the country air quickly awakened my lungs and welcomed me back. I stepped out of my car and looked around. Sculpted hedges led to the front door where guests were greeted with wind chimes and a doormat that read "A Step in the Reed Direction." I scooted my bag higher onto my shoulder and rang the bell, but there was no answer. I checked the time on my phone and walked around to the back of the house. My heart swelled. The dock was glowing with lanterns and Tyler was standing at the edge of it.

He lifted his arm to wave at me, and I dropped my bag and dashed toward him.

"Good to know you can still take direction," he said.

I stopped about five feet away from him. "I thought you'd be impressed."

"Sit down," he said and gestured toward the two Adirondack chairs he'd brought down from the porch.

Tyler lowered himself into one and sat perched on the edge of the chair, resting his elbows on his knees, facing me. He took both my hands in his.

"I have something to ask you, and I couldn't think of a better place," he started. "You are an exceptional woman, who deserves someone much better than me. But for some ungodly reason, you love me as much as I love you, and for that I'll be forever grateful," he said, pausing to wipe a tear from my cheek. "And if there's a chance in hell I can make you happy, then I'd like to spend the rest of my life trying." He pushed his chair back, got down on one knee, and pulled a box from his front pocket.

My hands flew to my mouth.

"Will you marry me, Chloe, and let me give you the family you deserve?"

I nodded fiercely and answered without hesitation. "Yes."

Tyler opened the box and unveiled an infinity band of emerald-cut diamonds. It was the most magnificent piece of jewelry I'd ever seen. He placed the ring on my shaky finger, and I leaped into his lap and held on to his neck for dear life while I sobbed with joy. My infatuation with him had never waned. I was as head over heels right then as I'd been the first time he touched me on that very dock.

"All I've ever wanted was you," I said, pulling back. "Please don't put yourself down. I hate when you do that. You've already made me so happy, and I can't imagine moving forward in life without you. I don't ever want to be without you."

He tightened his grip and rubbed my back with firm strokes. "I love you, Chloe. Your legs, your face, your hair, your vanilla-scented shampoo, your insane job. All of it."

"I love you, too, so much."

His lips met mine, and I was as excited as if he was kissing me for the first time. My heart beat with anticipation as he pressed me down onto the dock with the weight of his body.

Something about being at the lake filled both of us with a renewed sense of discovery. Tyler paused to gaze at me. His hands slowly traced my neck and jawbone as he regarded me with a combination of familiarity and curiosity. He stood and led me to the house. As soon as we stepped inside, I pulled him to the guest room off the kitchen where I'd lived for three weeks so long ago. Nothing had changed. He threw me onto the white bed, and we made love like two young college kids on summer break.

We spent the weekend there snuggled up in front of roaring fires and stuffing our faces. That Saturday we drove into town and picked up food from the local gourmet market and sat on the patio with wine and beer and cheese and talked for hours about what kind of wedding we would have. How long we should stay in our apartment. How many kids we'd have, and how much fun it was going to be trying for them. After Tyler's accident, when we'd first moved in together, we had talked occasionally about getting engaged one day. Even back then both of us were eager to get married and start a family, but I insisted I needed to get through law school and pass the bar first. Tyler had also wanted to feel more settled in his own career before getting married. It killed me to think he still felt trapped and unhappy with his job. His already strained relationship with his father had taken yet another hit when he'd broached the subject of switching jobs with him recently. He wanted to go to film school and get into commercial production like his cousin Mitch, but Tyler's father was insistent on his going to business school and reviving his grandfather's meatpacking business.

I used our time at the lake that weekend to encourage him to talk to his dad again. Dr. Reed had controlled Tyler's life for as long as he could remember, and defying his parents was nearly impossible for him. Their love was always conditional; something he'd begun to realize after the accident. It was difficult for me to watch him vie for his parents' respect at the age of twenty-six. It reminded me of the days when I babysat Sammy and Sarah, and they would write stories or make drawings and try to goad their parents away from their cell phones for even a moment to show them their accomplishments.

"Mommy is going to love this one!" Sarah would say to me, adding extra red glitter to every creation because it was her mom's favorite color. "Maybe she'll put this one up in her office?" She'd hope. Four hours later, I'd find the drawing torn in half on the floor of Sarah's bedroom. And no matter how much I gushed and squealed, it could never make up for her parents' disregard. I knew all too well that children of every age needed validation from their parents, and whether those parents were delusional recovering alcoholics or inconsiderate socialites, learning to thrive without it was an arduous process.

Sunday night, our last night at the lake, we sat on the dock wrapped in blankets.

"I really think you should talk to your dad again," I said.

"I know you do."

"I'm not trying to be annoying, but if you're unhappy, then I'm unhappy. And I know you want me to be happy, right?" I teased.

Tyler leaned forward and kissed me. "Very much so."

CHAPTER TWENTY-ONE

Tyler and I were married the following summer on that very dock. It was a small ceremony with fifty guests including Grace and Jack and her parents, Tyler's extended family, and a few friends. Cam declined due to a "work thing," but promised to send a gift within the allotted year's time.

I'd asked Grace's father, Ethan, to do me the honor of walking me down the aisle. A large, handsome man who adored his wife and his family and represented everything I ever hoped for in a husband, he was the embodiment of honesty and integrity.

I wished my mother could have been there, but she'd insisted on staying in Miami. She assured me that she would've loved to come, but that the authorities would most certainly be waiting to ambush her at the airport. She'd moved into an assisted-living facility in Florida where she employed a woman named Vivian to come in once a day to help with minor chores and errands. She refused to leave her house other than to check on her brother, who was being treated at a nearby hospital. I'd been down there only once to visit her since the move. We'd sat in her apartment for two days watching television and eating takeout because she wouldn't let me take her to a restaurant. I'd sent her an invitation to the wedding and offered to send her a plane ticket, but she was unwavering in her decision to stay put. She did, however, send me a white cotton cardigan from Dillard's.

The ceremony was held at the base of the Reeds' hill, overlooking the lake, and the reception took place at the Grand Geneva Resort where we were staying for the weekend along with many of the guests. Tyler's mom had been reticent to let us use the house for any of the festivities without her input, so my wedding had quickly become her wedding.

"We wouldn't want our guests in the direct heat, would we?" she asked and insisted on handing out parasols to everyone when they arrived.

She'd ask me questions as if my opinion carried any weight, but in reality every question was simply a declaration of the only opinion that mattered. Hers.

"You don't really want to serve ranch dressing with the crudités, do you?"

"You're not going to wear flip-flops on your weddin' day, are you?"

"Bless your heart, you didn't really think wildflowers were fit for a bridal bouquet, did you?"

I nodded and bit my tongue for most of it. As long as I was standing at the end of that dock with Tyler next to me, I didn't care what was on my feet or in my hands.

I had convinced myself that Tyler's parents were pleased with our union. Either that, or they'd simply learned to put a good face on it. Mrs. Reed had thrown us an engagement party at their country club where I actually overheard Dr. Reed bragging about my career path to one of his friends. He never said much to me, but he regularly asked about my job and listened to my answers with great sincerity and pride once I was officially a Reed.

Since our jobs only allowed for a short honeymoon, we flew to Cancún for a long weekend. Tyler and I drank margaritas and ate more guacamole than I'd thought humanly possible in those four days. We wore very little clothing, spent mealtimes in the hot tub, bedtime on the beach, and joked about how appalled his mother would've been with our lack of decorum.

To say that my job was demanding was an understatement, but I loved what I did. Having a front-row seat to other people's familial and marital drama was not only a fascinating study of human nature but also an opportunity for me to give those people some justice. It was more rewarding than I ever thought possible. Soon after I'd passed the bar exam and begun working full-time, Tyler had a heart-to-heart with his father and began taking film school classes at night while working at McCutcheon during the day. The year of our engagement we were like two ships passing in the night. Tyler had wanted to double up on his courses so that he could get his degree and start a business with his cousin Mitch, so e-mails and texts were our main source of communication during that time. Though I didn't get to see him as much as I would have liked, I was thrilled to see him on the road to finding his passion. When we did have a little downtime together, he talked to me at length about his courses and what he was learning. About the type of business he and Mitch wanted to create, and about the work they'd be able to produce.

Mitch was his first cousin on his mother's side, and four years older than Tyler. I met him and his girlfriend Hollis for the first time at our wedding. They were both creative types. Hollis was a jewelry designer who sold her wares mostly at art festivals and online. She had a degree in metalsmithing and art history, and was for sure the type that would hold a bouquet of wildflowers at her wedding one day. Mitch worked as production designer and graphic artist for an ad agency in Chicago, and was eager to get Tyler up to speed so that they could go off on their own.

That fall, after our wedding, Tyler finally quit his job at McCutcheon Meats, and he and Mitch opened their own commercial production company called It's All Relative. Mitch got a loan from the bank, Tyler used some money from our wedding, and I invested $10,000 from my personal savings account. His parents made no secret of what a bad idea they thought it was, but since Dixie Reed cared more about appearances than anything else, Tyler soon became the most celebrated and accomplished commercial director in the Midwest whenever she spoke of him. If all else failed, he had her counterfeit praise to fall back on.

The first two years of our marriage came with the typical challenges and rewards. We argued over what kind of dining room table to buy, and then made love on top of it once it arrived; we fought over who should do the grocery shopping, and then fed each other Chinese takeout at midnight. We worked too hard, too long, too late, and slept until noon on Saturdays, bickering over which one of us should do a Starbucks run. I excelled at work, and began to make a name for myself in my field. I built my client list, won all but two of my cases, and had referrals coming in from all over the state. It's All Relative began to grow its client base as well, and went from four employees to twenty-four in the course of eight months. We stayed in our apartment in the city for as long as we could stand it, but soon began itching for a bigger place. I had doubled my salary, and wanted us to start a family and own a home in the suburbs. We'd talked often over the years about what kind of parents we'd be.

"I'll be the disciplinarian," I'd say.

Tyler rolled his eyes. "The second they thrust their bottom lips out, you'll burst into tears and give them whatever they want."

I nodded slightly. "I do hate it when kids cry. But you're going to be a pushover too; I'm sure of it. Especially if it's a little girl."

"So then I'll have two girls running me around in my own house?"

"Damn straight."

"You're right: we do need a bigger place."

Tyler would be the fun Dad who'd wrestle his kids and tickle them until they couldn't breathe. The type that would volunteer for every coaching opportunity available to him—but not badger his kids like his own father had. I knew he was eager to be a good, attentive father, and even more so to have a son. We were both excited for the opportunity to prove to ourselves that we knew what good parenting looked like, despite our lack of examples.

So the week before my twenty-ninth birthday, we moved out of our apartment in the city, right back to where we'd come from, into a four-bedroom Cape Cod in Glenview. We hired painters and hung drapes. Shopped for new furniture and towels. I had the two smaller bedrooms upstairs painted in pale yellow and kept them unfurnished. We did the kitchen in a bright apple green and the foyer in a shade of flannel gray. I bought new hand towels for the guest bathroom on the first floor, and we finally found a place for some of our more unwieldy wedding gifts, such as the crepe maker and eight-piece fondue pot. Anytime I'd run to the grocery store, I'd come home with flowers and fill vases in every room. It was a small gesture, but it allowed me to create the dream home I'd never had growing up. By Christmastime we were settled in, and decided to host a small holiday-housewarming dinner. We invited Tyler's parents, Grace's parents, Mitch and Hollis, my paralegal Robert and his wife, Madison, and of course Grace and Jack, who'd married a year after Tyler and me.

That day I set our brand-new dining room table with the glass-ware and flatware we'd registered for. I made my first beef tenderloin, and Grace's mom, ever so thoughtful, brought two side dishes so that I wouldn't feel overwhelmed in the kitchen. I tore up loaves of sourdough bread and put them in a basket next to a dish with room-temperature butter. I lit candles in a pair of tall silver candlesticks that had been a wedding gift from one of Dr. Reed's colleagues. It was the most elegant party I'd ever hosted, and I was pretty damn proud of myself.

The evening went off without a hitch.

That is, until Mrs. Reed had too much to drink.

"Oh my stars! Beef tenderloin; aren't you ambitious," she said, taking a bite. "You know that Williams Sonoma offers a cooking class on all the *basics*. Wouldn't that be fun for you?"

Grace lifted her napkin to her mouth to hide her smile.

"My schedule is a little demanding, but that does sound...fun," I said.

"And Chloedear, the color in the kitchen is such an interesting choice. It looks vereh fresh, but I would've thought it better for a bathroom. You must really like green."

"I guess I do," I said. "It *is* very fresh."

She rested her utensils on her plate and folded her hands in her lap. "I have a copy of the *Better Homes and Gardens* color guide that I'll bring over; it's no trouble at all," she continued. "Also, I saw the most lovely bedroom set at Ethan Allen; it's their Quincy collection, and would look wonderful upstairs."

"We have a bed, Mom," Tyler said without looking up from his plate.

"Vereh well, but you can't be sittin' on that old davenport in the family room. I saw one with the most gorgeous floral print that I'll have sent over next Thursday. A proper floral print will look perfect under your front window."

I kicked Tyler on the shin under the table, but he said nothing. Grace's mom, Sydney, looked at me with wide eyes like she was finally starting to understand what I'd been telling her about Dixie Reed all these years.

"That's very generous of you, but not neces—" I started to say.

"And I've ordered you a subscription to *Southern Living* magazine," Mrs. Reed interjected before delicately patting her mouth with the linen napkin. "Tylah, dear, did you hear that Sadie recently married and moved into the most elegant three-story colonial up in Lake Forest? Her whole front drive is lined with magnolia trees. You're not too far from each other now."

"Excuse me," I said and pushed my chair away from the table. "I'm going to get dessert ready."

Grace followed and found me tossing things into the kitchen sink. She placed a hand on my shoulder. "She's awful; don't let her get to you."

I turned to face her. "Seriously, Grace, have you ever seen someone behave that way? And I don't know if Tyler is oblivious to it or if he just doesn't give a shit, but he should be defending me in there."

"I'm sure he's just used to the way she is, and has trained himself to ignore anything and everything that comes out of her mouth."

"I literally drove forty minutes out of my way to pick up Dr. Reed's favorite lemon tart. I'm just waiting for her to announce that she read an article in *Newsweek* about how citrus fruits are loaded with pore-clogging toxins."

"Shhh." Grace laughed. "Do as Tyler does, and just ignore her."

I sighed and returned to the table with some more bread.

Despite what Dixie Reed thought of the house, I loved it more than anything in the world. It represented so much to me: everything I'd worked for, time I'd sacrificed away from Tyler, a sense of normalcy. It was a place unlike anything I'd ever dared to imagine for myself, and would eventually hold everything that was precious to me. The layout was open and warm. The doorbell chimed instead of buzzed. There was even a wraparound porch and swing set in the backyard that we had asked the previous owners to leave behind when we purchased the home. All it needed was a baby.

But a year later, those swings were still empty.

CHAPTER TWENTY-TWO

Tyler and I began our quest for a child like everyone else. As soon as we were married, I went off the pill, and we had sex. Lots of it. We were newlyweds, still eager to grope each other in cabs and French-kiss at restaurants. And having spent the last few years doing everything I could to *prevent* myself from getting pregnant, I figured it would happen as soon as I threw out the birth control. I mean, my mother had spent an entire decade of my youth telling me how easily it could happen and how to avoid it; surely once I was unprotected, I would get pregnant with little or no effort.

Not so much.

For a while I was content to be busy with work, and convinced myself that it would happen when it happened. But once we'd moved into our new home, I became more and more anxious. That swing set became a daily reminder of my childless state, and I was fielding relentless questions from people asking when Tyler and I were starting a family. I spent hours online reading blogs and seeking advice from other women experiencing their own tribulations with infertility. I equally stalked and avoided friends on Facebook, amazed at how many of them were either pregnant or had just given birth. Newborns and pregnant women were suddenly popping up all around me and taunting me at every turn. Pointing at me and playing on my insecurities and fears like school-yard bullies.

And then Grace announced she was pregnant, further exacerbating my self-pity. I had never noticed how many pregnant women there were before. Worse was when women would complain about being pregnant. One day I was in the ladies' room at work, and the receptionist from the third floor waddled in and chatted me up as I was washing my hands.

"Ugh." She sighed. "If I have to pee one more time this morning, I'm going to scream."

I pursed my lips into a half smile.

"And my ankles are killing me; I can hardly walk."

I grabbed a white trifold paper towel from the dispenser and dried my hands. "I'm sure it'll all be worth it."

"Yeah right; soon I'll have three brats refusing to listen to me!" She laughed heartily.

I walked out of that bathroom without a word and into the one just below it on the second floor. I sat in a stall and cried. I hated feeling sorry for myself, and I hated being jealous even more. I had spent my entire life accepting the hand I'd been dealt, and teaching myself the skills that were necessary to change things. But there I was, given a situation that I couldn't study for, negotiate with, or purchase. Tyler would do his best to try to convince me to be patient. To remind me that it would happen for us when the time was right, but he wasn't nearly as anxious as I was.

So after five months of officially "trying" and being disappointed every time my period arrived—much like a surprise visit from my mother-in-law—I sought help from my gynecologist.

"I have a what?" I asked Dr. Leonard.

"You have a uterine abnormality," he told me. "It's quite common really, and varies among women. Yours is shaped more like a T than the typical pear shape."

I shook my head. His words were clearly spoken, but made little sense to me. All I heard was: "In addition to your size-ten shoes, you have a strange uterus. Basically, you're kind of freakish. You're abnormal. I'm sorry to be the one to tell you."

"What exactly does a T-shaped uterus mean? Is that why I'm having so much trouble getting pregnant?" I asked him. "Will I be able to get pregnant?"

"Generally speaking, uterine abnormalities don't affect your ability to become pregnant and give birth. However, it may be more difficult for you to carry your baby for the full nine months of pregnancy. It's really hard to say at this point."

I pondered his explanation, but couldn't worry about carrying a child before I actually conceived one.

"This is going to sound stupid, but is there anything else I should be doing to get pregnant other than having sex?" I asked.

He smiled at me and my T-shaped uterus.

"I've tried using ovulation kits once or twice, and lying with my feet elevated after sex," I continued. Little did he know I'd nearly perfected my post-intercourse headstand.

"You can always try artificial insemination if you're feeling discouraged."

And with that suggestion, our mission began—and our fun newlywed sex ended.

Over the course of a year, Tyler and I tried four artificial inseminations, during which time I became addicted to pregnancy kits. My doctor had warned me not to use them, insisting that the results would be skewed, but I was obsessed. The insemination process consisted of me sitting on the examination table waiting for José, the lab technician, to roll in the ultrasound machine, which was basically a dildo with a camera. By law, José was not allowed to insert it inside of me, so I was left to do the task myself…with José cheering me on. Once the wand was in position, my body would tense up like a cat being forced to wear a sweater. I became immobile and frozen, unable to move or breathe comfortably, just praying the whole thing would end quickly. Pride had become a distant memory...as had fun newlywed sex. Even as a young girl I had always been modest, never one to flaunt my cleavage or wear short skirts to accentuate my long legs. Yet, there I was at the ripe old age of twenty-nine with my legs spread and my crotch on display for anyone with a white lab coat.

Once the condom-covered magic wand was inside me, José would begin his hunt through my ovaries, looking for those golden eggs. He needed to confirm I was producing enough, and that they were big enough to do the job. After confirming my eggs were good to go, the technician would get them gussied up for their date with Tyler's sperm.

That same day, Tyler would also have had to go to the clinic and leave his "deposit." As embarrassing as the procedures I had to endure were, I'm not sure there's anything more humiliating for a man than walking past a crowd of people and into a room to leave a sperm sample.

"Good luck, honey!" I'd say, giving him a thumbs-up.

"I hope this kid appreciates my hard work," Tyler would joke.

"We'll make sure they know how much effort went into their conception."

"Maybe we should leave the porn out of it," he said.

"Agreed."

Once Tyler did his job, a nurse would take Tyler's sperm, wash them in the spin cycle, give them each a spritz of cologne and a tequila shot, and then load them into the turkey baster that would eventually be inserted into my waiting vagina. So this was how babies were made. After Tyler's sperm were inside me, the nurses would instruct us to have sex the next day in case there were any drunk, lazy sperm that didn't feel like cooperating. After each insemination, I bought pregnancy kits by the cartonful, and had them hidden everywhere in the house. I was willing to pee on anything that would give me the results I was looking for.

My moods swung wildly, but the one thing I could count on was getting my period each month—and losing hope every time. During this time, Grace gave birth to a beautiful little girl named Francesca. I planned her baby shower and hosted it at my home. While she sat and opened gifts, my heart broke with every little bib and pink layette she held up in the air for a picture. Grace and I had always talked about starting a playgroup and how our kids would be best friends, just like we were. Only, by then I was a year behind.

Although Tyler and I had both been tested for every possible thing that might be preventing us from having a child, the doctors had found nothing concrete and simply labeled our problem as unknown. He was as supportive as he could be, but I knew it frustrated him to see me upset and have his manhood questioned. And while he'd told me repeatedly that he was fine with all of the doctors' visits and procedures, I would occasionally catch him sighing and rolling his eyes when I'd mention some new test we had to endure. There was really no way to sugarcoat the fact that he had to masturbate in the doctor's office while everyone outside knew what he was doing. So aware that they were basically waiting to greet him as he exited the room, semen sample in hand. He and I had laughed about it at first, and he'd tried so hard to pretend it wasn't humiliating. Early on, we even made up a few nicknames for his sperm sample, such as Tea Time with Tyler and A Few Good Men, but those had long since been forgotten. Our sense of humor had started to fade by failed attempt number four.

"Good luck, honey!" I'd say, and Tyler would walk past me with no retort.

Alas, none of the inseminations worked, and we were told that in vitro fertilization or adoption would be our only options.

CHAPTER TWENTY-THREE

Kimberly James is on line two," my assistant Rachel's voice rang through the intercom. "She says it's urgent."

I placed my coffee down and glanced at the clock; it was a quarter after seven in the morning. What urgency could this woman possibly have at this hour? "Put her through, and send Robert in here, please," I said as I reached for line two. "This is Chloe," I answered.

"We need to go back to court!" Kimberly James shouted. "He dropped the kids off last night, and they were a wreck, an absolute disaster. Lukey had dirty socks and wet feet, and Lila had ketchup in her hair!" She paused, waiting for my appalled reaction, which never came. "Chloe, did you hear me? I want you to file a motion to modify his visitation today."

Being a divorce lawyer had its perks, and sharing your morning coffee with a lunatic was one of them. I took one of the many deep breaths I would take that day and answered her calmly. "I'm not going to file a motion to modify or terminate visitation just because your kids came home with dirty socks. And the reason I'm not going to do that, Kimberly, is because in order to do that you have to prove to the court serious endangerment or a substantial change in circumstances, not to mention this phone call alone has already cost you two hundred and fifty dollars. Filing a motion to go to court over this and have his visitation modified will cost you an additional twenty-five hundred dollars. Enough money to purchase new socks for the remainder of both their lifetimes, thereby never having to wash another pair."

"Put Robert on the phone," she demanded.

"Robert is my paralegal. He takes orders from me, not my clients."

Kimberly James hung up on me that morning, but it wasn't the first or last time. A minute later, Robert walked into my office carrying three file folders and two doughnuts.

I sipped my coffee with one hand and rubbed my temples with the other. "Please remove one of those doughnuts from this office, whichever one you're not eating," I said. "I have to be at the fertility clinic at nine, so can you file the *Anderson* motion at the courthouse this morning?"

"Sure," he said. "Everything okay?"

"We're starting our IVF process. I may need to have some blood taken and an ultrasound to examine my follicles, to see how many eggs I'm producing and how big they are. I'm not sure; it's our first consult. Glad you asked?"

Robert tossed his half-eaten doughnut in the garbage. "I'm full," he said.

I playfully flung a binder clip at him. "Just file the *Anderson* petition and see if you can chat up their lawyer about settling. I need some feelers put out there to gauge how serious his wife is about keeping the house. Also, do not take any calls from Kimberly James this week. I'll handle her."

"Okay, boss, good luck with those eggs today." He smiled. "Time to get cracking," he said before sauntering out.

I went back to rubbing my temples and checking e-mails when I heard Rachel's voice again. "Tyler is on line one."

"Thank you," I said and grabbed the phone. "Hi, honey."

"Hey, I can't make the appointment this morning," he said.

"Why not?"

"The Kraft team was supposed to come in at two o'clock, but they just rescheduled for this morning. One of them has to be on a flight this afternoon, I guess."

I sighed loud enough for him to hear. I hated feeling like I was putting added pressure on him, but it was our first IVF appointment, and I wanted him there. At the beginning of our relationship, I'd been the primary breadwinner. Responsible for most of the bills when Tyler was in film school, and footing the down payment for the house. He had always been supportive in other ways, though, like putting up with my long hours, sometimes watching me flash in and out of the apartment at midnight, only to shower, sleep, and return to the office by six o'clock in the morning. Or picking up the dry cleaning and doing the grocery shopping each week because I never had enough time for either task. But over time, as Tyler and Mitch's business became more successful, and he had more money in his pocket to pad his confidence, he had grown less inclined to appease me. It reminded me of how I used to feel when I didn't have my mother's attention anymore. When she'd stopped drinking and started focusing on random tasks like cleaning her closet and organizing her eye shadows, rather than cooking dinner for us or driving me to swim practice.

"Sorry, babe, can't make it today," he said.

I shook my head. I knew why Tyler was putting his job before this appointment; he was losing hope and despised having his virility under suspicion. Maybe I didn't need him there to hold my hand, but I wanted it. "Okay," I answered solemnly, hung up the phone, and shrugged it off. What had once seemed like the most romantic notion in the world—having a baby with the man of my dreams—had become a complex labyrinth of emotions, appointments, and self-doubt. It was a depressing, necessary evil, but what choice did I have?

"Chloe," Rachel said as she poked her head into my office. "Your mom is on line one."

"Thanks, Rach, I'll take it." She was instructed to alert me of all my calls. But my mother always required a lengthy excuse as to why I couldn't come to the phone, so Rachel routinely looked to me for said excuse. My mother had no understanding of working or what it took to hold down a job and answer to someone else. She never had. So if I were to take her call, I would need to be prepared to talk to her for as long as she wished, which was sometimes more than half an hour. Her highly detailed stories about people breaking into her home and rearranging her closet, only to arrange it back to exactly how she had it, were never brief.

Rachel regarded me with surprise and went back to her desk to put the call through.

"Hi, Mom, how are you," I answered, leaning back into my desk chair.

"I'm not well. Vivian noticed that some of my blouses had been moved from the back of the closet to the front, and I'm beside myself."

My mother was defined by the contents of her closet. All her material possessions were in there. Clothes: some brand-new, some hideously old. Jewelry: the nice stuff that had been handed down to her from her mother, right alongside the crap she bought at Chico's. Shoes, purses, Precious Moments figurines, and an entire vintage set of Fiestaware that she refused to keep in the kitchen.

"Did Vivian notice, or did you insist that the blouses were moved?"

"I pointed it out to her, but she agreed with me."

"You're paying her, Mom, of course she's going to agree with you."

Mom ignored my comment and instead went on for about twenty minutes, describing which items had been touched and which hadn't. I listened and did what Vivian did, agreed with her, because I wanted to hear her voice and do what little I could to ease her stress. When I told her we were starting the IVF process, she sounded excited about meeting her grandchild. Her granddaughter to be exact.

"I'll buy her a layette," Mom said.

"Well, you have some time."

"Yes, but I see them on sale all the time, and it doesn't hurt to plan ahead."

"You're right."

"Such wonderful news."

My mom was never skeptical or discouraging when it came to my getting pregnant. She always expressed the same pure excitement about the baby. She never acted as though I wouldn't have a child, which was exactly what I needed to hear just then.

CHAPTER TWENTY-FOUR

I arrived at my fertility doctor's office at a quarter to nine. As I opened the door, heads turned in my direction automatically. I located an empty chair, snatched a copy of *Parenting* magazine from a side table, and began to wait. Stone-faced women sat, lined up on wooden chairs around the perimeter of the room. Heads down as though they were outcasts at a high school dance. Although every one of us was there for the same reason, no one dared to speak to one another. And while I couldn't know their exact circumstances, I shared their pain. A few husbands sat, obedient and impatient, pretending to look busy on their cell phones. The occasional sound of a nurse calling someone's name was often the only reminder that we were there for a purpose. Since I was alone that morning, I thought I would shake things up. Engage someone in conversation. For God's sake, weren't we all suffering the same fate? It would seem that a room filled with women feeling inadequate and insecure would be the ideal venue for idle chatter.

To my left was a couple in their late thirties. Other than scrolling through his iPhone, the husband was nearly comatose, while the wife was slumped over, reading on her Kindle. Every time a nurse called someone else's name, he'd sigh angrily through his nose, and she'd lean farther away from him. The days of hope and holding hands were over for them. To my right was a beautiful young woman sitting alone and cleaning out the contents of her purse. She glanced over at me once she realized I was studying her.

I held up my copy of *Parenting* magazine. "Seems kind of cruel, doesn't it? That they should flaunt their subscription to this and *American Baby*," I said, alarming most of the room by breaking the code of silence.

She let out a muffled laugh. "My thoughts exactly. It kills me to flip through those things."

"I'm Chloe," I said, extending my hand.

"I'm Alexa. Nice to meet you."

We chatted quietly for about fifteen minutes. It was refreshing to talk to someone there. Though I'd always been eager to hear about other women's experiences, I hadn't dared to ask many people about it.

"Would you like to grab coffee sometime?" I asked her.

"I would love that," Alexa said. "I'm free most afternoons around three o'clock."

"Lucky you, what do you do?"

"I'm a writer," she said.

"Wow, that's fantastic. What do you write?"

"I have a weekly column in the *RedEye*, and I've also written two novels. I'm working on my third right now. How about you?"

"I'm a divorce lawyer," I said. I could've sworn a few heads perked up at those words.

"I bet you have some good stories to tell."

"You have no idea."

"Well, why don't you give me your cell number, and I can give you a call tomorrow," she said. We exchanged numbers just as a nurse called my name.

"I have to be in court until four, so maybe after that?"

"Sounds great."

I followed the nurse to an examination room, removed the jacket of my black pantsuit, and waited for the doctor.

After twenty minutes of me growing irate with impatience and texting my office like the disgruntled husband in the lobby, the doctor came in.

"I'm Dr. Wilder. Sorry for the wait," he said.

"It's okay," I mumbled.

He looked at the calendar in front of him. "Let's see here, so today's your initial consult. Then it's about two to three months before we do the procedure. We're going to get your menstrual cycle back on track with the pill, and then you'll start your series of shots. It looks like July will be your month. We close down the office for ten days each month to do the procedures, so it's important to stay on schedule."

"So mine will be in July?"

"Correct. Then during that time you'll come in every other day to have an ultrasound and get some blood work done. Once your follicles look good, you'll take your final shot to release the eggs and then come in for the extraction."

I swallowed. "I hear that's painful."

"So is childbirth." He smiled in a way that annoyed me.

After walking me through the rest of the process, Dr. Wilder concluded with what would be expected of Tyler.

"I hate to ask, but I assume he's on board with this?"

"Yes, of course," I said. "He was supposed to be here, but had a last-minute thing at the office."

"Wonderful. Well, it was great to meet you, Chloe, and we'll get you started. Be certain to follow the instructions to the letter and let the nurses know if you have any concerns."

CHAPTER TWENTY-FIVE

The next day after court, I met Alexa for coffee. I was grateful to have a new friend during that rough time. Grace was always amazingly supportive, but there had been an uncomfortable strain between us ever since she got pregnant that was admittedly my fault. I never wanted to make her feel like I was jealous of her baby or not happy for her; I just couldn't talk to her about every detail of this process while coveting the adorable, rosy-cheeked baby girl in her arms.

"How has this whole thing been on your husband?" I asked her, cutting right to the chase. "I'm always eager to know how other couples are dealing with the stress."

She shrugged and then tilted her head. "It's been hard, but mostly because I feel so incompetent. We both do. He's been really supportive and reassuring, so much so that sometimes it actually makes me feel worse. Weird, right?"

I sipped my coffee and furrowed my brow. "Not weird at all. I completely know where you're coming from. It's like, sometimes you want him to be pissed off so that you don't feel like you're the only person who's angry at everyone and everything."

"I get tired of the guilt. Which is entirely self-imposed, but I can't help feeling like this is all my fault. He comes from a family of six, and we really want a big family. I feel like I'm the one thing getting in the way," she admitted.

"Hard as it may be, you need to get over that. The worst thing you can do is dwell on why it's not happening or whose fault it is or isn't. You need to think positively…at least that's what everyone's always telling me. Easier said than done, I know." I smiled.

She sighed. "You're so right. I'm sorry."

"Don't apologize to me! I know where you're coming from, and I know how hard it is to talk to people who don't get it. I have literally forbidden some of my girlfriends from asking me about it. If you are my friend and you got pregnant by having sex…do not try and make me feel better with your kind, understanding looks and concerned questions. Just keep your trap shut and send a gift when you receive my birth announcement," I said, laughing.

"How about your husband?" she asked.

I took another sip and thought about Tyler. "He's been handling it about as well as I'd expected. It's hard for him…he doesn't deal well with any sort of controversy. He sort of shuts down and goes into denial when his pride is tested. I think that's the hardest thing for men; it's like this whole process is mocking their manhood. It's a real hit to their egos when they can't easily procreate all over the place like they thought they could."

We sat for two hours and shared personal stories and details I hadn't even shared with some of my closest friends. I told her about my family and my strained relationship with Tyler's mom. I confided in her about my fears that I would never get pregnant and that Tyler would leave me, causing his mother to rejoice.

"It must be hard having a strained relationship with your mother-in-law," Alexa said.

I shrugged. "Oh, I'm sure she thinks we get along just fine. Honestly, I've gotten used to it, and Tyler's mother is no threat to my marriage. That's all I really care about. He and I both share in the task of tolerating her."

"Good to know," she said.

I pushed my chair back from the table. "Well, I really enjoyed this, thank you. If nothing else, I'm shameless enough to admit that hearing your problems actually make me feel much less alone with my own," I said. "Now if you could please put on twenty extra pounds like I have, then I'll like you even more."

"I'm sure that won't be a problem. Please keep me posted on your progress."

"I will, and you do the same," I said.

When I got back to the office, Rachel told me there were three messages for Robert to call Kimberly James. I crumpled them up and headed to my desk. Around six o'clock, there was a knock at my office door.

"Come in," I said.

The door swung open, and Cameron Sparks was standing there with a coconut cake.

CHAPTER TWENTY-SIX

C am!" I squealed, running over to give him a hug. "You're a sight for sore eyes. Come in and take a load off."

Cam took a few of his signature, slow cool-guy steps over to the nearest chair, and I sat down in the one beside him.

He handed me the cake box. "It's not from Fresh Factory."

"Fresh Market," I corrected him. "And you're forgiven, but I need a coconut cake like I need another neurotic pill-popping client."

"Is she single?"

"Almost!"

"That's my girl," he said.

I placed the box on my desk and then sat back and crossed my legs. "What on earth are you doing here?"

Cam had moved to Los Angeles to be closer to his business partner and to get his MBA from UCLA.

"I'm in town visiting a friend."

"Who?"

"You."

I shook my head and laughed. "A text would have been nice."

"I'm kidding. I'm in town with my buddy Rick. He's our accountant, and we're here to meet with some investors about a casino project."

"Sounds fancy."

"If you like casinos."

"And I know you do," I said.

Cam lifted his feet and rested the heels of his shoes on my desktop. "Talk about fancy: look at you with your own office and everything."

I looked around at my office. It wasn't big, but it was mine. The firm I worked for looked more like an advertising agency than a law office. There were glass walls and furniture from Design Within Reach and Room & Board. Books and law journals were housed in white laminate cabinets instead of dark oak shelves and dusty bookcases. Marble floors and brightly lit corridors replaced Berber carpet and green desktop bankers' lamps. Some clients didn't trust a lawyer without a three-piece suit and a cigar, but most of mine appreciated our contemporary look.

"Can I take you to dinner tonight?" he asked.

"As long as you don't mind eating dinner at nine o'clock. I have a few things to wrap up before I can get out of here."

"Nine o'clock is good. Steaks or sushi?"

"Sushi sounds great. There's a spot a few blocks from here."

He pulled his feet off the desk and reached over to pat me on the knee. "I'll be back at nine to pick you up."

"I'll meet you down in the lobby. The building locks the elevators to guests at seven o'clock."

"The lobby it is."

When Cam left, I was just reaching for my phone to call Tyler and let him know I wouldn't be home for dinner, when it occurred to me that he hadn't called to ask about the doctor's appointment. I held my cell phone in my hand and slid back down into the chair. He should have called.

By seven o'clock I'd answered over one hundred e-mails and listened to forty-three voice mails. Although Rachel left every day at six, the office was still filled with people, and most of the attorneys stayed well past nine each night. Just before I was about to head down to the lobby, Robert stuck his head into my office to say good night.

"You heading out soon?" he asked.

"I am, actually. A friend from law school is in town, and we're going to grab dinner."

"Nice," he said, adjusting the strap of his computer case on his shoulder. "I filed the *Anderson* papers, and I can call Kimberly James tomorrow if you'd like, so she'll back off."

"Pfft," I said as I threw my phone, lip gloss, and wallet into my purse. "I don't think anything will make her back off."

Robert stood in the doorway, watching me gather my stuff. He looked as though he had something else to tell me.

"Was there something else?" I asked.

"Well, it's just that…yeah, I do have some news to share."

I stopped what I was doing and put my hands on my hips. "So help me God, if you are leaving me…"

He let out a small awkward laugh indicating this was hard for him. "I'm not leaving you or the firm. In fact, I need my job now more than ever." He paused. "Madison is pregnant."

The look on his face killed me. Not because he and Madison had what I wanted, but because he was so hesitant to tell me. That he knew how much I was struggling and how hard it was for me to hear the good news and be happy for them. For Robert and Madison and for everyone else who was able to procreate without injections and blood work and ultrasounds and condescending physicians. The thing was, I was happy for them, just also sad for me.

I dropped my hands from my hips and clasped them in front of my chest. "Robert, I couldn't be happier for you. I can tell by that look on your face that you didn't want to tell me, and I hate myself for that."

He smiled. "No, I knew you'd be excited for us. I just didn't want to break the news this morning as you were on your way out the door to the fertility clinic."

I stepped out from behind my desk and gave him a professionally acceptable congratulatory hug.

"When is she due?" I asked, pulling away.

"Around Thanksgiving."

"Lots to be thankful for, Rob. Please give her a big hug for me."

"Consider it done."

As I was waiting for the elevator to head downstairs, I got a call from Tyler.

"Hi, honey," I answered.

"How'd the appointment go?"

I gently shook my head. "It was hours ago, Ty."

"I know, I'm so sorry. I knew you were going to be mad."

"I'm not mad, I'm disappointed. This is a huge deal, and my work isn't any less demanding than yours. I just need to know you're going to be with me on this from here on out. I'm going to have to give myself injections and be at the clinic every other day once we get started. It's going to be very taxing on both of us."

"I know, and I love you. I'm so sorry about today. You know I am."

I sighed. "I know," I assured him. "Robert and Madison are expecting."

"That's great news...you okay?"

Tyler more than anyone knew how I grappled with people's baby news. One day we'd received two invitations to different one-year-olds' birthday parties in the mail. I cried when I saw them sitting on our hall table. One invitation was jungle-themed with the sweetest picture of a baby lion cub, and the other was bright pink and glittery. My stomach sank before I was overcome with guilt. Why couldn't I be happy for people anymore? Why was my immediate reaction to recoil and drink a self-loathing smoothie? Ever since then, I'd put Tyler in charge of opening the mail and had him RSVP no to anything that arrived in a pastel envelope.

"I'm fine. I felt like such a jerk, though, because I could tell Robert was reticent to give me the good news. I've turned into this horrible bitch who hates pregnant women."

"Come home," he said.

"I can't. Cameron is in town, and I'm meeting him for dinner," I said.

"What's he doing here?"

"Some work thing."

"I'm not invited?"

It hadn't occurred to me to invite Tyler. "Come meet us," I suggested. "We're grabbing sushi, which I know isn't your favorite…"

"I'm teasing, Chloe; go have fun and say hello for me."

"Okay, see you later, love you."

"Love you."

I met Cam in the lobby, and we jumped in a cab and went to Naniwa on North Wells Street. As soon as we sat down, he ordered a large hot sake and a scallop appetizer.

"So you're doing IVF," he said, pouring the sake into tiny ceramic glasses that looked like they belonged to a child's tea set.

"We are," I said.

"You are."

"Tyler and I are doing IVF."

He crossed his arms and leaned back in his chair. "I hate when people say, 'we're expecting' when it's really just *her* that's expecting.

Please, do me a favor: when you get pregnant, just tell people that *you're* expecting."

I raised a brow and held it there. "When and if I get pregnant, I'm going to tell everyone that Tyler and I are expecting, and every time I do, I'm going to smile and think of how annoyed you'd be."

He shrugged. "So what are you hoping for, boy or girl? And don't just say a healthy baby."

"Let me guess, you hate when people do that too?" I asked. "At this point, I'm just hoping to get pregnant. Aside from work, it's all I talk about, think about, read about, and dream about. I thought a person could simply have sex with their husband to make a baby, but apparently my middle school P.E. teacher was a big fat liar."

"Mine was a big, fat retired army sergeant who hated skinny, smart kids."

"Sounds like we're even then," I said. "Are you going to order for us?" Cam always liked to order for the table. Whether there were two or twelve people out to dinner, he reveled in that responsibility.

We sat for two hours reliving old stories about our grueling law school days and swapping new stories about our respective careers. Cam could work from anywhere and was itching to move again.

"Do you think you'll ever come back here to Chicago?"

He shrugged. "It gets too cold here, but we'll see. Maybe when you have a kid. Someone's going to have to teach it how to play Minecraft."

Once we were through, he ordered another large sake and the check.

"I can't tell you how great it is to see you, Cam. Have you got your sights set on any lucky girls out west?"

"A few."

"No one worth mentioning?"

"Not really," he said. "I'm still sorry I missed your wedding by the way. Did you get my gift?"

Cam had sent Tyler and me our most original gift. A blown-out ostrich egg, said to bring good luck and prosperity into the home. "Of course I did. Didn't you get my thank-you note?"

"I may have. How's the egg working for you?"

"Pretty well, actually."

Cam and I walked out to the street, and he hailed two cabs. One to take me to the train, and one to take him back to his hotel. We embraced, and the smell of him instantly took me back to a time I remembered fondly—when I'd felt so much more relaxed and like my real self.

"Thanks, Cam."

"Anytime."

A week later a package arrived for me at the office with a card attached that read *Try these. —Love, Cam.*

Rachel helped me open the large box, and we discovered a pair of heavy iron candlesticks with an image of a flutist just beneath the candle plate.

"What is it?" I asked.

"Kokopelli," she said, reading a small pamphlet that she'd pulled out of the box. "Says here that he's the God of Fertility. Who's Cam?"

I lifted one of them out of the box, tilted my head, and smiled. "Just a really great friend."

CHAPTER TWENTY-SEVEN

I was scheduled to begin my IVF shots the second week of July, so Tyler and I decided to take his parents up on their invitation to spend the Fourth of July weekend with them in Lake Geneva beforehand. We arrived at the house around six o'clock that Friday, with dessert and wine in hand. Tyler and I had wanted to get a room at the Grand Geneva for the weekend, but his mother insisted we stay at the house with them. Sammy and Sarah, who had just turned sixteen, had each brought a friend, so that made for eight people in a four-bedroom house.

Time spent at the Reeds' home in Lake Geneva was always a respite for me. I'd fallen in love and gotten married there, and I breathed easily and slept soundly in that house for the most part. Tyler's mom made dinner that first night and served it out on the patio. The table was laden with a feast of oven-fried chicken (she'd given up panfrying it in grease after reading an article about Paula Deen being diagnosed with type 2 diabetes), mashed potatoes, summer squash, and macaroni and cheese.

"How is work going, Tylah?" his mother asked after everyone had sat down and filled their plates.

"It's going good; we got two new clients last week. Some record label and a division of Kellogg's that's introducing a new zombie cereal for kids called Brain Berry. Their tagline is 'Bringing breakfast back to life.'"

"Zombie cereal. Well, I nevah. Did you hear that dear?" she asked Dr. Reed, who looked up from his iPad.

"What's that?" he asked.

"Tylah has two new clients."

Dr. Reed nodded in approval and grabbed a roll.

"Did I tell you that Mitch and Hollis just got engaged?" he asked his mother.

"I did not know that. How lovely. She's seems like such an interesting girl."

"She's really great," I chimed in.

"When's the weddin'?"

"He mentioned something about getting married in Vegas. I think they're going to do a small ceremony out there in a few months," Tyler said. "Work's been crazy though, so I'm not sure when he's going to be able to get away."

Tyler's mom gently slapped the tabletop. "I'm so tickled to hear how busy you are; that's just wonderful news. Isn't it, Chloe?"

I looked up from the chicken leg I was gnawing on and wiped my chin. "Yes, it's fantastic," I said and leaned in to give Tyler a greasy kiss. "I'm so proud of him. He's worked really hard for this."

"And how is work going for you, dear? You poor thing, you hardleh have time to cook a proper meal for your husband with those long hours."

A foot-long sub and a bag of Baked Lay's seemed proper enough to me. I cleared my throat and heard Grace's voice in my head. *Just ignore her.* So I tried, and changed the subject.

"We're starting our IVF treatments next month," I said excitedly.

Dixie Reed tilted her head and studied me. She raised a finger to her lips and narrowed her eyes. I glanced at Tyler when she failed to comment, but he was on his fourth piece of chicken, texting someone.

"What's that?" Sarah asked me, and I nearly reached out and hugged her for breaking the silence. But before I could answer, her mom finally spoke.

"I'm sure Chloe doesn't want to discuss that type of thing at the dinnah table."

"Oh, I don't mind," I said and turned to Sarah. "It's a fertility treatment we're doing to help us have a baby."

Mrs. Reed stood and gathered her plate. "Who would like some warm homemade apple pie and vanilla bean ice cream?" she asked. "Sarah, darling, please clear the dishes."

I rolled my eyes and mouthed to Sarah quietly. "I'll tell you more later."

Sarah and her friend cleared the table, and I went inside to rinse everything in the sink. Mrs. Reed came in as I was putting the glasses back in the cabinet.

"Chloedear, we always want to put the glasses upside down on a shelf; nevah right-side up." She corrected me from behind and walked out.

"I'm excited for you and Tyler to have a baby," Sarah said to me.

"Me, too. Can we count on you to babysit?"

"I would love that! Can I?"

"Of course you can."

By the time we'd finished with dessert and cleanup, the kids had retired to their rooms with their friends and their iPhones. Teenagers require nothing more.

I was exhausted, but had two motions to write by Monday, so I went to the foyer where I'd left my computer case. When I turned around, I found Mrs. Reed right behind me.

"I thought we could have a little chat," she said with her Betty Boop lashes all a flutter.

"Of course."

Nothing ever changed in that house, which was one of the things I loved most about it. The white wicker furniture, the talking pillows, the squeaky floorboards on the screened-in porch, and Dixie being condescending. I followed her to the exact spot where she'd warned me to stay away from her son years earlier. The irony of him being my husband now made me smile as we sat down across from each other. I'd changed so much during that time, while she hadn't changed one bit.

"It sounds like Tylah is vereh busy with his business."

"He is, yes. We both are."

"And we would hate to see him under any added stress, what with his work becoming more and more demandin'."

"I think he thrives on being busy; it's a real rush for him."

"He's always been so ambitious, that one, we wouldn't want anything to slow him down. I'm sure if you can make things nice and peaceful for him at home that will help a great deal."

"I try to," I said, glancing toward the door, praying for him to walk up and rescue me.

"You know God will nevah give us more than we can handle, and it sounds like the both of you are just too busy right now to be thinking about starting a family."

I forced a smile. "That's precisely why we're taking God out of it," I said, but my joke fell flat. Like a homemade apple pie tumbling off a windowsill. Facedown. "Wouldn't you and Dr. Reed like to have a grandchild?" I added.

"Of course we would, if it's blessed by God. You cannot force these things."

So God was going to deliver my baby? Maybe he's also the one who sends the stork? I thought while she went on. Proved a fool once again: believing all I had to do was have sex to conceive.

"We don't want to mess with fate, now do we? Perhaps if it's not working out for you…it's just not the right time. And who knows what havoc those drugs can wreak on your body and how they'll disturb a little one growing in there. I read a story once of how this lovely couple ended up with five premature babies, and two of them were connected. It put a terrible strain on their marriage."

I took a subtle yet deep breath and folded my hands in my lap. "It's all perfectly safe, and we're starting next week."

She smiled. "Please do let me know when Mitch and Hollis's wedding is. I'd be delighted to send them something off their registry."

CHAPTER TWENTY-EIGHT

A week later I began injecting myself with a cocktail of drugs that included Menotropin, also known as "nun pee." Not only was I unable to make a baby, but I was being forced to take protein hormones from the urine of celibate, postmenopausal women. Specifically nuns, I was told. My shame had no bounds at that point.

Giving yourself a shot in the stomach, or anywhere else for that matter, is about as unnatural as giving yourself a haircut. I was waging a civil war in my brain: the first couple times, my body actually recoiled from my hand. During that first week, I was instructed to take the three shots at the same time each day. So every morning at six thirty I would make the bed, give myself three shots in the stomach, have my coffee, and leave for work by eight. Every other day, I ran to the fertility clinic during my lunch hour for an ultrasound and blood work so that they could monitor the progress of my follicles. A word I never thought I would say or hear so many times in one lifetime. On the eighth day of my monitoring, they told me everything was looking good and sent me home to take my "trigger" shot at six thirty. Exactly thirty-six hours later, they would extract my eggs and set them up on a group date with Tyler's sperm. The trigger shot, which needed to be injected into my lower back at the designated hour, would eventually release my eggs. This one, I could not administer myself.

It was our third wedding anniversary. However, instead of celebrating with champagne and chocolate-covered strawberries, my husband was slowly approaching me with a syringe. His hand was steady, his eyes fierce and determined as I backed myself up against the kitchen counter. There were tears in my eyes, but that didn't faze him. My hormones were in the hands of a fertility specialist, and there was almost nothing that didn't bring me to tears those days. I knew I had to have that final shot in my lower back. I knew the chopstick-sized needle would hurt. I knew I would have to endure more weight gain and pregnancy symptoms, even though I wasn't officially pregnant. My jeans had gone from a size six to a size ten in seven months, and I knew I had to endure the retrieval procedure—which I'd heard was an evil, painful surgery—where the doctor sucks the eggs out of your ovaries and leaves you eggless and doubled over with cramps. I also knew Tyler would have to take that embarrassing walk to the "donor room" equipped with pornography, baby oil, and hand sanitizer again. But I still didn't know for sure if any of it was going to work. This was not how I'd imagined us making a baby. None of this had ever crossed my mind when we got married and decided to start a family. We'd been so focused on using protection and *avoiding* getting pregnant before we were ready.

"Come on, Chloe," Tyler said, holding the syringe steady. He looked like he'd rather sit through five hours of needlepoint instruction from his mother than do what he was about to do. "This isn't any fun for me either, so don't drag it out."

I nodded, closed my eyes, and then turned around and lifted my shirt. I tensed up and moaned through closed lips as he sunk the needle into me.

"It's done," he said, patting me on the shoulder.

"Thanks, honey," I whispered and opened my eyes. Tyler turned me back around, cupped my chin in his hands, brought his face to mine, and kissed me twice on the lips.

"I'm sorry you have to go through all of this," he said. "If we'd been heroine addicts like I suggested a while back, that shot would've been no problem."

I managed a smile. "If we'd been heroine addicts, I'd probably have seven kids by now," I said bitterly.

The next day was Saturday, and I went to Target to pick up some cleaning supplies, an errand that should've lasted all of fifteen minutes, but instead turned into two hours of me stalking innocent women and children throughout the store. It was like standing in the middle of a bakery when you're on a diet. There were children and families everywhere. Some kids were happily swinging sippy cups in their front cart seat, while others were getting yelled at for touching things or whacking their siblings. I closely observed every single one of them. But the worst for me was a young girl with no wedding ring and a barefoot baby resting clumsily on her hip. She looked frazzled and overwhelmed, and I immediately labeled her child as an accident. She'd probably gotten drunk, slept with some guy, and ended up with more than she'd bargained for. Maybe she loved him, and he broke her heart? Maybe she'd only known him for three horny hours? It didn't matter, because she was my biggest nemesis. The girl who had no desire for or intention of getting pregnant, but won the baby lottery whether she liked it or not. The girl who had the one thing I couldn't obtain on my own no matter how hard I studied or worked. I wanted to run up to her, place my hands on her shoulders, and tell her that while she might be overwhelmed and questioning her fate, she should cherish the gift that she'd been given. She should know how hard it was to create a child, and she needed to appreciate what she had.

But who was I to judge? I left the store that day brokenhearted and empty-handed, and called one of my favorite moms in the world: Grace's mom, Sydney. She'd shown me the true meaning of a mother's love and had always treated me as nothing less than beloved family. She was also the one woman I knew who had everything in common with that young, ill-equipped girl in Target.

CHAPTER TWENTY-NINE

Ten minutes after peeling out of the Target parking lot, I entered Grace's childhood home and found her mom in a familiar position: unloading the dishwasher.

"This is a nice surprise, Chloe," she said, even though I'd phoned ahead. "How's your mom?"

It was always the first thing she asked me. "She's doing okay. It's awfully hard to talk to her on the phone these days—or in person for that matter. She doesn't always have a grasp of what's going on or why I'm calling. I never know what awaits me on the other end of the line, but she has a woman who checks on her every day and keeps me up to date."

She smiled, lips pursed. "I'm so sorry."

I nodded and then grabbed an apple from the wire basket in front of me.

"What's Tyler up to today?" she asked.

"He's golfing."

"Good for him. Grace mentioned that you and she were going to get together in a couple weeks for dinner."

"Mmm hmm," I mumbled mid-chew.

Sydney closed the dishwasher and walked over to me. "She also told me you've been swamped at work. Have your doctors told you to take it easy at all? I want to make sure you're taking care of yourself," she said, sitting down next to me. "How are your treatments going?"

I'd been struggling to conceive for so long that there was almost nothing else I thought of or talked about. I'd begun to avoid phone calls from my friends because I couldn't bear the tone in their voices when they'd ask me how I was doing or how things were progressing. I blamed everything on work, telling people that I couldn't make plans because I was overwhelmed at the office. I knew everyone was simply trying to be supportive, but it had become painful for me to put on a happy face and pretend like I wasn't dying inside every time someone would ask when Tyler and I were going to start a family. I wanted to give people good news as much as they wanted to hear it, but I had nothing.

"I took the trigger shot last night," I said.

"That's exciting."

"I guess. I'm just so nervous and anxious…and tired. In addition to being narcoleptic, my brain is exhausted. I can barely concentrate on anything other than work and these treatments. I haven't made dinner, cleaned the house, filed my nails, or even had sex with my poor husband in weeks." I paused. "Tyler asked me to pick up some shoes for him a week ago, and I literally can't do it. Either I forget to do it or I sit on the couch thinking I should go and do it, but instead can't bring myself to get up."

Grace's mom sighed and gave me that look that I loathed. That look where her head tilted, her forehead contracted, and her eyes glistened with pity. She wanted nothing more than to make everything better for me, and seeing her genuine concern made me miss my own mother. Or at least the fact that my mother wasn't the one sitting across from me, yearning for my happiness.

When Grace's mom was a senior in college, she'd slept with a guy at a fraternity dance and found out she was pregnant during final exams eight weeks later. No belly shots or lubed-up ultrasound wands for her. Just good ol' drunken sex to get the job done. He had not responded kindly to her when she initially told him about the pregnancy—in fact, he ran for the hills and disappeared altogether. It had taken her years to tell Grace the truth about who her real father was, and it wasn't until we graduated from college that she got the chance to meet him in person. According to Grace, the meeting was both revolutionary and uneventful. Unlike me, Grace had always wanted to connect with her biological father, but more out of curiosity than anything else. Not because she longed for a father. No, there was no void there.

Grace's mom was famous for finding the most creative ways to warn us about premarital sex, without making Grace feel like the embodiment of a young girl's regretful decision.

Girls, you're so young. Don't get yourself into a situation that will stifle your youth.

Not every situation works out like mine did. In fact, very few have a happy ending.

Don't be afraid to ask me for help.

If you're having sex, you better be using protection! Are you having sex? Wait, don't tell me.

If you are having sex, you should be using protection…for many reasons.

You're using protection, right? Never mind, don't tell me.

"You're doing everything you can do, Chloe. I'm so sorry that you have to go through all of this, but imagine how much more you'll appreciate the good news when you get it." She smiled and squeezed my hand.

"What if I don't get it?" I asked, but being pessimistic had never done me any good. It only forced people to give obligatory compliments and words of encouragement. "I honestly don't think I can go through this again," I said, lowering my head into my hands. My body had become a voodoo doll, subject to needles, pills, and probes. I was sore, bloated, fatigued, depressed, and the thought of starting over was unbearable.

"I have no doubt that you will have your child. One way or another, you and Tyler will be blessed with the baby you deserve," she said softly.

"I hope so, and I'm trying to be more optimistic. Tyler has been great, and all I've been doing is moping around feeling sorry for myself."

I had completely lost sight of the things that were going well in my life. Tyler's business was thriving, I was kicking ass in court, and our marriage was solid. However, I couldn't help but go to that dark, insecure place in the back of my mind where I wondered whether our relationship would survive if I were ultimately unable to get pregnant. Sure, he was wonderfully supportive now, and confident to a fault, but what would happen to us if there was no baby at the finish line? Would Tyler still want to grow old together with no children? Thoughts like that kept me up at night and were the one thing I couldn't talk about with him.

"Thanks for the chat. I'm sorry to drag you down with me today," I said.

"Chloe, I think you think you're a bigger downer than you really are. Do people feel bad about what you're going through? Naturally. But no one wears the burden more than you do. I don't want you to feel like you can't talk to me. And while I wish everything could go smoothly for you in life, it's simply not possible. As much as I hate seeing you like this, it would make me feel worse to think you're trying to protect me in some way by not talking to me about it." She lowered her gaze to make eye contact with me. "Okay? So don't you worry about upsetting me with any of it. I'm a big girl."

"No, you're a little shorty," I said and laughed. Grace and I used to tease her all the time since she was easily six inches shorter than both of us.

"Very funny. I'm glad to see you haven't lost your winning sense of humor."

I jerked my head up and threw my hands in the air. "Oh, and did I mention I'm taking nun pee?"

CHAPTER THIRTY

When I came home that night, I found Tyler cleaning out the garage. His shirt was off, and his tattoos were shimmering with perspiration. When he waved at me as I pulled into the driveway, he looked every bit the gorgeous football hero that I'd fallen in love with. I still wanted him so badly, but our quest for a family had muddied our romance. For years now, sex had come with a price. An expectation and a disappointment. It became something we did out of obligation, not passion.

"You're going to shock the ladies next door. You know Saturday is bridge night," I said and gave him as kiss.

He flexed his right bicep and grinned. "You've been asking me to do this, so I thought I'd get it done before your surgery tomorrow."

"Thank you."

"How's Grace's mom doing?" he asked.

"She's good. I went and whined to her so that you'd be spared."

"Everything's going to be fine, Chloe. Tomorrow is just the beginning for us. I promise you, I have a good feeling about it."

I nodded. "I know. I'm honestly doing everything I can to think positively. I wish I didn't have such a crazy couple of weeks at work though. I mean, as if there's ever a good time, but people's schedules are so stringent—the courts, the fertility doctors—I feel like something is going to suffer, and neither can afford to."

Tyler removed his gloves and wrapped his arms around me. I rested my head on his warm chest and just stood there for two minutes, hoping that everything would go smoothly in the morning.

"What's going on at work?" he asked.

"I have the *Anderson* case coming up. We filed to get the wife exclusive possession of the house during the divorce proceedings so that her kids could have some peace and stability. At the moment, the husband just comes and goes when he pleases, and deliberately starts fights with his wife, which causes the kids to get hysterical and pee in their pants."

"What an asshole."

"You have no idea what these people put their children through all in the name of spite. If it means they get to be right or they get to see their spouse suffer, then they could care less about how it affects their children. It's hard to believe how many people will throw their kids to the curb, just to have the last word."

Tyler pulled away and met my eyes. "You'd be out of a job if there were no pricks out there."

"Very true."

We closed the garage door and ordered a pizza. Afterward, I went out to the trunk of my car and brought the candlesticks that Cam had sent me into the house.

"What are those?" Tyler asked as I sat them down on the kitchen island.

"Cam sent these to me. They're fertility candlesticks."

Tyler lifted one up and rolled his eyes.

I gently took it back from him. "And if you think I'm above lighting them, you're sadly mistaken."

"If they make you feel better, then knock yourself out. What time do we have to be at the clinic in the morning?"

"Seven," I said. "They should let me know how many eggs they got while I'm in recovery. It's supposed to be really painful."

Tyler sat on one of the stools. "You and your eggs will do great."

"Then you have to do your part," I said, looking apologetic.

"Don't worry about me, kid. As long as they have *Big Tit Bitches 4*, I'll be just fine."

I buried my nose in my hands and laughed and prayed and shook my head skeptically. No one understood what we were going through. Every day I fielded calls and court documents for people who showed no regard for their children. Sometimes I thought that every parent should be subjected to what we were going through if they wanted to have a child. Maybe then they wouldn't take their kids for granted. I knew I wouldn't.

The next morning we arrived at the clinic at a quarter to seven and were immediately ushered into a room for the procedure. Tyler held my quivering hand until Dr. Wilder asked him to stand aside. Having my eggs extracted was as painful as I'd expected, but I did my best to grin and bear it and remind myself why I was doing it. Afterward, Tyler went to leave his deposit and uphold his end of the bargain. When we were both done, we sat together in recovery for about an hour or so until the nurse came in.

"We were able to get twelve eggs, which we'll begin fertilizing today. We'll call you with the results tomorrow," she told us.

"How many typically survive?" I asked her.

"It depends. Everyone is different, but we'll have a better idea in the morning. You'll come back in three to five days to have the transfer. At that point you'll discuss with the doctor how many to have put back in."

Tyler and I both nodded. "Thank you," I said.

"My pleasure. Just go home and take it easy, and we'll see you in a few days," the nurse said and left the room.

"You ready?" Tyler stood and asked.

"Yeah." I said, and we left.

The phone was ringing when we walked in the house. I checked the caller I.D. before answering. "It's your mom," I said.

"Just leave it. I'll call her later. She probably wants to know how the surgery went."

Despite her misgivings about IVF, she had done her best to be supportive once she realized we were going to go through with it. Far be it for her to act rude. It wouldn't be proper. My own mother had also lent her support in the form of a loaf of banana bread, sent through the mail. Parcel post.

"I'll call her back," I said, feeling generous and familial. It was never lost on me that she would be my child's only reasonably sane grandparent.

"Hi, Dixie," I said when she answered the phone. "We were just walking in and missed your call."

"Chloedear, how are you? How did the procedure go? I ran into Joyce McNary at the market this morning, and she told me her niece ended up with triplets after having five eggs put back into her. I simply had to tell you to be wise about it."

"Thank you. I'll defer to the doctor later this week when we have the transfer done. They were able to pull twelve eggs today, but we'll be lucky to have one or two viable ones left in the end."

"And how is Tylah doing? I'm sure this must be such a drain for both of you."

"Would you like to talk to him?" I asked. Tyler overheard me and began to wave his arms. "Um, you know what, he just jumped in the shower, but he's doing fine. Very supportive. He's been wonderful," I said, winking at him. "Thanks for calling. I'll talk with you later."

"Good-bye, dear," she said and hung up.

I went to lie down on the couch, and Tyler brought me an iced tea. We put a movie in, and he eased his body in next to mine. I rested my head on his abdomen while he gently massaged my lower back. I was asleep ten minutes later.

CHAPTER THIRTY-ONE

No rest for the weary—or the divorce lawyers. Monday morning I had to be in court to argue why my client, Melinda Anderson, should be allowed to live in peace with her children during her divorce from her husband, Blake Anderson. Blake had cheated on Melinda with a woman named Christina, whom he'd met at a sales conference in Phoenix. Christina was married to a guy named Richard, who'd called Melinda and told her that he'd found her husband, Blake, having sex with his wife—doggy style—on a trampoline in their backyard. Melinda had been sitting in the car line at her sons' school, waiting to pick them up when she got the call. Sad? Yes. A shame? Yes. Unfortunate? Sure. Out of the ordinary? Not a chance.

Cheating spouses were often the catalyst for my clients' divorces, but typically not the real reason for the demise of their marriages. Apathy, addiction to prescription drugs, and self-loathing—among other things—often led people to rebel against their family and ultimately do something unforgivable. That's when they'd come to me. For peace, justice, and merciless revenge. In my entire career, only one couple, out of hundreds, had agreed that they never should've married in the first place, and that was okay. She didn't want anything from him, and he didn't want anything from her. They split their assets, agreed to joint custody of their one child, and never looked back.

But not Melinda and Blake Anderson. As if crushing her with an extramarital affair wasn't enough, he was hell-bent on destroying what was left of her dignity, her reputation, and her checkbook, with no regard for the emotional harm he would be inflicting on their children. Blake had refused to leave their home, despite the fact that he had extensive family in the area and Melinda had none. Blake also owned three other rental properties in Chicago, but insisted on staying in their house and making everyone miserable. He started fights and berated the children simply to goad Melinda. Only to chastise and scream at her when she came to the kids' defense. The two boys were unable to sleep, began wetting their pants, and refused to be alone with their father. The courts had initially ordered a "bird-nesting" scenario, in which one parent would leave, and the other would enter for his or her allotted time with the kids. But this had only resulted in more confusion and uncertainty for the children who'd expressed anxiety about where their mother was going and when she would return.

Since mediation had failed, there I was in court, almost twenty-four hours after my own personal egg hunt, listening to Blake's attorney address Dr. Michael Whalen, the court-appointed evaluator, on the stand. I popped three Advils before he began.

"Dr. Whalen, could you please review your findings on the two parenting styles?"

"Certainly. Shall I read from the report?"

"Please."

"The children are primarily attached to their mother and enjoy a close, warm, and trusting relationship with her. Mrs. Anderson has been the boys' principal caretaker since birth, and they rely on her to meet their needs for physical and emotional sustenance. The boys feel happy and secure in her presence and experience anxiety to varying degrees when contemplating separation from her. Collateral contacts report that she is an exemplary parent in many ways."

"And Mr. Anderson?"

Dr. Whalen cleared his throat and took a sip from his glass of water before continuing. "Mr. Anderson is not as patient, and loses his temper easily. Although the manner in which he disciplines may not rise to a level that would cause undue alarm, from the boys' perspective it is so very different from what they experience with their mother that they perceive him to be frightening and off-putting. Additional findings reveal that Mr. Anderson is highly self-focused and preoccupied with meeting his own needs—often at the expense of the needs of others. Making it challenging for him to spend extended periods of time with children, who are by nature unrelenting in their demands and need for attention."

"And what children aren't?" Blake's attorney commented snidely. "There's nothing in your report that says anything about any of the parties being at risk; is that correct, Dr. Whalen?"

"That's correct."

Blake's attorney removed his suit jacket and went back to pacing in front of the bench. "Would it be fair to say, if you considered there to be an imminent risk to either Mr. or Mrs. Anderson or the children, that that would have been contained in your report?"

"Yes, of course."

"Would it also be fair to say, if you learned of circumstances during your evaluation that caused you to believe that one of the parties or the children were in physical jeopardy, that that would have been contained in your report?"

"Yes."

"Is it reasonable for us to conclude, because those things are not referenced in your report, that you did not come up with any findings showing that either party or the children were endangered during the course of your investigation?"

"That's correct."

"No further questions, your honor." Blake Anderson's attorney waved at the judge and took a seat while I stood and approached the witness stand.

"Good morning, Dr. Whalen. On this matter of a shared residence, I believe you stated in your report that you did not believe a shared residence was in the best interest of the children during the pendency of this case, correct?"

"That is correct."

"Is it your opinion that there are certain benefits for the children that come from sharing a residence, bird nesting as it's called, as they were doing? And if so, what are these benefits?"

"Well, from their perspective, they get to stay in one location, not packing a bag, going back and forth. Life is consistent. The only thing that changes is Mom's there some of the time and Dad's there at other times."

I walked back over to where my paralegal, Robert, and Melinda Anderson were seated and grabbed a piece of paper from the table. "Are there certain benefits, specifically for the children, of Mr. and Mrs. Anderson having separate residences?"

"Yes, I believe so."

"And what might those be?" I asked.

"I can only think that because the parents are uncomfortable with the circumstances and are at times anxious about the arrangement, that that's something the children pick up on from time to time."

"Would you agree that it would benefit the children to begin to deal with the reality, which is Mom and Dad are getting divorced, and they're going to have two toothbrushes and two houses and two bedrooms—two of everything, eventually—and that the parents are causing additional, unnecessary stress and anxiety by postponing the inevitable? That the children would ultimately benefit from two separate households?" I asked, standing right in front of him.

"Yes, I would agree," Dr. Whalen answered.

"No further questions, your honor."

Judge Kathleen Donahue acknowledged me. "Do you have any additional witnesses?" she asked.

"Yes, Judge. I'd like to call my client, Melinda Anderson, to the stand."

Melinda walked over with a wad of tissue in her hand and took a seat next to the judge. I asked her the routine foundational questions regarding her name and marital status, and then went for pay dirt.

"On the evening of May fifth of this year, did anything unusual occur in the home?"

Melinda's eyes welled as she sat straight and began to speak. "Well, the night began like every other night with Blake yelling and screaming because the kids were being loud and wouldn't get in the bath. I asked him if he could give me a hand with them, and he flipped out. He grabbed my arm and twisted it so hard that his fingernails broke the skin and left bruises. It wasn't the first time he'd grabbed me, but it was the first time I was really scared." She sniffed.

"Please continue," I said.

"Then he stormed out of the room, screaming obscenities at me, and I followed him to the kitchen where he grabbed a knife from the butcher block and shoved it in the drywall next to the stove. His face was beet red, and I actually believed he might hurt me or the kids that night."

Although I continued questioning her for another hour, I was confident that we'd established our case. After an additional thirty minutes of cross-examination, the judge called for a short recess.

I walked back to the table and sat down with Robert and Melinda. She was red-eyed and weepy, and had lost fifteen pounds from her already slim frame since we'd started the divorce proceedings. I squeezed her hand, and we sat in silence while the judge put her reading glasses on, gathered a small stack of documents, and disappeared into her chambers. The only sounds came from someone coughing a few rows behind us. Half an hour later, Blake's attorney and I rose as the judge walked back in to give her ruling.

"The court finds that Melinda Anderson testified credibly regarding the negative effects of her and her husband jointly occupying the marital residence during the pendency of this litigation. I agree with Dr. Whalen's conclusion that the bird-nesting arrangement has caused unnecessary stress and tension for everyone, and that Mrs. Anderson's well-being and safety may be in jeopardy." The judge removed her glasses and looked at Blake before continuing. "Further, given the testimony of both parents and the court-appointed evaluator, I'm ordering Mr. Anderson to complete a twelve-week parenting workshop. Effective immediately," she said and let her comment hang there for a moment.

Afterward, Melinda gave Robert and me a hug. "I can't thank you enough, both of you. My kids will finally be able to have some peace," she said.

"I'm happy that it worked out. You're free to have the locks changed at your earliest convenience," I told her, and she nodded. "Robert and I have to get back to the office, but we'll check in with you soon about the next steps."

Robert and I shared a cab back to the office. "It was nice to see her get some relief," he said to me.

"It is."

"With Madison pregnant, it really puts things into perspective. I've sat through countless numbers of these things, but with my own kid on the way, it's all the more unbelievable to see people using their children as pawns like that. God forbid Madison and I ever get divorced, but you have my permission to kick my ass if I ever do anything remotely unforgivable."

"Don't worry. I'll do more than kick your ass," I assured him. "How is she doing?"

"Great, really good," he said. "And how about you? Am I allowed to ask about the IVF stuff?"

I smiled. "You are allowed. I'm getting knocked up in three days, actually."

"That's awesome, Chloe. I know it's going to work."

"You do?" I laughed. "Thank God, someone does; can you tell my eggs that?"

"I'd be happy to," he said as we paid the cab driver and entered our office building.

CHAPTER THIRTY-TWO

Three days later, Tyler and I were back at the clinic. Me on my back with a catheter, and Tyler perched next to a monitor as Dr. Wilder injected two fertilized eggs back inside of me.

"Consider yourself pregnant," he said.

I shot him a look of surprise. "Really?"

"Well, what I mean is that you should act like you're pregnant. No alcohol, get moderate exercise, take your vitamins—things like that."

As if I knew what it was like to be pregnant. Wasn't that why I was there, legs splayed for him? I rolled my eyes and laid my head back down on the white paper.

"We'll have you come back in one to two weeks to do a blood test. Until then, I would stay away from the in-home pregnancy tests as they tend to be very misleading with both positive and negative results."

"Okay," I said, but I'd already planned on peeing on them all weekend.

Tyler and I left the office, holding hands with high hopes. Then we went home and lit the candles.

When I was young and my prayers were consistently ignored, I quickly grew tired of religion. But since Tyler's parents were staunch Catholics, I had taken it upon myself to create a new relationship with God—one that I could turn to in situations that required divine intervention.

About a week after my transfer, I was driving home from the train station when I passed a church on a street that I had driven down a hundred times before. I stopped in front of Saint Francis. It was eight o'clock at night, but the front doors were wide open. Something inside me told me to go inside and pray.

I approached the entrance tentatively, not wanting to disturb any services that might be going on, but once I entered the foyer, there was pure silence. I walked through another set of double doors into the nave. I stood alone at the end of the aisle and marveled at the church's splendor. The large altar looked as though it had been prepared for the next service with wine and communion set on top. Large stained-glass windows circled the room in hundreds of colors, depicting some of Christ's joyful and most trying moments. I took a few steps and sat on the edge of one of the wooden pews for about five minutes before finally pulling down the padded bar near my feet and kneeling. Just as I was about to formulate something... anything to say, I felt a tap on my right shoulder.

"I'm so sorry to disturb you," said a man in a black-and-white clerical collar.

I leaped to my feet, knocking my knee on the little built-in box that held the Bibles. "Oh, no bother, I was...the door was open, and I just came in for a second." I stood and hovered over him. I instinctively slumped my shoulders and bent my knees once I became aware of his smaller stature.

"It's no trouble, my dear," he said, folding his hands in front of him. "I was only going to tell you that you are early. Tonight's evening service was moved to nine o'clock to accommodate the youth group event. It's their annual spaghetti dinner tonight."

"Thank you, Father."

"I'm Father John. Is there anything I can help you with?"

I sat back down and thought, *Here's my chance.* My one-degree of separation from God. This man standing calmly before me had an "in" with possibly the only person, or deity, who—according to Dixie Reed—was necessary to help me achieve my dream of having a child. Instead of formulating an intelligent and thoughtful request, I did what I'd done that entire summer: I burst into tears.

Father John did not move a muscle as I wiped my face. I wanted to tell him that I wasn't weak. That I was an accomplished and successful lawyer, and that he needn't feel sorry for me—but I said nothing. Once I had composed myself, I moved over, and he joined me on the pew.

"I see you are not yourself," he said. Maybe he did know me after all.

I took a deep breath. "My husband and I are trying to have a baby, and it's been very hard on me, as you can see," I started. "I must confess that I'm not much of a churchgoer, but something drew me in here today."

"This is God's house, open to everyone who needs it."

"Thank you. I was going to say a prayer, but I wasn't sure how to phrase it," I told him. "Should I just ask for what I want? Like meeting Santa?"

Thankfully, Father John had a sense of humor. "There is no wrong way to pray," he said, speaking in short, majestic statements.

I see you are not yourself.

This is God's house, open to everyone who needs it.

There is no wrong way to pray.

Things he could've said to anyone for any reason, yet I felt intrinsically moved by his words.

I looked him in the eye and smiled as he stood.

"Tell God what's in your heart. He is always with you," he said and smiled. "Stay as long as you wish." Father John turned and walked away toward the other end of the pew. Once I was alone again, I knelt and prayed.

Hey God,

Thank you for inviting me into your home. I know this is a little weird, well, maybe it's not since Father John says you're always with me…in which case, you probably know why I'm here. As you know, Tyler and I have been trying to have a baby and, well, that old-fashioned method you created hasn't really worked out for us. So we're now among the weary masses trying to conceive a child through science, and deep down I'm losing faith. My patience is nonexistent, and my hope is fading fast. I work with people who take their children for granted every day, which you also must know, and it's getting harder and harder to do my job…which I love, by the way. There's a new bitterness about me that I hate. I don't want to cringe when I hear of other people's pregnancies. I don't want to judge other parents, waiting for my chance to do it better. I don't want to wait any longer for my baby, and I don't want to let Tyler down.

I'm sure I can't just waltz in here and ask you for my baby, because if that were the case, I'd have to ask for world peace and a cure for cancer first. I guess what I'm asking for is some more strength. I need to be able to carry this burden, and it's gaining weight with every day that passes. Please just equip me with what I need to get through this. As much as I want this baby, I want to be able to forge ahead and do whatever is in my power to make this possible for Tyler and me.

Thank you for listening. And last, I'm not above a little immaculate conception…just saying.

My phone rang as I was inching my way out of the pew. I silenced it immediately when I didn't recognize the number on the screen. When I got outside there was a new voice mail, so I pressed play.

"This message is for Chloe Carlyle Reed. This is Officer Gregory of the Florida State Police calling. We have your mother, Jane, in custody."

CHAPTER THIRTY-THREE

I ran to my car and dialed Officer Gregory's phone number.

"This is Chloe Reed. I just got a phone call about my mother; can you tell me what's going on?!" I shouted into the phone when he answered.

His voice was very methodical and void of inflection. "Good afternoon, Mrs. Reed. We responded to a call from the Publix grocery store on Collins Avenue earlier today. It appears that your mother was screaming obscenities at the cashier when the store manager intervened and called us. She then began threatening the manager once our officers arrived on the scene."

I almost ran back inside the church yelling, *one more thing!*

"Anyway," he continued. "She's calmed down considerably, but she's going to need someone to come down to the Sunny Isles station and post bond."

I closed my eyes and exhaled. "What's she being charged with?"

"Disorderly conduct—it's a misdemeanor, but she'll need someone to come get her and pay a five-hundred-dollar bond. In cash."

"Oh my God, okay, well, I live in Chicago, so I obviously can't get down there. Let me call her caregiver and see what I can do. Can I at least wire the money to the station to cover the bond?"

"You'll have to call the bond desk about that."

"I don't suppose you have their number?"

"Nope."

I hung up with him and searched for Vivian's number on my phone. She answered on the first ring.

"Vivian, oh thank God you're home. It's Chloe, Jane's daughter, and I just got a call from the police station that Mom has been arrested."

She gasped. "Oh no, Ms. Jane, no—what happened?"

"I guess she got belligerent with one of the cashiers at Publix…"

Vivian made a *tsk tsk* sound on the other end.

"Is something wrong?" I asked.

"I told her the women there were not talking bad about her, and she never believes me."

I dropped my head back onto the headrest. Poor Vivian now had this to add to her list of things to manage when it came to my mother. "I'm going to wire the money to the station. Could you please get down there to pick her up? She has no one else, and I'd hate for her to have to jump in a cab after that ordeal."

"Yes. I will get her and bring her a Diet Coke."

I smiled. "Thank you, Vivian."

Just as I hung up, I got a call from Tyler.

"Hi," I answered.

"Where are you?"

"Sitting in my car outside the Saint Francis church—where I just had a heart-to-heart with God—and fielding calls about my mother's arrest. You?"

"Your mother got arrested?"

"Yup," I said, accentuating the *p*.

He sighed. "And you're going to church now?"

I knew Tyler could see my own mental demise through the phone. "I have my blood test in a couple of days, and I thought I could use a little extra help." I'd already taken twelve pregnancy tests since the two eggs had been replanted in me. Eight were positive and four were negative. I confessed only two of them to Tyler.

"Come home," he said.

Two days later I went back to the fertility clinic to get a blood test that would confirm whether I was pregnant.

"Okay," the nurse said as she placed a cotton ball on my arm after removing the needle. "You're all set. We'll call you tomorrow with the results."

"Who calls, you or Dr. Wilder? I heard the nurses call with bad news, and the doctors call with good."

She laughed. "I've heard that, too, but I promise you that is not our policy. I can't say who will call you, but you will definitely get a call either way."

I hopped off the table. "Do you happen to know what time? Because I'll be obsessing until I hear from someone."

"I can't say for sure, but we typically get the results back by noon. But don't hold me to that."

Back at the office, I threw myself into my work with a vengeance. I answered e-mails, ran two meetings, wrote two petitions, and even returned Kimberly James's phone calls from the day before. I got home late that night and nearly burst into tears when I saw that Tyler had waited up and cooked dinner for me. Spaghetti with our favorite vodka cream sauce, an iceberg salad with Thousand Island dressing, and vanilla ice cream for dessert.

At ten the next morning, my cell phone rang. I looked away from my computer and saw THE CLINIC on my phone. My throat tightened.

"Hello?" I answered.

"Chloe, this is Dr. Wilder. I have some good news for you."

CHAPTER THIRTY-FOUR

I hung up the phone and leaned back in my chair. I placed my hands on my flat stomach and smiled. It worked. The candles, the prayers, the IVF. Everything had come together and brought us a baby. I didn't want to be cruel and make Tyler sweat it out, but I wanted to surprise him with the good news in person. His production offices were in Old Town, about fifteen minutes from mine in the Loop, so I jumped into a taxi and went to find my baby daddy.

I spun through the revolving door of his building and took the elevator to the third floor.

"Hi, Megan. I'm here to see Tyler," I said to the receptionist. I began to walk right past her when she stopped me.

"Hi, Chloe, how are you? Do you mind waiting one sec while I grab him for you? The Brain Berry clients are back there."

I glanced over her head. "I really wanted to surprise him. I'll be very discreet."

"Um, well, let me just get him for you."

"Okay," I said, throwing my arms up in defeat. As much as I wanted to surprise him, I wasn't going to let her ruin my mood. A minute later, Tyler walked up to me behind Megan.

"Did you hear?" he asked, smiling. "You wouldn't be here if it was bad news."

"I might be," I teased, but there was no hiding the elation on my face.

Tyler lifted me off my feet and spun me around. "Oh my God, I'm so relieved," he said kissing me on the cheek.

"Me too."

"Have you called your mom?"

"Nope. I ran straight over here. I haven't told anyone."

Tyler latched onto my hand and led me back to his office where we spent the next hour making phone calls—and making people's day—with our good news.

I texted Cam when Tyler was on the phone with his mom.

The candlesticks worked. We're expecting! I hit send and smiled. Every Monday morning for the next four months I got a phone call from my mother at nine o'clock. The conversation was almost always the same.

"Hi, Mom," I'd say.

"How are you feeling?"

"Good, thank you."

"Are you taking your vitamins?"

"I am."

"Are you staying away from alcohol?" she'd ask.

"I am, yes."

"Are you staying away from caffeine?"

"I'm trying."

"Is everything okay with the baby?"

"Yes, so far so good."

"When is the next doctor's appointment?"

"I have one every few weeks, so I'll be going back early next month."

"When is the baby due?"

"Still on April twelfth."

"And what date are you coming to visit me?"

"I'm coming the weekend of December tenth." Among the many relationships I'd ignored throughout my quest to have a child, the one with my mom had suffered the most. She refused to come visit me in Chicago, and I had put off visiting her in Florida more times than I could count. I knew that if I didn't get down there before the baby was born, I'd never do it.

"Okay, be good."

"I love you, Mom; talk to you later."

I battled a mild case of morning sickness for the first couple of months, but once that passed, I felt great—and very fortunate. The only thing weighing on my mind was Tyler. He and I had so much to celebrate, but so little time together. We were both working ridiculous hours, and I hardly ever saw him. He often had commercial shoots that were scheduled at night, and I had early court times in the morning. We communicated through texts and Post-its. As often as not, I found myself walking in the door at nine o'clock at night, hungry and tired, throwing a Hot Pocket in the microwave, leaning against the counter, and wolfing it down by myself.

Tyler had missed two ob-gyn appointments because he never got my messages. So for my twenty-two-week appointment on Wednesday, December 8th, I called him ahead of time to make sure he'd be there. He'd been at work until past midnight working with Mitch on some animation for a new client, and I knew he was exhausted, but my gyno appointments were always at nine o'clock. I routinely booked their first appointment of the day so that I didn't have to wait, and so that I could get back to work as soon as possible. But at nine fifteen I was still waiting to be called in, and Tyler had yet to arrive.

At nine thirty I was called into the examination room. I dialed Tyler's phone as I followed the nurse. There was no answer, so I called the house phone. When our voice mail picked up, I called his office, but Megan said he hadn't been in yet that morning. I shook my head, silenced my phone, and threw it in my bag.

Once I had finished with Dr. Wilder and his staff at the fertility clinic, I had gone back to my ob-gyn, Dr. Leonard. He walked in that morning with the ultrasound technician after I'd changed into the robe that was left for me. Open in the front. I knew the drill by then.

"Good morning, how have you been?"

"Pretty good," I said, my mind sullen and elsewhere.

"Everything seems to be progressing nicely; nothing out of the ordinary for you, I hope. Any pains or spotting?" he asked.

"Nope."

"All right then, I'm going to have Avery do the ultrasound and take a few pictures. We should be able to get a gender for you today if you'd like. Let her know if you'd rather she keep it a secret."

I sighed. I'd completely forgotten that we were going to find out if the baby was a boy or a girl today. The thought made me even angrier with Tyler than I already was. I wanted to strangle him for ruining that moment. I had pictured myself lying there, holding Tyler's hand, our eyes gazing at the screen with anticipation—a nail-biting, cinematic-worthy event—waiting for what I thought would be a highlight of my pregnancy. As we'd endured the arduous process of fertility treatments, the last thing we'd focused on was the sex of our baby. We just wanted a baby. Any baby. All we dared to dream about was having one that was healthy. But I knew that Tyler wanted a son more than anything. There had always been so many things I wanted for Tyler. For him to be happy with himself. For him to love his job. And for him to have a son. I still wanted nothing more than to bring that joy into his life. But this still wasn't how I'd imagined finding out. All alone with a random technician.

"Let see here," Avery said as she began the ultrasound. "It looks to me like there's no question with this little one. Would you like to know the baby's gender?"

"Yes," I said.

CHAPTER THIRTY-FIVE

After braving the snow in heels and brushing my car off, I returned to the office and called Hollis. She and Mitch had eloped in Las Vegas the weekend before, and I'd set up a dinner at NoMI, a swanky restaurant nestled in the Park Hyatt on Michigan Avenue, for the four of us to celebrate that night. But since my mood had taken a nosedive after sitting at the doctor's office alone all morning, I called her to cancel.

"I'm so sorry, I'm just not feeling up to it tonight. I'm supposed to leave Friday morning to visit my mom, and I haven't even begun to pack."

"Of course," she said. "Don't be silly, we can get together any-time."

I'd purposely left my cell phone at the bottom of my tote bag and in vibrate mode all morning, so I wasn't shocked when Rachel popped her head in my office around noon to tell me that Tyler was on line one.

My heart ached as she waited for my response. I wanted so badly to talk to him. Being silent and stubborn was difficult for me, but I had a point to make and couldn't think of any other way to make it. His absence that morning had emptied me of the joy that was rightfully mine. Robbed me of celebrating with friends and toasting to love and life.

"Take a message," I said.

Rachel left without hesitation but came back a moment later looking apologetic. "He really wants to talk to you."

I shrugged. "Then he should've shown up to our appointment this morning," I told her. "Sorry, I shouldn't put you in the middle. Tell him dinner's canceled tonight and that I'm leaving for court and will call him from my cell."

She smiled. "Will you?"

"Hell no."

Tyler never called back, which only intensified my resentment. I had wanted and needed—and expected—him to grovel. I was already asleep when he came home that night, and gone at the crack of dawn the next morning. By the time I left the office the next day at four o'clock, it had been over thirty-six hours since we'd spoken.

Thursday evening I was upstairs in our bedroom packing a bag to leave for Florida in the morning, and it was still snowing. Half of the flights out of O'Hare had been canceled, but mine was still on schedule. A weekend with my mother had never looked better.

I heard Tyler enter the house around seven o'clock. My car was in the garage, so he knew I was home. He walked into the master bedroom carrying flowers. I knew from experience that he didn't do apologies very well. The sight of him crushed me. I wanted to forgive him in that instant and run into his arms. But I didn't move.

"I fucked up," he said profoundly.

My breathing intensified.

"Chloe, I'm sorry, but avoiding each other isn't going to do any good."

I stared at him, barely recognizing the look on his face. He was apologizing, but his eyes were inscrutable. His words did not match his cool demeanor. I had so much to say, yet so little faith that any of it would have an effect on him.

"I hardly know what to say to you. My anger has been
for nearly two days. You have no idea how upset and disappointed
I am. Do you? What could you possibly have been thinking? How
could you miss the appointment and then ignore me for a whole
day afterward!?" My voice rose at the end.

He threw his head back and began to walk toward the window.
"I said I fucked up, and I'm sorry. I tried calling you yesterday, and
you wouldn't take my call, so I figured you didn't want to talk to me."

I stood up from the floor where I was folding clothes to better
convey my rage. "Are you kidding me?!" I yelled. "We are not in
high school, Tyler. This is a marriage, a partnership, a goddamned
commitment! We're having a child together, and you're running
around acting like one. I have *never* been so angry with someone
in my life, and it kills me that it's you of all people! How could you
behave like this?"

"Don't freak out at me; I got stuck in a conference and tried to
call you, but you wouldn't take my *fucking call*!" he yelled. Then he
stormed out of the bedroom, slamming the door behind him.

I sat down on the bed, sobbing, thinking, this can't be happening. We'd come so far and overcome so much together. Why
was it breaking down during what was supposed to be our happiest time? Weren't we supposed to be rubbing cocoa butter on my
stretch marks and laughing over celebrity baby names as we chose
the perfect moniker for our own little one? I was no good at living
with hostility, and there was no way I could leave town with things
like this between us. At that moment, I didn't care about being
right. I didn't care about making a point and watching him suffer. I
just wanted to move forward and make amends with my husband.

I took a hot shower and went downstairs to find Tyler in the
kitchen, opening a box of pizza. He looked at me when I entered
the room.

"This is ridiculous," I started quietly. "I'm leaving tomorrow. Can we at least have dinner together?" I asked.

"I'll be in the den," he said over his shoulder as he left the room.

I sat at the kitchen island with my laptop and inhaled four slices of pizza without tasting a single bite. I hated arguing with Tyler almost as much as I hated following him around trying to make things right between us. I argued for a living and preferred to leave it at the office. Tyler was stubborn, and regardless of whether he was the instigator or not, he often made it seem like everything was my fault.

Once I'd finished eating, I joined him on the couch with my computer. While the noise from the TV was a welcome distraction, it also served as a reminder of how little we spoke to each other. At ten o'clock, Tyler's phone rang, and he walked into the kitchen to take the call. He grabbed a beer from the fridge, and I could see him pause near the sink to finish his conversation. He didn't return until he'd hung up.

"Who's calling so late?" I asked when he returned.

Tyler took a sip of his beer. "It was Mitch. He and Hollis are in Atlanta, and he wanted to make sure I had the call times for tomorrow," he answered. "The extras need to be there two hours early to get into makeup for the zombie cereal thing, and the three principal actors don't need to be there until noon. Mitch wanted to make sure I had the correct schedule because he's usually the one to send out the call sheets, and they need to be e-mailed tonight. So I've got to take care of it, and then I need to be on set in Hinsdale by six thirty tomorrow morning."

"Mitch and Hollis are in Atlanta?" I asked. "What for?"

"I'm not sure. I think maybe his mom is sick. She lives there. They probably went there to see her," he said, thumbing a message on his phone.

"His mom is sick?"

He looked up at me abruptly with an annoyed expression on his face. "I don't know, okay? All I know is that he's in Atlanta, and I have to get these call sheets done and get to bed." He turned back to his phone.

I closed my laptop, grabbed my glass of water from the coffee table, and began to head upstairs. "I'm going to bed, too. My flight is at ten tomorrow morning, so I guess I won't see you until Monday," I said over my shoulder. "Good night."

"G'night, Chloe, love you," he said, looking over at me. "I'm sorry, I really am. Things are crazy at work, and I'm just…planning for this shoot tomorrow is really working me over. There are so many balls in the air, and I just want to make sure everything goes well."

His eyes were heavy, and I could see that he was anxious to be left alone. I nodded and went to bed.

Tyler was gone by the time I woke up the next morning. The snow was still falling. I checked my flight from home to confirm that it was still on schedule, but by the time I got to the airport, it had been delayed due to the storm. Two hours later, it was canceled altogether.

I was about to call my mom when my phone rang. It was Rachel.

"My flight was just canceled," I said as I picked up.

"I know, I just got an e-mail alert from the airline," she said.

"I should have known, but this morning when I checked, it said the flight was still on time. Oh well."

"Well, Kimberly James's husband's lawyer called this morning and asked to move the deposition to Monday, so at least you'll be in town for that now," she told me.

"Okay, tell him that's fine," I said, swallowing through a dry throat. I glanced at a clock on the wall and realized it was just about time for one of my ravenous hunger pangs to set in. I spied a Cinnabon and started speed walking.

"Do you want me to send a car back to come get you?" Rachel asked.

"No, thanks, I'll just jump in a cab," I said. "In fact, I think I'm going to bring Tyler his fridge today. We had a fight last night, and I'd like to do something nice for him."

Tyler had come home a few times complaining that his soda had been stolen from the main refrigerator in their communal lunchroom, so I'd asked Rachel to order a mini-fridge for him a couple of weeks earlier. Robert had put it in my trunk, but I hadn't had a chance to deliver it yet.

"Sorry to hear that. What were you fighting about?"

"It's not worth getting into. But he's been ridiculously stressed out about this commercial he's working on. I know he'll be on set in Hinsdale all day, so I'll bring it by his office while he's not there. It'll be a nice surprise for him when he gets back."

"That's sweet of you," Rachel said. "Are you sure you don't want me to send a limo?"

"I'm sure, thank you. The fridge is in the back of my car, so I'll just jump in a cab and head home first. I should be in the office by three," I said. "See you then."

On the ride home I called my mother and told her my flight had been canceled. Her reaction was the same as if I'd told her I had eggs for breakfast. As the cab pulled onto my street, I noticed our cleaning lady's car parked in front of the house. She wasn't due to come until Monday.

"Karina?" I called out as I entered through the side door. "Hello, Karina?" I shouted up the front stairs a second time.

She appeared at the top of the stairs wearing rubber yellow gloves. "You coming home today?" she asked me.

"No, what are you doing here?" I knew her to be on time, but never three days early.

"Tyler, he text me and ask if I come today."

I shook my head. "When did he do that?"

"Yesterday morning."

We stared at each other with nearly the same bewildered expression.

"It's okay?" she asked.

I nodded, confused, and got in my car.

By the time I arrived at Tyler's office, I was beaming with excitement. But first I needed to find one of the guys from his office to help me with the large box. I parked in front of the building, left my hazards on, and started walking toward the revolving doors. The sight of Mitch stopped me in my tracks.

"Hey, sexy momma," he greeted me with a hug as I froze.

I took a step backward and nearly tumbled off the curb. "I thought you were in Atlanta with Hollis?" I asked him, confusion setting off fireworks in my head.

"Atlanta?" he said, looking equally baffled. "Why would I be in Atlanta? We have the Brain Berry shoot this weekend," he said and put his arms straight out in front of him to mimic a marching zombie.

A deadly chill ran through me.

CHAPTER THIRTY-SIX

My chest tightened and my breathing intensified as snippets of last night's conversation with Tyler began flashing through my head. I struggled to recall the specifics and make sense of it. Had Mitch even called him last night? My "pregnancy brain" had failed me on more than one occasion, but there was no doubt in my mind that Tyler had told me Mitch and Hollis were in Atlanta. In fact, he'd gone out of his way to include details regarding Mitch's mother's health and the urgency of getting the call sheets out to the team before morning. When I had talked to Hollis the day before, she hadn't mentioned it, but if his mother were ill that would certainly be reason enough for them to head down there at the last minute. I gently clutched my stomach and decided against asking about his mother.

"Whoa, you okay?" he asked, sensing my discord and reaching out to touch my shoulder.

I nodded and looked down at my trembling hands. "I'm… I'm…it's just morning sickness."

"You poor thing," Mitch said. "Tyler's upstairs. Why don't you go lie down?"

My head jerked up. "Tyler's upstairs?" I asked.

"Yeah," he confirmed, narrowing his eyes. "You sure you're okay?"

I nodded.

"All right then, I gotta run. See you later."

"See you," I said. I continued to stand motionless outside the doors that led into Tyler's office building. He'd lied to me, and every ounce of my being knew he wasn't hiding anything good. There was no congratulatory gift in his trunk for me. No velvet box waiting on the kitchen counter next to a vase of roses to greet me upon my return from Florida. Something was very wrong. I took the elevator to the third floor and walked straight past Megan at reception as she attempted to greet me. Tyler was right where Mitch said, yet not where he was supposed to be. He looked at me like I was one of the zombies.

"Hi," he said, standing up hastily. "Are you okay? What are you doing here?"

"What are *you* doing here?"

His eyes fluttered as he ran his hand through his hair. "I work here," he said.

Was he really going to toy with me? "I thought you were supposed to be on set all day in Hinsdale."

"I'm on my way there now," he replied.

I locked eyes with him for a moment before he glanced down at his desk. "I just saw Mitch downstairs and asked him how his trip to Atlanta was."

Tyler fumbled with his computer and put his keys in his front pocket while I stood across from him, resisting the urge to heave a stapler at his head. "Do you have something you need to tell me, Tyler?"

"No."

"Are you serious? I just bumped into Mitch, and he assured me he was nowhere near the state of Georgia this week."

He shook his head. "I never said he was in Atlanta."

My eyes went wide. "Have you lost your mind? Yes, you did say that; you even went so far as to tell me his mother was sick, remember? It was just last night!" I screamed. He went to close the door.

"Are you sleeping with someone?" I asked.

"No."

"Why was Karina cleaning the house today?"

Tyler walked back to his desk chair. "I have no idea."

"I was at the house a half hour ago, and she told me you asked her to come today. Let me guess, she's lying too?"

He said nothing.

"What the hell is going on? Are you cheating on me?" I asked, incredulously. "Answer me!"

"No!"

My mind began to race, as memories of other questionable activities came to mind. Like why his phone bill and credit card statements didn't come to the house anymore. And why Hollis had replied, 'Oh, it hasn't been too bad,' when I commented to her about our husbands' many late nights lately.

"Why doesn't your cell phone bill come to the house anymore?" I asked him.

"Because the company pays for it now."

"No, they don't. I still see the canceled checks online. I just don't see the bills. Let me see your phone."

"You're not going through my phone."

"Then let me see the phone bills."

"I don't have them."

I shrugged calmly. "Fine, then I'll subpoena your phone records when I get back to the office."

I watched him sink slowly back down in his chair. He glanced at me, then looked away and thought hard before speaking. "What do you want me to say?" he asked.

"I want the truth, because right now I don't believe a god-damned word that's coming out of your mouth. You have sixty seconds to tell me what's going on, and why you're lying to me before

I leave here and subpoena all your calls and texts for the past six months. And you know I'll do it."

"I have nothing to hide."

"Then give me your phone."

Whether his back was up against a wall or he was trying to prove something to himself, I don't know, but he handed me his phone. I held it in my hand, not quite sure what I was going to find and then slid my thumb across the screen to unlock it. I tapped the phone icon and a list of his recent calls popped up. I scrolled through them. Many of the names I recognized from his work. Some were nicknames. Some were just numbers. Only one was a woman.

"Who's Morgan?" I asked.

"A friend," he said too quickly for my taste. His expression was nervous, but I could tell from his body language that he was trying desperately to appear indifferent. His hands were shoved in his pockets, his shoulders slumped, and his eyes were darting around the room.

"Why have I never heard her name before?"

He shrugged.

Did he really want to be cross-examined by me? Was he seriously going to put me through this? I may have been emotional and hormonal and high-strung, but I was no fool. He had to know that by now.

"Do you think I should believe you?" I asked.

"You should believe what you want."

"Do you think you're acting like someone who has nothing to hide?"

"I'm not one of your clients."

"Don't be so sure," I said, keeping my gaze fixed on him. The entire left side of my chest had begun to cramp up, and the pain was unbearable. It took every ounce of mental fortitude not to double over as I stood in front of my beautiful husband and dodged the ugly lies he was throwing at me. My subconscious was fighting with reality, making it hard to concentrate. I wanted to believe him. I needed to believe him. I needed to know that what he was saying was the truth. But deep down, in the pit of my stomach, I thought, *He's cheating on me.*

My knees buckled, and as I reached for a chair, he scrambled toward me. I smacked him across the face with the back of my hand as I sat down. "Don't fucking touch me," I mumbled.

Tyler stepped back and began pacing.

I caught my breath before speaking again. "Who is she?" I asked. "And do not make me ask twice."

He didn't make me ask twice, but he did make me wait for an answer. "She's a makeup artist, and she's just a friend."

"I didn't realize you wore makeup," I said, and he had the nerve to roll his eyes at me. "Well, I can't think of any other reason you'd need to talk to a makeup artist so often. How long have you known her?"

"I don't know, maybe a month or so," he said.

"Don't pretend like you don't remember the first time you fucked the makeup artist and cheated on your pregnant wife. I want to know exactly how long it's been!"

Tyler said nothing. My hands were shaking. I had no idea how to process the horror film that I was starring in. All I could think about was my baby. Our baby. Had I become a single parent in that instant? Why in God's name would he ruin everything we'd worked for?

He finally spoke. "We met a while back, on a shoot for Gatorade, and then I saw her again a couple months ago at the Burger King gig," he said, wiping his brow. His eyes shifted back and forth from me to his cell phone, which I'd placed back on his desktop.

"And when did you begin sleeping with her?"

He didn't answer me or deny anything. He just sighed. When his phone buzzed, alerting him to a text message, he lifted his head and reached out to grab it, but I got to it first. I heaved it at the wall behind his head and watched it shatter into pieces.

"Goddamn it, Chloe!"

I was unfazed. "Answer my question before your laptop suffers the same fate. When did you begin having sex with Morgan the makeup artist? Was it before or after we got our test results? Were you fucking her the day after we celebrated the pregnancy or the day before? Did you tell her all about what a wonderful father you're going to be?" I stood, disgusted, and grabbed my purse. I turned to leave, and then paused with my back to him and my hand on the doorknob. "Next time she's sucking your dick, tell her it's a boy," I said and walked out.

CHAPTER THIRTY-SEVEN

I ran outside and around to the side of his building, then collapsed on the ground and vomited. Dirt and gravel dug into my palms and knees as I spit and sobbed and caught my breath. I managed to get inside my car and drove four blocks before pulling over. Tears and snot and sweat drenched the front of my shirt. My body convulsed as I thought about Karina at the house, scrubbing the bathtub on Tyler's insistence. Had he planned to bring that woman into our home while I was in Florida? *Of course he did, you stupid, clueless fucking idiot!* In one fell swoop my husband had turned me into my mother. A delusional, heartbroken, insecure woman looking for a crutch.

Sitting in the car, I cried for myself and for my mom. In a matter of minutes my confidence, my intelligence, and the future I'd envisioned for myself had been ripped from my grasp. I wanted to drive my car into a brick wall. I hated myself for feeling that way and for letting that happen. How could that have happened?! I threw the car door open and vomited two more times on the side of the road. Saliva dripped from my chin.

I drove to the dumpster behind our local grocery store before heading home and kicked the mini-fridge out of the back of my SUV. Eyes wide and snot running down my nose like a crazy person, I watched it crash to the ground and drove away. After spending another forty minutes sitting in my car, I cleaned myself up and went into lawyer mode. My mind was frantically trying to piece things together and figure out where to begin my investigation. Tyler was too stupid to have covered all of his tracks, and I was intent on unearthing every one of them. As soon as I got home, I asked Karina to leave, changed my clothes, and started tearing through his desk drawers looking for clues. Ever since we'd been married, we'd always split the bills. He paid the utilities and two of the credit cards, while I paid the mortgage and the American Express. We'd always kept separate bank accounts. My idea.

About halfway through the pile, I found the Visa statements. I scrutinized every charge. Starbucks, Shell, Home Depot: nothing seemed out of the ordinary for him until I turned the page and saw RedEnvelope. I rifled through the stack and found charges for lingerie, flowers, candles, a watch, and more. He'd spent nearly $2,000 on gifts for her over a three-month period. I sat on the floor and shook my head. He wasn't just sleeping with this idiot, he was courting her, *dating* her. My husband was dating someone else. I dropped the papers and wrapped my arms around my baby. I knew it was more than I could bear, but I couldn't stop. I went to the phone and dialed his voice mail. It took me only two tries to guess his password: 1-0-1-4, our address. What I sat through next was probably the hardest to endure. There were two new messages from a woman with a Southern drawl—just like his mother, I couldn't help but note.

"Hey babe, it's me, where are you? I just missed your call. I'm on my way to my mom's; call me back."

"Where are you? Call me, so I know what time we're meeting, 'kay?"

After replaying them several times, I deleted the messages. Clearly, I had some decisions to make, and a more detailed conversation with Tyler was inevitable. I wanted answers, and I was owed answers, but I wanted them on my terms. I paced the entire first floor of the house while my brain ping-ponged back and forth between wanting to cry and wanting to bury him. I needed to do something or talk to someone, but I was too humiliated to call anyone. Who was I going to call, my mother? The mere thought of breaking this news to her brought me to tears again. Everyone who was close to me knew nearly every detail of what Tyler and I had gone through, not only to be together but also to become parents. Even some of my clients knew about my fertility treatments because there had been times I'd had to cancel meetings or phone calls to rush in and have my ovaries checked. It had gotten to the point where being honest with people around me became easier than trying to pretend I had some mystery disease that kept my physician on speed dial.

Tyler didn't come home after work that day. The next morning I called a locksmith and had the locks changed. He certainly wasn't going to be allowed to come and go anymore as he pleased. He never called me to deny anything, nor did he bang on the front door pleading to talk with me and work things out, so I spent the entire weekend curled up in a ball under my covers. I ignored all calls and texts and never opened my laptop. The smell of food was repellent, so I drank water and forced myself to eat pretzels for the baby. I cried, I ached, I anguished. But mostly I sat in my quiet bedroom in a numb state of disbelief. I played every scenario over and over in my head and couldn't come up with how we had gotten to this point or where to go from here.

The deposition on Monday for Kimberly James required a commanding performance, so Sunday night I managed a shower and checked my phone. Thirty missed calls from Grace, Rachel, Robert, Cam, my mother, and various clients. Ninety-eight e-mails, forty-five text messages, and fourteen voice mails. None of them from Tyler.

Monday morning I walked into the office and waved at Rachel. She quickly stood up when she saw me.

"Hey, you okay? I tried to reach you all weekend. I was worried when you didn't come in Friday," Rachel said as I shuffled past her desk in a fog.

"It was a long weekend," I said. She followed me into my office.

"What's going on? Is everything okay with the baby?" she asked. I nodded.

"Do you want to talk about it?"

"Yes, but not right now," I said.

"Gotcha. Did you get the message that the deposition was canceled?"

"No, but that's good news."

"I believe there was an issue with Kimberly and her husband over the weekend. She left you a voice mail, I think."

"Okay, I'll check them now."

Rachel left while I went through the motions of being normal. I did everything I usually did. I placed my tote bag on the floor next to my chair and removed my laptop from it. I carefully pulled the white plastic lid off my Starbucks venti skim latte so that I didn't have to drink hot coffee through that unforgiving little hole. I powered up my computer and let my e-mails load while I took a sip. I grabbed my cell phone and plugged it into the charger cord that lay on my desktop. Everything was normal, only everything had changed.

About fifteen minutes later, my phone chimed. It was a text from Tyler.

We need to talk, it read.

I almost laughed when I saw it. I snorted and shook my head at the mere thought of him lying to my face, ignoring me for three days, and ruining my life, only to come up with that bit of genius. That was the best he could do?

Six hours later I responded with my own sentiment.

How could you?

CHAPTER THIRTY-EIGHT

Tyler texted me back right away, but he didn't answer my question.

When can we talk? I want to do this in person, he wrote.

Do what in person? Did he think for one second that he was in control anymore? We weren't going to talk until I was ready to talk. Until I had mapped out exactly what was going to happen. He knew I could make life hell for him, and he was right. He also knew how much I loved him, and yet he had taken advantage of my vulnerability and mocked me by doing the one thing I had always been afraid a man would do to me. I was strong in every aspect of my life, but never where Tyler was concerned. All I had ever wanted was for us to have a family, and I had been convinced that giving birth to Tyler's son would make him love me the way I loved him. It was the one thing that would bind us forever and ensure that he would look at me with the same admiration I had for him. I was only a couple months away from changing everything for the better. How could he have done this to us?

When I'm ready to see you, I will let you know, I answered.

I need my things, he replied.

I guess you should have planned ahead, I texted back and turned off my phone.

Hard as it was, I had to try to think logically, like I was my own lawyer. And while I doubted Tyler was eager to come groveling back to me, I needed to know what his intentions were. But first I had to be certain of my reaction. Assuming there was an apology waiting for me, did I want it? Would it matter? Could we save our marriage? He'd broken my trust and my heart; I didn't know if I could ever forgive him for that. And if he could do something like this at the height of our euphoria, then he was certainly capable of doing it anytime. That said, I didn't want to be alone. His texts brought tears to my eyes.

Robert knocked on my door and entered simultaneously. He paused his familiar, determined stride when he saw my face. "Are you okay?"

I stared at him, ready to nod, and then shook my head instead. "I will be," I said as a few tears rolled down my cheek.

"Sorry, the door was open…"

"It's fine; please, sit down," I said and gestured to the two arm-chairs across from me.

Robert sat down and placed three file folders on my desk. "Madison has me well versed in the art of nodding and agreeing, so if you want to talk about it, I'm all ears." He smiled.

Robert and I probably spent more time together than he and his wife did. I imagined he was subjected to long tirades about why he couldn't leave work before nine o'clock at night, and why he had to be back in the office no later than seven in the morning. Only other lawyers ever really understood—not only how taxing those hours were but also what they meant. Hours spent at the office were our lifeblood, our credibility, our means of proving our worth. He probably did his best to explain this to his young wife, just as I'd done with Tyler for so many years, but it was hard for our spouses to feel that they weren't a priority. That they didn't come first. Did that mean I deserved to be cheated on?

"Tyler is cheating on me," I said outright. "He's fucking some makeup artist."

Robert slid down in his seat. "No," he whispered.

I sighed. "Yup, so it looks like you just got yourself a new client."

"He told you that?" Robert asked.

"He didn't have to."

Robert's cheeks puffed up with air, and then he exhaled a long breath. "Oh my God, I don't know what to say, I'm so sorry."

"Yeah, me too."

"How did you find out?" he asked.

"I caught him in a few lies, and he didn't have the time to cover his tracks," I told him. "Remember how I was supposed to visit my mom this weekend?"

He nodded.

"Well, my flight got canceled, and I went to drop off that fridge I bought him at his office as a surprise, because he was supposed to be out all day on a shoot. The fridge is now rotting in a dumpster somewhere. Anyway, he was planning on spending the weekend with this woman in our house while I was away."

Robert rolled his eyes. "Unbelievable," he said shaking his head. "What are you going to do?"

"I really don't know. I haven't even spoken to him since I found out on Friday. In fact, he just texted me for the first time in two days. He wants to talk, but I'm afraid of what he's going to say," I admitted.

"Can you forgive him?"

"I don't know. Maybe if it was a onetime thing, you know? A colossal mistake for which he was regretful and apologetic...then maybe. But it's been going on for months. He's been sending her gifts, and God knows what else," I said. "Something tells me I may not have a say in the matter."

Robert shifted in his chair, and I caught him glance at my stomach before crossing his legs. "He's an idiot."

I nodded.

"I wish I knew what to say, Chloe; I'm in shock," he started. "I mean after everything you've gone through with the baby and everything…I just don't get it."

"Me neither."

"Is there anything I can do to help?" he offered. "Do you need a place to stay?"

"No, thank you, I'm fine at the house. I had the locks changed, and I'm guessing he finally realized it when he went there this morning to get his things."

"He should know better than to mess with you," Robert said.

"Yeah, anyway, I just got a message from Kimberly James that her husband accosted her at Sports Authority yesterday, and she called the police. He was arrested and charged with battery. She wants an emergency order of protection filed today covering her and giving her sole possession of the children. Can you take care of that for me?"

"Of course," he said and stood.

"Thanks, Robert, and please don't feel sorry for me, okay?"

"Too late," he said and smiled. "I know this can't be easy. Just let me know if there is anything I can do. If you need him to take a long walk down a short pier, just say the word."

"I will, thank you."

Late that afternoon, I filed for my own divorce. Not because I'd made up my mind and decided I wanted a divorce, but because I needed a court case number to be able to subpoena Tyler's phone records.

And so began my new obsession.

CHAPTER THIRTY-NINE

Every night for the next two weeks I came home from work, curled up on the couch and cried. I cried so hard one night that I was convinced I was having a heart attack. When the paramedics arrived at my house, they said my symptoms were more congruent with those of a panic attack and asked if I'd had any recent significant changes in my life.

I avoided all calls that weren't work-related, and only communicated with friends and family via text. Some knew bits and pieces of what happened; some knew nothing at all. I found out from Hollis that Tyler had been staying on their couch, and that Mitch had given him a stern scolding. She'd told me that Tyler broke things off with Morgan, and that Mitch had forbade the company from ever hiring her again. But it was all too little too late as far as I was concerned. The damage was done.

Once I got my hands on Tyler's text records, I sat and read through every single one of them. They made me sick to my stomach. It was like bad amateur porn. Cheesy and appalling and hard to look at.

I can taste your cologne on my tongue.
I need you.
I'm so wet right now thinking about last night.
Did you get the pictures? xoxo
Can you meet for "lunch" again?

My tits still smell like you.

I knew I was torturing myself, but I didn't care. I deserved it for being so stupid. I wanted to hang them all over the walls of my bedroom as a reminder of how naïve I was. Maybe reading them every morning would give me the strength I needed to end my marriage.

Eventually, I confessed my situation to Grace. She wept on the phone as I recounted what I knew and read her a few of the texts that Morgan had sent my husband. She ached with me like everyone else I'd told. Everyone but Dixie Reed, that is.

Mitch and Hollis kicked Tyler out after three weeks, and he eventually went to stay with his parents. I'd texted him that I still wasn't ready to talk or see him, and he honored my wishes. About five weeks after I learned of his affair, his mother showed up at my office one Thursday morning.

"Your mother-in-law is here," Rachel said from the door. "What should I tell her?"

"Send her in." I paused. "And then save me in ten minutes."

I sat up straight and waited for her to enter. I refused to stand or greet her with a hug like I normally would have. There was no way she was there to sympathize with me, so I braced myself for a standoff.

"Chloedear, bless your heart, you're positively glowing," she said.

"Hi, Dixie," I said and gestured to an open chair.

She took a seat and removed her gloves. "How are you feeling?"

"Pretty good now that the morning sickness has subsided."

"I see you finally have a proper baby belly." She smiled.

I looked down and folded my hands over my stomach.

"I hope you don't mind my barging in here like this, but I was in the city for a hair appointment, so I thought I would stop by and check in on you and my grandson."

"It's no problem at all," I said, keeping my comments deliberately short.

Dixie nodded slightly and looked around the room before speaking again. "As you know, Tylah is staying with us, and he would vereh much like to come home to you."

I raised a brow. "I knew he was staying with you, but I was unaware he was so eager to come home."

"Oh yes, and I think you both would be better off puttin' this whole thing behind you."

This whole *thing*? My body temperature began to rise. "That's easier said than done, now, isn't it?"

She shifted in her seat. "I don't think so. We all know how hard marriage can be when we add certain challenges to the mix. Remember how I warned you that messing with fate might test your relationship?" she dared to remind me. "Tylah's a good man, and he knows he made a mistake, but he loves you and the baby, and it's time he came home."

I looked down at my hands and closed my eyes for a second. "Well, I'm not ready for him to come home. And I'm not sure I'll ever be ready after what he's put me through. I'm guessing you know very few of the details, and I'll keep it that way, but your son has not behaved like someone who loves me or values his marriage. Trust me."

Dixie began to fidget and shake her head. She probably hated having her grown, married son back in his childhood bedroom, leaving dirty laundry on the floor and shaming the family. Again.

She continued, "Well, I know we wouldn't want to raise a child all on our own now, would we? Imagine what this poor little boy is going to have to endure without a father around. Surely you will think of him when you're making your decision."

"Surely my son wouldn't want me to compromise my integrity either."

Just then, Rachel stuck her head in. "Sorry to interrupt, but you have that conference call now…on line two."

I glanced at the blinking phone. "Thanks, Rachel. I need to take this," I said to Tyler's mom. "Thank you for checking in on me, Dixie."

"Of course, dear." She stood, smiled at Rachel, and left.

"It's actually your friend Cam on the phone," she said. "Perfect timing."

"He always knows when I need him. Thanks."

I lifted the receiver and pressed line two. "Hello?"

"I'm coming to Chicago tomorrow."

I smiled and felt truly happy for a moment. "That's the best thing I've heard all week." Cam knew my situation. Mostly through texts and e-mails because I loathed recounting the details over the phone. He'd confessed that he had never been a huge fan of Tyler's, but that was so easy to say given all that had happened. "What brings you to town?"

"I have some business. There's a convention in Rosemont on Saturday."

"Do you want to stay with me? I would love it. My house is so empty and quiet, and you know how I crave a little chaos."

"Sure," he said. "Couch or crib?"

"We have a fluffy queen-sized bed in the guest room with your name on it. I'll even put magazines in the bathroom for you."

"Wow."

Cam landed in Chicago the next night and took a cab to my house. I ordered Chinese food, and we sat on the floor in front of the TV like old times.

"So what's the plan?" he asked me. "I know you have a plan."

I let out a small laugh. "Oh, I *had* plans."

"Come on, seriously, I'm going to make you talk about this because I know you don't want to."

"And I'm going to make you go to a hotel."

"Do you know what you're going to do?"

I scooped a forkful of skinny noodles into my mouth and chewed before answering. "I'm not sure what will eventually end my marriage, Tyler's affair or my pride."

"Has he apologized? Does he want to make things work?" he asked.

"I really haven't given him a chance to. I mean, let me rephrase that, he's had plenty of chances, but I haven't been willing to hear him out. Not yet."

"Why not?"

I stretched my legs out in front of me and placed my plate on the coffee table. "I don't want to talk over the phone, and I'm not ready to see him in person. I can't tell you how hard it was to look at him when I realized he was lying to my face. I'm not sure I can stomach it again."

Cameron nodded. "I get that, but you're having a kid together in a few months. You need to get this over with, either way, and move forward. Do you know if he's still seeing the girl?"

"According to his cousin's wife, they're over."

Cam dug through the plastic bag that held our food and pulled out two fortune cookies. "Which one do you want?" he asked. "Make it good."

I pointed to the one in his right hand, and he opened it for me.

"The object of your desire comes closer," he read and pointed to himself.

I rolled my eyes. "Give me that," I said, snatching it out of his hand. The words were exactly as he'd said them. I smiled and met his gaze. "It probably means the baby."

"Probably."

I placed the small piece of paper in my lap. "I'm sure you and every other guy out there are dying to be with a divorced single mother."

"I never said that I was or I wasn't. I was simply quoting Confucius."

"I'm glad you're here," I said.

"I promise not to play on your vulnerabilities." He smirked. "Too much."

"Thank you."

"I mean it, you know I want what's best for you. But mostly I want you to have what you deserve, and you deserve to be happy. You need to be able to move on. Either you're getting divorced or you're going to forgive Tyler and move past it."

"You make it sound so easy. Maybe the answer is in the last cookie? Let me have it."

Cam tossed the fortune cookie at me, and I cracked it open over my plate. It read, "A good way to keep healthy is to eat more Chinese food."

CHAPTER FORTY

I woke up the next morning and dialed Tyler's cell phone. It'd been too long since I'd heard his voice, and he answered on the first ring.

"Hey," he answered. I could hear the hopefulness in his voice in just that one word.

"I guess we should talk."

"I'm ready, tell me when and where. Can I come by the house later?"

"Cam's in town, and he's staying here, so why don't you come by the office tonight around six."

He took a moment before answering. "I'll see you at six."

My hands were trembling when I hung up the phone.

Cam was at the kitchen island with his laptop and a cup of coffee when I went downstairs.

"I called Tyler," I said.

"And?"

"And he's going to come by the office tonight so that we can talk."

He nodded. "What are you going to say?"

"I'm hoping to listen mostly. I'm not going to put any pressure on myself to make a decision."

"Good luck with that."

My workday was typically busy. I did my best to not watch the clock, but at five thirty, I began to get anxious. I told Rachel that

Tyler was coming by, and asked her to stay a little late to make sure that no one bothered us once he'd arrived.

She walked him in at five minutes to six.

"Thanks, Rachel," I said and smiled at her. She shut the door on her way out.

Tyler walked over to give me a kiss, and I let him.

"Have a seat," I said, and then shook my head at how formal that sounded.

Tyler sat in one of the chairs across from me, and his eyes went straight to my belly. "You look great," he said.

"Thank you."

"How do you feel?"

"Pretty good."

Tyler leaned forward and clasped his hands, dropping them between his legs. He looked great himself. His hair was shorter and messy, and he was wearing the North Face winter coat I'd bought for him the year before.

"Do you want to take your coat off?" I asked.

"Oh yeah," he said and shed his jacket behind him on the chair before leaning forward again. "Thanks for letting me see you."

I smiled.

"I've been thinking a lot about what to say to you, and I just want to start with an apology. I'm really, really sorry for what I've done." He struggled with the words, but I could tell he was being sincere.

I gently scratched the side of my nose. I could already tell I was going to cry at some point during this conversation and was regretting meeting at the office.

He continued, "I don't have an excuse for what I did. You have to believe me when I say I never wanted to hurt you."

I tilted my head and rolled my eyes as passively as I could. "Why did you go through with the IVF if you were unhappy? Why would you put us both through all this if it's not what you wanted?"

He sat in silence for a moment before answering. "I didn't want to add you to the list of people I've disappointed in my life."

"Oh, *please*, you do not get to play the victim here." I raised my voice, and then took a deep breath. "I'm sure you're sorry, and I get that you think you can't come up with an excuse, but I'm going to need some sort of an explanation for why you did this before I can even begin to consider forgiving you and moving forward. I don't want excuses, I want answers." I paused. "I said I was going to subpoena your phone and text records, and I did." The reality of my comment hit him hard. He sat back in the chair, and his expression went blank. He probably had no memory of the things he'd texted to Miss Morgan, while I on the other hand, felt as though every single word had been engraved into my brain with a knife. "Maybe, if this had been a onetime thing, God, even a two-time thing, it would be easier for me to chalk it up to stress and pressure or whatever else you thought you were going through at the time. But this has been going on for months. You've bought gifts for her, and sent naked pictures to her, and she can smell your cologne on her tits." He cringed. "What if I hadn't caught you? Who knows how long this would've gone on?" I paused. "I realize we need to make a decision, but from where I sit now, I'm not willing to forgive you, and I don't know if I ever will."

Tyler looked defeated. He let out a long sigh and kept his eyes fixated on the floor in front of him. I wanted him to stand and beg and plead and make a case for us, but I knew it would never happen. Not because he didn't want us to be together, but because he was incapable of fighting for what he wanted. He would take my words and assume I was putting up a wall between us. He would assume that I wanted to be left alone, and that he should wait for my next cue. He would never believe that he could prove his strength and love to me by knocking that wall down and being the man I so desperately needed him to be right then.

But I refused to push him into it. He had to do it of his own volition for it to mean anything.

Tyler's lips were closed when he looked up and smiled at me. "I understand. I just want you to know that I'm not seeing her anymore, and that I'm going to rent an apartment if I can't come home."

And that was it? He'd given up already?

"Okay, I'm sorry, but I'm just not ready," I said.

"It's fine, I get it. I hope we can still talk. I'd like to know how things are going with the baby."

"Of course."

Tyler and I stood and hugged. I was going to have to get him a new cologne if we were going to stay together.

I walked him to the elevator. As I returned to my office, I didn't shed a single tear.

CHAPTER FORTY-ONE

I came home that night to find Cam in the kitchen, unloading an enormous feast from Morton's Steakhouse. Two filets mignons, creamed spinach, lyonnaise potatoes, stone crab claws, and key lime pie.

"Good lord, this is all for the two of us?"

"You're eating for two, so it's technically three of us. How did it go with the big guy today?" Cam asked, pouring himself a glass of wine.

"He's getting an apartment. He said he was sorry, and I believe him, but I'm not ready to forgive. And he was hardly begging to come home."

"So you need more time."

"Yeah, and I need to start interviewing nannies. How do you feel about kids?"

"They give me hives, but for you, I'd be willing to take Benadryl."

I sat down next to Cam and marveled at the meal before us. I was starving, and so grateful that someone was looking after me, even if only for one night.

"Cam?"

"Chloe."

"Why are you here?" I asked.

He stopped slicing his steak and turned to face me. "Why are you asking me that, all weird and dramatic?"

"It's just that you've hardly left the house, and haven't mentioned the convention or anything."

"You think I have ulterior motives?"

I laughed. "Sort of."

Cam placed his fork and steak knife down next to his plate. "I'm here on business, and I'm here for you."

I stared into his eyes for a good long moment. "Thank you."

"You're welcome. May I continue eating?"

"You knew I needed you, didn't you?"

"I knew you needed someone, and I knew you weren't going to ask for help."

"You know there couldn't be a worse time for me to afford to get confused," I said.

"That makes no sense."

I looked away and took a sip of my ice water. "I mean, having you stay here, bringing me food and taking care of me. I don't want you to leave," I said, brows raised. "But I have to be able to focus on what's right for me and the baby."

"Look, I'm here because I care about you and I was worried about you. That's all. I'm not trying to swoop in on my white horse and take you for my own. Do I want you to go back to Tyler? No. But you should know that no one is going to think less of you if you decide to take him back and try to make your marriage work. You do realize though, that if you're going to accept his apology, you're going to have to do it and live with it, because holding on to the betrayal will kill you."

"I know."

"You thought you were going to get some lustful confession out of me, didn't you?"

I laughed again, and it felt really good. "I just don't want to feel guilty for leaning on you, that's all."

Cameron pulled me close to him, and I rested my head on his shoulder. "Does this make you feel guilty?" he asked.

I smiled. "No, it feels fucking great."

While Cam went to his convention that Saturday, I had a nanny candidate come to the house for an interview. She was a referral from Alexa, whom I'd met at the fertility clinic. Alexa's first IVF treatment had not been successful, and she was gearing up for round two that winter. After she'd sent me the name of her sister's nanny, I packed up the candlesticks that Cam had given me and sent them to her.

Before the nanny arrived, I googled "Interview Questions for Nannies" and felt like an idiot when I read through them and realized I hadn't thought of a single one of the recommended questions. I'd only come up with:

Are you opposed to eleven-hour days?

Can you work until nine o'clock if need be?

Have you ever been arrested?

Do you drink alcohol?

Do you believe you're being followed by imaginary federal agents?

But thankfully the much more practical people at BabyCenter .com had an entire work sheet with a list of more important questions like:

Do you have any formal early childhood development or childcare training?

Would you be willing to take CPR classes?

How do you comfort children and deal with separation anxiety?

I printed out a copy of the questionnaire and had her fill it out when she arrived. Born and raised in Montego Bay, she looked like she was in her late thirties. Her thick Jamaican accent and unflappable approach immediately put me at ease. I tore up the stupid questionnaire, trusted my instincts, and hired her on the spot.

No problem, man.

Cam went back to California, and Tyler moved his stuff out and into an apartment in the city. He and I kept in touch and met for lunch or dinner every few weeks. It wasn't especially comforting to see him, but I felt that I should at least make the effort. Some nights I would cancel; others I would pick somewhere loud with lots of TVs to distract me. I bided my time by going to work and trying to pretend everything would be all right one way or another. Outside of the office I was incapable of making even the most minor decisions, so I didn't.

When I was thirty-five weeks along, his mother threw me a baby shower at her country club. It was a little awkward given the circumstances, but she insisted. Grace came with me, and we sat among Dixie and her friends as they drank cocktails at noon, ate grilled chicken Caesar salads, and showered me with blue gifts.

Afterward, Grace drove me home, and we sat on my couch and caught up. There hadn't been much of a chance for a heart-to-heart with Dixie Reed hovering about nervously.

"How much time are you taking off work?" she asked me.

"I'm going to take the whole three months. I'm sure I'll be working from home as soon as I feel up to it, but I'm going to try not to go down to the office or the courthouse at all during that time."

"Good for you, you deserve a break. What's the latest with Tyler?"

I shrugged. "Good. Weird. I don't know. Once he moved out, it was like starting my whole life over."

"I was worried that was going to happen."

"What?"

"That you'd become complacent and used to the idea of being alone."

I looked out the window in front of me. "You think I should take him back."

She smiled slightly. "Honestly, I do. I know he put you through hell, and you know I'm not discounting his behavior whatsoever, but then I look at you and your beautiful boy growing inside," she choked up. "I just know how hard it is to raise a child with two parents, let alone one." She paused and lowered her chin. "Do you still love him?"

"Yes," I said quietly. "I just never realized how hard it was to forgive. I mean, let's be real; I grew up being disappointed by the one person who was supposed to love me more than anyone. I could've written a book on "How to pull yourself up after being let down," but with Tyler, it's different. The betrayal is still so raw and deliberate. At least with my mother I could chalk it up to mental illness. Tyler knew exactly what he was doing. Over and over again." My blood boiled every time I rehashed it.

"I don't mean to sway you either way, I promise. You're one of the best people I know, and you're going to thrive as a mother with or without Tyler. That much I know for sure."

After Grace left, I went upstairs to change into some comfier clothes. I had to be in court early the next morning, so I spent a couple hours reading through a deposition and preparing my petitions. Afterward, I ate half of a leftover sandwich from the fridge and decided to take a bath. I ran the water, undressed, and climbed into the tub. Just as I leaned forward to adjust the temperature, the water between my legs turned bright red.

CHAPTER FORTY-TWO

The next second, I was doubled over with cramps. I let out a loud moan, tightly closed my legs and managed to turn off the water with my right hand. I sat in the tub, rocking back and forth, clutching the right side of my body as unfamiliar sounds emerged from my throat. I didn't even realize tears were streaming down my face until I tasted them on my lips. When I looked down again, the blood was pouring out of me, heavier and faster. I held onto the side of the tub and craned my neck, looking for my cell phone on the bathroom counter. It wasn't there. I got to my knees, pulled a towel down from its hook and threaded it between my thighs like a diaper. My entire body tensed as I inched my way out of the tub and crawled on one arm into my bedroom. I yanked the house phone down off the dresser and dialed 9-1-1.

"Nine one one, what's your—"

"Please, I need help! I'm pregnant and bleeding profusely, and it won't stop. My address is 1014 Maple Drive. I'm upstairs on the floor and I can't move; blood is everywhere, please help me!" I hollered with terror, and then I moaned wildly as the pain in my side intensified.

"Try and relax, ma'am; the paramedics are on their way. I've sent the call, and they will be there shortly."

I hung up and dialed Grace's cell phone.

"Hey you," she answered.

"I'm bleeding! Please come back! I'm lying on my floor, and I think I'm losing the baby!" I sobbed and choked, unable to breathe.

"Oh my God! I'm on my way, call 9-1-1 now!" She said and hung up.

One of the longest minutes of my life passed.

Two of the longest minutes of my life passed.

Three of the longest minutes of my life passed.

I heard a loud bang below as the fire department kicked in the side door that led into our kitchen. A second later, three firemen and two paramedics were standing over my blood-drenched naked body. They went to work at lightning speed, covering me and placing me on a stretcher. I moaned louder, and my head rolled uncontrollably from side to side.

"Please help my baby, please help the baby. I'm pregnant, oh my God, why is this happening, please don't let me lose the baby." My pleas and primal screams were on replay for the entire ride to the hospital. Once in the emergency room, the staff moved even more quickly than the paramedics.

"Do you know how far along you are?" a nurse asked me.

"Thirty-five weeks."

She rushed me up to the maternity unit, where one nurse began to monitor the baby's heart rate, and another eagerly tried to get an IV into my arm. Dr. Leonard walked in in scrubs, consulted with the team of nurses, and then came to my side.

"Your placenta has separated, and you're losing a lot of blood. The baby is in great distress, so we have to do an emergency C-section," he said and disappeared.

My cries and screams were so foreign to me that I could've sworn I was living through someone else's nightmare. I was raced down the hall into another brightly lit room filled with people and monitors. An anesthesiologist came to my side, injected something into my IV, and that was the last thing I remember.

I blinked and then closed my eyes.

I blinked again but couldn't keep my lids open.

The room was empty and silent.

My head was heavy against the pillow.

My arms were weak. I couldn't move them.

My eyes were still closed when someone took hold of my hand.

I forced them open and saw Tyler standing over me.

CHAPTER FORTY-THREE

Thank God," he whispered and gently tucked some stray hairs behind my ear. His eyes were weary.

"Where's the baby?" I asked.

"He's in the NICU. He's perfect. They had to resuscitate him and put a breathing tube in, but he's doing great. A real trooper like his mom." He squeezed my hand and didn't let go.

"I need to see him."

The door swung open, and Dr. Leonard walked in with a nurse. "You're awake. Good. How are you feeling?" he asked.

"A little sore. Can I see the baby?"

"Give yourself another hour of rest, and then we'll have one of the nurses wheel you down there," he said and then turned his attention to one of the monitors behind me.

"Why did this happen to me?"

He gave a small shrug. "A placental abruption can be caused by any number of things, or nothing at all. The good news is that you did the right thing, and you're both going to be just fine."

"He's only thirty-five weeks though?"

"He'll probably spend a week or two in the NICU. We have to keep an eye on his lungs since he's a little early and has a breathing tube now. But he's doing really well."

I choked up. "I can't thank you enough for everything you've done."

He smiled. "It's my pleasure. Take it easy, and I'll check back on you tomorrow."

Tyler let go of my hand and pulled a chair over to the bed. "You okay?"

I nodded.

"You gave us all a big scare. I thought I'd lost you. I've never been so scared in my life."

"I don't know what happened. I was getting in the tub and started bleeding." I paused to fight back tears. "It was awful."

"Everything's okay now, shhhh, don't get upset; you need to relax."

I turned my face away from him and closed my eyes. His adoring green eyes were more than I could handle. "I assume Grace called you?" I said softly.

"Yeah. She called your mom, too, and again when you safely came out of surgery."

"Is she still here?"

"She left as soon as I arrived because Jack is out of town, but she's going to come back in the morning."

"What time is it?"

"A little after ten."

My body was weak, and my mind was struggling to piece things together. Once I'd sat down in the bath, everything happened so quickly. It was hard to grasp that my baby was now outside of my body and in good health. I had been so convinced he wasn't going to survive.

"So what are we going to name this little guy?" Tyler asked.

To me, there was so much permanence and importance that came with naming a child. I would've loved to have had someone in my life that I could've named my son after, but I wasn't about to honor Tyler's father, Jim, with a namesake. And I never liked when boys had the same name as their dad…too confusing. So I'd spent a few hours online in recent weeks looking for a name with no significant associations whatsoever. Just one that made me happy.

"His name is Connor. Connor Samuel Reed." I had no intention of robbing my son of his right to his father's last name.

Tyler smiled. "I love it. And Sammy will be thrilled."

An hour later, I buzzed the nurse and asked her to take me down to the NICU. Tyler followed us as she pushed me in a wheelchair to the elevators. We were buzzed past security and asked to sanitize our hands and arms. I could feel my heart pounding as I was wheeled past the row of clear-plastic bassinets. As she stopped in front of Connor's, I placed my hand over my smiling mouth and gazed at him. He was perfect, just like Tyler had said. He was covered in tubes and surgical tape, but he was absolute perfection.

"Can I touch him?" I whispered to the nurse.

"Of course," she said.

I slowly eased myself out of the chair and stood over him. I gently placed my pinky finger into his grasp and leaned over to kiss his tiny face.

"How long will he have to be here?" I asked.

"At least a week. Until he's eating and breathing on his own."

Tyler held up his phone and snapped a bunch of pictures of my son and me. We fed him some formula, changed a diaper, and then headed back upstairs to my room. Tyler fell asleep on the daybed by the window.

The next morning, Grace and her mom greeted us with coffee and doughnuts.

"I can't tell you how worried I was; I've never been so terrified in my life," Grace said. "When I saw your back door had been kicked in and you were nowhere to be found, I seriously almost had a heart attack."

"I'm so sorry," I said.

"Don't be silly. I was just so glad they got you to the hospital in time."

"Thank you for calling my mom. What did she say?"

"Well, I played down the severity of the situation at first, but I thought she should know what was happening. I told her you were rushed to the hospital with contractions and that I would call her back when I had more details. By then I knew you and the baby weren't in any more danger, so I let her know, and she was very relieved. You should call her as soon as you can. She really wants to know his name."

"I will, after you all leave."

"I also called Rachel because I remembered you were due in court today. She said to give you a big hug, and that she would make some calls for you."

"You're the best; thank you so much."

"When can you take him home?" Sydney asked me.

"In a week or so."

"We can't wait to meet him," she said.

"You're allowed to see him, but you have to be accompanied by Tyler or me."

"No, no, no, you rest; we'll see him soon enough."

Tyler showed them the pictures on his phone, and they cooed with joy. After Sydney and Grace had left, I asked Tyler to hand me his phone so that I could call my mother.

"Hello?" she answered.

"Hi, Mom."

"Hi, honey, I've been waiting for your call. How are you? How is the baby?"

"He's perfect, Mom; his name is Connor Samuel Reed, and he's the most beautiful little boy I've ever seen." My mom was unaware of Tyler's infidelity. I hadn't had the heart to tell her, and had decided to keep her in the dark until I'd made my final decision.

She gasped. "Connor is the most wonderful name in the world. I'm so proud of you."

I smiled. "Thanks, Mom. I'll have Tyler e-mail you some pictures, and you can have Vivian help you download them on your computer."

"Oh, I don't know if I'll be able to do that."

"Just let Vivian do it for you. I'll call her and let her know, okay? You don't have to do a thing."

"When will I be able to see the pictures?"

"As soon as you check your e-mail. They should be right in the e-mail message and if you need help, we'll get you some."

"All right. I'm so excited to see him."

"He came a few weeks early, and he's in the infant intensive care unit, so don't be alarmed by all of the tubes on him. He just needs a little extra help for about a week, but he's going to be fine."

"He's in good hands," she said.

"Yes, he is. I love you, Mom. I'll call you later." I handed Tyler's phone back to him.

He placed it in his pocket and grabbed his jacket off the back of a chair. "I'm going to go over to the house and have the door fixed. What can I bring you?"

I hated relying on him, but was very grateful he was being attentive. "If you could grab my phone, my phone charger, and the suitcase next to the closet. I had packed up some hospital stuff a couple weeks ago. Oh, and my laptop; it's in the kitchen."

He nodded. "Do you want a sandwich or something?"

"Sure, whatever's easiest."

After Tyler left, I slept. The nurses came in to check my vitals periodically, but I was mostly alone until Tyler returned with my things.

"My mom sends her love," he said as he placed my belongings on the table next to me. I smiled and thanked him.

Just then a nurse walked in with two dozen yellow roses in a rectangular glass vase. Tyler took them from her, set them on the windowsill, and handed me the card, which I read to myself.

A mother like no other. Love, Cam.

I smiled. Rachel must have called him.

Tyler was staring at me, wondering who had sent them.

"They're from Cam," I said. Tyler's eyes narrowed, but he made no comment.

Tyler came every day and spent several hours with Connor and me. As comforting as it was, pretending to play happy family and acting as though we belonged in a Norman Rockwell painting was a little awkward. But I was physically weak and my hormones had reached new heights, leaving me little energy to consider doing anything other than play along.

I was discharged five days later. Connor would be there another week before getting the green light.

CHAPTER FORTY-FOUR

Tyler and I picked our son up from the hospital two weeks before he was even supposed to be born. His nanny, Felicia, started as soon as he came home, allowing me some extra time to recover. Tyler came by after work every few days, bringing dinner and any other things I needed from the store. It wasn't meant to be a long-term solution, but I couldn't think beyond the day to day at that time. One night during Connor's second week home, Tyler was accompanied by his mother and his siblings.

Dixie gasped with delight as she leaned over the crib. "He is precious. Just precious," she said, shaking her head in disbelief. "We're going to need to schedule his baptism as soon as possible. I'll call my parish in the morning."

"That's not necessary. I'll take care of it," I said.

"You're going to call the parish?"

"I'm not going to use your parish. We're going to have him baptized at Saint Francis."

Dixie studied my face and made no further comment. I diverted the focus back to Connor. "Who wants to hold him?"

Sammy and Sarah deferred to their mother, so I lifted my sleeping baby out of the crib and handed him to Dixie. She sat in the rocker and sang to him for about three minutes until he woke up screaming. It was mostly a drama-free visit because my mother-in-law kept her attention on the baby—and off my shortcomings.

Once everyone left, I gave Connor a bath, fed him, and rocked him back to sleep.

Tyler was waiting for me in the kitchen when I came downstairs, so I grabbed a bottle of water from the fridge and joined him at the breakfast table. Empty bottles were drying on a rack next to the sink, and there were three cases of formula on the island along with other groceries that needed to be put away. There was so much to do, but I could tell he needed to get something off his chest.

"Do you want something to drink?" I offered.

"No, thanks."

"I can make some coffee if you want."

"I'm good," he said. "Is Connor asleep?"

I nodded.

"We need to talk," he said.

I nodded again.

Tyler placed his hands on the table, and we sat in silence for a couple of minutes.

"I guess I should start," he said and released a deep breath through his nose. "First and foremost, I don't know if an apology is even the right thing to do again at this point, or if it would help repair what I've done to us, but I am sorry for putting us both through all this pain. More than I can express."

"Try," I said.

"I know I screwed up bad. Looking back, I…I really don't know what I was thinking. I mean, I wasn't thinking. I've been losing sleep for weeks trying to figure out a way to explain myself to you and explain why I did what I did, but it all sounds so meaningless. I guess I was frustrated with everything that was going on with the IVF, and you were always angry with me about something. I thought once you got pregnant, you'd be happy and things would get better, but it only got worse."

I leaned back and crossed my arms. "Please don't put this on me. When the going got tough, you bailed. Own up to it. Don't act like my behavior was the reason for this. I may not be perfect, but I loved you like no one else, and I have *never* failed you in hard times. You don't get to shirk your responsibilities here. If you behaved like a pathetic, spineless, uncaring fool—even for a moment—then have the decency to acknowledge that. Don't act like I should feel sorry for what you were going through."

"I'm not blaming you or asking you to sympathize with me."

"That's sure what it sounds like."

"Jesus, I'm trying to give you some indication why I might have done what I did. Isn't that what you've been asking me for? I don't have an explanation, and even if I did, there's no excuse. That being said, I love you, and I want to make this marriage work. I know I fucked up, but I also know that if you can forgive me, we can get through this together. It's the best thing for Connor, you know it is."

Tears sprang to my eyes at the mention of Connor's name. My poor sweet little guy, swaddled away in his bedroom, had never asked for this. He deserved to grow up in a house with two loving parents and a swing set in the yard. That had been my plan for him, and now I was going to have to explain how everything went wrong.

"I'm so sorry," Tyler said again when he saw my face.

I took a deep breath. I had so many questions, like how could he have done this? Why did he let it go on for so long? He said he never meant to hurt me, but did he think of my feelings at all during that time? Was he ever in love with that woman? But in that moment I realized there was nothing Tyler could say that was going to make it better. He'd broken my trust and my heart in one fell swoop. What words could he possibly muster to make things better?

"It's easy for you to bring Connor into this now, but you should've been thinking of him all along, and you weren't. Even if I wanted to, I'm not sure I know how to forgive you or how to move on. I can't imagine ever forgetting those texts she sent you or erasing the image in my head of you touching another woman."

Tyler ran his hands through his hair. "Don't say that. I know we can get past this. I have no interest in being with anyone but you. Ever. This whole fucked up mistake shouldn't be the reason for us to get divorced. She meant nothing to me. I was an idiot. I love you and Connor so much. Please let me make this up to both of you."

I began to cry. He'd said the same things so many times that they were just words at that point, devoid of any meaning. "I love you, too, Tyler, you know that. You've always known that, but I just don't think I can get past it. Not now anyway. I need more time, and I need to be left alone."

"What about the baby?"

"I'm not saying you can't see the baby, but you just coming and going as you please and trying to play house isn't working for me. It's too much. I'm not ready."

Tyler stood. He was frustrated, and I couldn't blame him, but I couldn't bring myself to feel sorry for him. I didn't trust him anymore. How could I crawl into bed with him and give myself fully again to someone I didn't trust?

The next morning when Felicia arrived, I went to Target to pick up some diapers and pajamas for Connor. I skipped through the aisles and headed straight for the baby section. I slowly pushed the cart past rows of bath toys, stuffed animals, onesies, lotions, tearless shampoo, burp cloths, and more. It was heaven to me. I'd tried to join the Mommy Club for so long, and now I was in. I could now be part of conversations about sleepless nights, pee-stained blouses, and fussy eaters. Other mothers could look to me for my infinite wisdom on soy-based formulas and a cure for cradle cap.

Wasn't that all I had ever wanted? To have a child of my own. Maybe it was too much to ask to be in love as well.

I glanced around and saw only four other women in the baby aisles. None of them had their husbands with them, but it was nine o'clock on a Tuesday morning. I filled my cart with more than I needed, headed home, and decided to call Cam.

"Hey you," I said when he answered. It'd been the first time I'd talked to him since my life had been turned upside down by Connor's unexpected arrival.

"How's mommy life?"

"Pretty fantastic," I said. "And a full-time nanny doesn't suck either."

"When do you go back to work?"

"In a couple months, but I have a ton of work to do from home. The e-mails and voice mails haven't stopped just because Connor decided he was ready to make his debut ahead of schedule."

"Can I come meet him? I was looking at flights for next week."

"Of course, we would love that. In fact, I have a favor to ask while you're here."

"You name it."

"I'd like you to be Connor's godfather. His baptism is next Friday."

Cam cleared his throat. "Does that mean I have to raise the kid if you die in a fiery car crash?"

"You did not just say that."

He chuckled. "I would be honored."

"You're a shit."

"Hey, that's your son's godfather you're talking to," he said. "Who's my god-spouse?"

"Grace."

"And what's going on with Tyler?"

"I can fill you in when you get here, but not much has changed…with him anyway. He's been coming over a lot and been really helpful, but I haven't taken him back."

"Sounds weird," Cam said.

"It is."

CHAPTER FORTY-FIVE

Cam arrived the following week and took his place at the Saint Francis altar next to Grace during Connor's baptism. My mother had decided to fly in as well, so Cam got himself a hotel room in the city. During her short stay with me, she mentioned that there was a man named Ricardo whom she'd met in her building and was going to marry. He hadn't proposed yet, but she assured me there would be a wedding within the next few months. When I called Vivian to find out more about him, she told me he was the doorman and never said anything more than "good morning" to my mother or anyone else. But Mom seemed happier than ever, so I went along with her fantasies. I was delighted to have her around, if only for a couple of days.

It was a motley crew, what with my mother and Dixie Reed in the front row of the church and my estranged husband by my side. But sitting there, staring at my son being held by my two closest friends, I was truly at peace.

Afterward, I had everyone over to the house for lunch. My mom insisted on staying upstairs with the baby. She said there were too many people around, and he was certain to catch something. Rather than argue with her, I let her spend the day with her grandson because she was leaving for Florida the next morning. Anyone who wanted to see the baby had to douse him or herself with hand sanitizer to get past her.

When everyone left, there was little I could do to hide the fact that Tyler was among the departing guests. My mom gave me a curious look as he said good-bye to her and left the house.

"What's going on?" my mother asked me. "Why is Tyler leaving?"

I scratched my head and sighed. "Tyler and I are separated."

She shook her head, deeply confused, but said nothing.

"I should've told you before, but I wasn't sure what was going to happen between us, and I didn't want to worry you."

My mom took a seat at the kitchen table and cast her eyes downward. "Chloe, I know you think I can't handle a lot of things, but you're wrong. You are my daughter, and I deserve to know when you're going through something."

"I know, thanks, Mom," I said and sat next to her.

She lifted her chin and looked into my eyes. "What happened?"

The words were on the tip of my tongue, but I needed a moment before I could utter them. "He cheated on me," I said. "When I was just a few months pregnant. He hasn't lived here since I found out."

Mom placed her hands in her lap and sat back in the chair. "You know I've been through the same thing?"

"Yes, I know."

"It's very painful."

I nodded.

"Is he still with this other woman?" she asked.

"No, he's not. He's apologized many times, and would like to come home and try to work things out, but I can't seem to get over it. It's all I think of every time I look at him," I said.

She stared at me with a severe look in her eyes. "If I'd been given the choice, I would've taken your father back," she said before grabbing her cigarettes and heading outside.

I sat in silence, stunned not by what she said, but how she'd said it. With that one statement, that one confession, she was telling me what to do. She would've gone back to my father after he humiliated her, because she was weak and insecure and codependent… and nothing like me.

I drove her to the airport the next morning, taking a thirty-minute detour just in case there were any agents who were tracking her departure. When I gave her a hug good-bye, I realized I was really sad to let her go.

Cam brought dinner to my house that night, and we ate in front of the TV once Connor was asleep. About halfway through our movie, there was a knock at the back door. Tyler was standing there when I opened it.

"Sorry I didn't call first, but I had to drop something off at my parents' house, so I thought I'd stop by."

"Oh, it's fine. Cam's here actually. We were just finishing up dinner."

Tyler looked over my shoulder, and then back at me. "Am I interrupting something?"

"No."

"Then why does it feel like I am?"

I shrugged. "I have no idea."

Tyler's expression soured as Cam came up behind me.

"Hey man," Cam said.

Tyler looked at him and said nothing.

"Do you want to come in?" I asked Tyler as I stepped back from the doorway.

He shook his head and kept his eyes on Cameron. "No."

"Tyler, we're just hanging out. Connor's asleep; come on in," I said.

Tyler looked at me for a second, then stepped into the house and punched Cam in the face.

CHAPTER FORTY-SIX

Cam collapsed as Tyler turned and left.

"Oh my God!" I screamed, dropping to the floor next to him. "Cam, oh my God, Cam, are you okay?!" I slapped him gently to try to elicit a response. "Cam, please!"

As soon as he moaned and lifted his hand to his head, I ran to the freezer and grabbed an ice pack. I frantically wrapped a dish towel around it and ran back to his side.

"Here, put this on your eye." My hands were shaking as I handed him the cold towel. "I am so sorry. I have no idea what just happened."

"My face has an idea," he mumbled.

"I cannot believe he just did that, oh my God, I am so sorry."

"You know any good lawyers?" he asked. "I'm just kidding, I'll be fine. You think a smart-ass kid like me never got hit in the face before?" Cam sat up, holding the ice pack to his face.

"Let me see it," I said.

He removed the ice, and I winced. "Well, it looks like your upper cheekbone, but at least it's not your eye."

"Yay," Cam said and placed the ice back on his face.

"I'm not trying to make excuses for him, but he's going through a lot, and I guess seeing you here must have pushed him over the edge."

"Clearly," he mumbled and leaned back against the cabinets.

"It's inexcusable. I'm mortified. He obviously feels threatened by our friendship, and since I'm letting you stay here and not him… he must have just snapped."

"You don't have to defend him," Cam said.

I nodded. "You're right. It was a dick move that you did not deserve in the least. Can I at least apologize like fifty more times?"

He shrugged. "Follow me with a cold beer, and I'll forgive you."

Cam made his way back to the couch, chugged his beer, and fell asleep. When Felicia arrived the next morning, I drove him to the airport. Though his face was bruised, his spirit wasn't broken.

"Never a dull moment," I said as I hugged him.

"Not with you."

"I always hate to see you go, especially after getting clocked by my husband."

He smiled. "Don't worry about me, you have enough on your plate."

"You're still cute, even with a shiner."

"I know," he said.

As he exited the car, I grabbed his bag out of the back and met him by the passenger door. I set it down at his feet and was about to give him a hug when he kissed me. He didn't say a word—just leaned forward, gently grabbed the back of my neck, and kissed me. My eyes were still closed when he pulled away. "You still taste like spearmint," I whispered before opening them.

"Thanks," he said, grinning like a naughty teenager.

I leaped into his arms and held him in a long embrace. It was hard not to beg him to stay, but I needed time to think and settle things in my life first. Maybe another time. "When will I see you again?" I asked.

"Just click your heels together three times and say, there's no one like Cam, and I'll appear."

I smiled. "It might be sooner than you think."

"I'm always here for you. Just say the word."

I nodded and hugged him one last time before getting in my car and bursting into tears.

I went home, answered a few e-mails, and took a conference call at two o'clock. I let Felicia go early that afternoon, and took Connor for a long walk in the stroller. We walked about ten blocks, to where Jack and Grace had just put a bid in on a house. She'd recently gotten a job teaching at Glenview Methodist Preschool and would be moving back to town within the year. By the time I got back to the house, Connor was awake and hungry. I fixed a bottle and fed him outside on the front porch before heading upstairs to put him to sleep.

He is an angel, I thought, as I sat smiling with my son in my lap. His dark blue eyes were on me, doing their best to focus and preserve the image of my face. I looked away for a moment and glanced out his bedroom window, which overlooked the backyard.

"Only a few more months and you'll be out there on those swings," I told him.

He smashed his tiny lips together and then stilled, his top lip protruding out over the lower one.

I rocked in the chair and sang "Twinkle Twinkle" and the alphabet song before gently placing him down into the crib. When I turned to leave, a framed photograph of Tyler and Sammy and Sarah caught my eye. It was on Connor's bookshelf, next to a blue piggy bank. Dixie had brought the photograph for Connor the first time she came to visit. I lifted the picture off the shelf and gazed into Tyler's eyes. I'd fallen for him through panes of glass so many years before; however, at that moment he was a stranger to me. I placed the frame back down and walked over to the crib. Everything I loved was right here.

I tiptoed out of Connor's room and headed into my bedroom, where I began tearing through some old boxes at the back of my closet in search of some other photos to add to his bookshelf. Just then something fell from a shelf above and landed at my feet. I laughed as I bent down to pick it up.

I carried it back down the hall to the baby's room.

"Looks like I won't be needing this anymore," I said and hung the "Find Your Bliss" pillow on my son's doorknob.

The End

EPILOGUE

I lifted Connor out of his car seat, set him on the ground and watched him sprint into Tyler's arms. I grabbed his overnight bag from the front seat and walked toward them.

"Everything's in here," I said, handing the bag to Tyler.

"Thanks. We'll be just fine."

I gave Connor a kiss on the head—which was all I was permitted by my precocious one year old—and headed for the airport.

I arrived at LAX at ten o'clock in the morning that Friday and hailed the first cab I saw. Grinning from ear to ear, I gave the driver the address and sat on the edge of my seat during the twenty-five minute ride.

As soon as the cab pulled away I walked up to the front door of the bungalow style house and rang the bell.

Cam answered with a smile and a bowl of Lucky Charms in his hand.

"Well, well, well," he said. "What are you doing here?"

"I came to bring you home."

ACKNOWLEDGMENTS

Much like everything I write, this book is filled with truths. The stories of infertility, infidelity, alcoholism, mental illness, and much more were inspired by those of some very generous and amazing women.

I would like to thank Stephanie Bass, Marilyn Mages, Erin Hanley, Alexa Wagner, and Robin Miller for sharing details of their personal stories with me.

Thanks to my fabulous beta readers: Wendy Wilken, Beth Suit, Iris Martin, Meg Costigan, Tammy Langas, Kelly Konrad, Jamie Struck, Rebecca Berto, my mom, and my mother-in-law. Your enthusiasm and honest feedback were encouraging and irreplaceable.

Thank you to my family at Amazon Publishing, especially the totally tubular team of Liz Egan, Carly Hoffmann, and Christina Henry de Tessan. And thanks to my agent, Deborah Schneider, for always having my back.

Also, to everyone who has read my books and supported my work over the years, I have no words to express my gratitude. I am so honored to be part of a community of authors who praise and support one another. I'm so humbled every time someone sets aside their life to read one of my stories, send me an e-mail, or leave a review on my behalf. I don't take any of it for granted.

Last, behind every great author are two great men...or something like that. A megahearty thank-you to my husband, Jeff, and my son, Ryan, for their unwavering support and confidence in me.

ABOUT THE AUTHOR

 A graduate of Purdue University, Dina Silver has spent the past fifteen years feeding her red wine habit by working as a copywriter in the advertising industry. After seeing the bulk of her professional prose on brochures and direct-mail pieces, she is delighted to have made the transition to novelist. She now hopes she'll become a screenwriter one day.

She lives with her family in suburban Chicago, where she spends way too much time on Facebook and Twitter when she should be working on her next book. *Finding Bliss* is her third novel.

Discover more at www.dinasilver.com.

22539251R00157

Made in the USA
Charleston, SC
26 September 2013